To my number one fan & friend, Glenda
In appreciation of all your
support and encouragement

Michael J Smedley

A Subtle Revenge

Michael John Smedley

Lulu Online Publishing

Copyright © Michael John Smedley 2008

The right of Michael John Smedley to be identified as the
author of this work has been asserted by him in accordance
with the Copyright Designs and Patents Act 1988

All rights reserved. No part of this publication may be
reproduced, transmitted, or stored in a retrieval system, in
any form or by any means without permission in writing
from the author, nor be otherwise circulated in any form of
binding or cover other than that in which it is published and
without a similar condition being imposed on the subsequent
purchaser

This novel is a work of fiction and any resemblance to real
people, alive or dead, is purely coincidental.

A Subtle Revenge

(Part 2 of The Decker Trilogy)

Chapter One

It must be a rare and unusual happening for an entire community to know the exact moment in time that a person died. Yet the village of Rowell knew the precise moment Maxwell Bull went to greet his Maker. It was one minute into the New Year on 1st of January 1990 in the stables of his country house.

No one saw him die but they all heard the sound that signalled his passing.

The solitary jumbled clang of the stable bell as its rope tightened around his thick neck and despatched him to oblivion. Spot on midnight as the last chime of the old church clock marked the passing of the old year, the villagers expected to hear the Manor House stable bell commence to ring in the new. Traditionally its clear sonorous peal echoed around the little Peak village, reaching every corner, entering every home, bringing its message of hope and joy to all their ears.

Old villagers claimed that the practice dated back two centuries or more. However research by a local historian proved its innovation to come from more recent years. The bell had first been rung by a grateful father, George Bellingham, in celebration of the safe return of his son from the horrors of World War One. The Bellingham family had long departed the great house but the tradition lingered on.

Throughout the village there was stunned amazement. Could it be that the new owner of the great house situated on the fringes of Rowell had broken the custom of generations? He had… and the consequences proved fatal. That last jangled sonorous ring was the very last sound ever to be heard by Maxwell Bull.

*

Police Sergeant Edward Decker answered the emergency call at twelve minutes past midnight. A small group of stunned villagers stood outside the entrance to the stables. Their deathly white faces slack with shock. A case of instant sobriety forced upon them by the horror of violent death. It acted as a very effective remedy for every ones' New Year inebriation.

The stables had been built in rustic brickwork designed to match the large square country house. Its bell tower, added as a belated afterthought, rose from the centre of the building. On either side a split loft had been created with bales of hay stored on one side and riding tackle on the other. There were three boxes on each side of the central passageway providing accommodation for six horses. Rising up from the central passageway, a wooden ladder provided a means of access. It rested against the side where the riding tackle was stored.

From the central tower, with its time-blackened solitary brass bell, hung the rope ... stretched taut by the weight of the late Maxwell Bull. There was little doubt that the man was dead for the weight of his body mass and the length of its fall had all but torn the deceased man's head from his body.

A professional hangman, had one still been employed, would have calculated the victim's weight and the distance it needed to fall in order to break his neck quickly and cleanly. Correctly secured the hangman's knot brought instant death, snapping the vertebrate cleanly. The knot around the victim's neck was a simple slipknot, formed by passing one loop of the rope through another. Its effect had been one of strangulation as it tightened and bit through the soft fleshy tissue.

Sergeant Decker, who lacked a strong stomach when it came to violent death, steeled himself for a cursory examination of the body. He touched nothing. Used just his eyes to take in the scene. His studied gaze took in the head of thick hair, the strong but fleshy features and the powerful heavy body beginning to run to seed.

It was the victim's hands that puzzled him. He examined both carefully. Across the palm of each hand the skin was torn away. Rope-burns! On the inside of each thumb, above the joint, there was a deep cut from which a trickle of blood had oozed and then congealed. The rope-burns Decker could understand. The cuts to the thumbs mystified him. There seemed not to be a logical explanation or reason for them. Would a man committing suicide grab for the rope? Decker asked himself the question. In that final despairing moment would his instinct for self-preservation overcome the destructive urge for death? Very likely... which explained the torn flesh on both palms. But a murderer, surely, would have tied his victim's hands behind his back to prevent such an act. The hands had been free. There was no evidence of rope marks around the dead man's wrists or any other indication that he had been bound.

Leave it to forensics, the Sergeant told himself, ... *They are the experts.*

Nevertheless while he waited for the *SOCO* team to arrive he made a careful search of the stable floor, climbed the creaking ladder to the loft, and found... nothing!

*

The following day, the second of January, life returned to normal. People went back to work after the long Christmas break. The newspapers were published ... and the scandal broke.

A large sum of money; one million pounds was reported as missing from the funds of the North Pennine Health Scheme. Maxwell Bull had been its Chief Executive.

Now, it seemed, the reason for his demise was obvious. The media was quick to form an opinion, and equally as quick to shape that of its readers. It had to be the suicide of a guilty man. Without a shred of evidence to prove otherwise Police Sergeant Decker's superiors came to the same conclusion. The forensic team found minute particles of rope adhering to the cuts on the insides of Maxwell Bull's thumbs. They matched the hempen strands of the bell-rope. No other marks were found upon his body. It was suicide. It had to be, a neat and final statistic for the police records and a satisfying solution that saved paperwork, manpower and resources.

Only in Edward Decker's mind did a niggling doubt persist.

*

They met in the snug of the Cock Inn at Briseley T'ill. Made strange bedfellows, the Chief Constable of the County police and Sergeant Edward Decker who resided in the village where his superior had been born. Despite the disparity of their positions a firm friendship existed between the two men.

Nigel Rowthorne, Repton school, Oxford graduate, former county cricketer in the days when there had still been amateurs and professionals, and ultimately, as fate had decreed, Chief Constable of the County, was a fellow member of the Briseley T'ill village cricket club. He was a vice president and a life member, an honorary position awarded without reservation to every former playing member. It was a unique bond that helped to cement the unlikely friendship forged between the two men.

'So let me guess what is on your mind.' the Chief Constable said, 'The Bull suicide... am I right?'

'As usual.' Decker answered, 'It just does not fit the man. It's totally out of character. He was definitely *not* the type.'

'Intuition? Or what?'

'No. Knowledge. That man had tremendous drive and personality. He was ruthless. Knew exactly what he wanted, and nothing, but *nothing* on earth was ever allowed to stop him. I can't believe a man like that would ever contemplate suicide.'

'Ah! That good old local knowledge at work again, Eh! You may be right. I have to admit I have never felt completely happy about the suicide verdict.'

Reflectively Nigel Rowthorne twirled his empty glass. Decker took the hint and signalled to the barman for two more pints.

'I know I'm right.' Decker said with conviction, 'What is more I have a personal interest in this one. I'm a member of the North Pennine Health Scheme myself and so is seventy percent of the Police Federation. The missing money... some of it is ours.'

A sudden explosive noise burst from the Chief Constable, a spontaneous laugh that he hurriedly converted into a cough. 'In that case,' Rowthorne said, 'and on behalf of the Police Federation, you had better look into the matter.' He paused a moment, 'Just a word of warning though, be discreet. For all their apparent strength and solidarity, financial institutions depend upon a very fragile commodity - confidence. Shatter it. Damage their reputation, and they can collapse overnight.'

Then with a steady hand he raised his glass, emptied its contents in one long smooth swallow, and departed.

Chapter Two

The office of the North Pennine Health Scheme had once been a large private Mansion House and lay four miles south of the village where Sergeant Edward Decker lived. It had originally stood in spacious grounds of its own, but time, progress and the demands of the Inland Revenue upon its original owners had reduced the estate to less than one acre. Most of the remaining land had been converted into a car park leaving just a long narrow lawn surrounded by a high stone wall at the rear of the building. Weed riddled flowerbeds lay to the right and the left of a semi-circular gravelled drive at the front of the building.

Decker was convinced that the answer to Bull's death was to be found there. A cursory examination of the deceased man's private life revealed little to suggest a motive for murder. He was single, without any known emotional ties either male or female. He lived with an older sister and employed a housekeeper to look after the two of them. As far as could be determined both sister and housekeeper were totally dependant upon Bull, materially and financially. It was highly unlikely that either would benefit by his early demise.

The reason and motive *had* to lie within the Health Scheme.

Bull had been a compulsive achiever, a man driven to succeed at any cost. Such men are ruthless, and in the course of reaching the top… enemies are made.

*

Decker's feet crunched on the gravelled drive leading to the large oak door of the converted Mansion House. Once inside the reception area he flashed his warrant card and asked to see the person in charge. A plump rosy-cheeked receptionist offered him a seat while she put through a brief call. The Sergeant refused the seat, preferring to take stock of his surrounding.

'Mrs Bergen will be with you shortly sir.' the receptionist announced.

Rachel Bergen, Edward Decker guessed, was in her early forties, a neatly dressed woman in a grey suit, grey hair, grey eyes and a calm demeanour. Petite.

Anxiety reflected in her eyes.

'Hello. I'm Rachel Bergen, the General Manager.' She said in a quiet controlled voice, 'Your visit is not unexpected. You are...?'

'Decker, Sergeant Edward Decker.'

'Aah!' Her sigh was soft and drawn out, 'Well! It's obvious why you are here. Shall we go up to my office?' She paused a moment, then asked, 'Tea or coffee?'

'Tea would be fine.' replied the policeman, 'Milk, no sugar.' Rachel Bergen turned towards the receptionist, 'Arrange that Jane will you? Thank you.'

An elegant oak staircase, wide enough to take a regiment six abreast, led to the first floor. Halfway up at a spacious landing where the staircase turned back upon its self was mounted an enormous gilt-framed mirror. It reflected the light of a glittering chandelier hanging over the well of the staircase. The effect was to create an illusion of space. Dark oak panelled walls added an air of wealth and solidarity to the house.

By contrast the office of the General Manager was stark and plain. The walls were bare of pictures or decorations of any description. It was as though its occupant only thought of the room as a temporary residence. As though she was reluctant to stamp it with a symbol of her personality.

Decker thought it very odd, and wondered why?

*

'Now what can I do for you Sergeant?' asked Rachel Bergen, 'I take it that your enquiries are to do with the death of our late Chief Executive, Mr Maxwell Bull?

'They are.' Decker acknowledged, admiring her lack of preamble and the ability to get immediately to the point. 'First I would like a list of *all* those currently employed by the North Pennine Health Scheme, and then, assuming that you keep such information, a list of all former employees. Say, over the last five years? Can that be done?' She flashed him a look that plainly asked, how can you doubt my efficiency and turning to a filing cabinet took out two separate files, which she laid before Decker on her desk. 'Present employees,' Rachel Bergen laid a petite manicured hand on the first file and pushed it slightly forward, 'and former employees.'

Decker took careful notes from the first file. It appeared fairly straightforward. There were twenty-three employees who worked in the building, predominately young women. Only four were men.

It was the second file that astounded him. The one listing the names and last known addresses of the scheme's former employees, during a period of less than five years, sixty-one personnel had departed the company.

Now that is unusual, mused the policeman turning over the numbers in his head. Mentally he worked out the statistics of it. On average an employee had departed *every* month! *In a recession when people turned cartwheels to hang onto their jobs? It doesn't make sense.* Of the staff employed *before* Maxwell Bull took over no one remained. Why?

*

Mrs Bergen watched quietly as he worked his way through the pile of information. She poured tea from a chromium-plated pot into china cups and sipped hers with an air of quiet reflection as she patiently waited. Finally she asked, 'May I ask what it is you are looking for Sergeant Decker? If I can assist...?'

The policeman looked up from his work and scratched the side of his nose thoughtfully. Most people he read easily. His ability to assess their character quickly and accurately had been developed over many years and from long experience. A little like extra sensory perception. But this woman... he was not at all sure.

'Just routine,' Decker replied endeavouring to sound nonchalant, 'We're obliged to look at everything after a suspicious death.'

'You don't believe he committed suicide do you?' said Rachel Bergen bluntly. 'He wasn't that kind of man. Not the Maxwell Bull I knew. He would never have killed himself in a million years. His ego was far too big to allow it. Even if he did steal the money, which I don't believe, the man would have brazened it out. That man could sell refrigerators to Eskimos. He had such self belief that he'd talk his way out of any situation.' There was no sorrow in her voice. No regret. Rachel Bergen was just stating a firmly held conviction… but with the faintest trace of venom showing.

'Are you suggesting he was murdered?' Decker asked tactfully.

'Isn't that what you really believe?'' Bergen countered sharply, 'But why?'

'A million pounds sounds like a pretty good motive,' suggested the policeman, 'The missing money?'

For a moment she bristled with anger then in a flash was calm again. 'It is *not* a million pounds. That's just silly newspaper talk, adding noughts where they don't belong to spice up the story. The actual amount was a mere two hundred and fifty thousand, that's all.'

She made the amount sound less important than grains of sand upon a beach. A quarter of a million pounds still sounded a good enough motive for murder and the policeman suggested as much.

'Well! Yes it is,' she replied, 'But in the context of our business it isn't a large amount. I mean, if Mr Bull planned to steal from the scheme, why stop at a quarter of a million and why now when we have just battled our way out of trouble? It's not logical. It does *not* make sense.'

'*Just* got out of trouble?' remarked Decker pointedly, 'Would you care to explain?'

She looked away from his eyes. He could almost see the thoughts racing through her mind. At last Rachel Bergen came to a decision and with regained composure faced him again. 'Look! What I'm about to tell you is strictly confidential. About a year ago the scheme ran into severe financial difficulties.' she explained, 'The North Pennine Health Scheme was the subject of an investigation by the DTI, that's the Department of Trade and Industry. It was very *very* serious and may even have resulted in the company being wound up. But, well, it was decided to increase the membership fees. There was a sticky patch up until August or thereabouts and then everything looked as though it would be alright.' Mrs Bergen sighed heavily, '…and now this.'

*

Decker remembered the inflationary price increase. There had been only the minimum of warning. He'd been surprised, for his monthly contribution had jumped by over sixty percent. The increase had been linked to a big improvement in the type and number of benefits offered by the Health Scheme. But how genuine were they? Doubtless every other member had been miss-lead to believe this was the reason for the sharp increase. Obviously it was far from the truth.

So what had gone wrong? Why all the secrecy? Had there been a massive cover-up? It was beginning to appear that way. Perhaps the mess was deeper and smellier than he had originally supposed. The whiff of corruption tickled the Sergeant's nose.

*

Further probing into the affairs of the scheme brought to light some curious facts. Between 1985 and 1989, in a period of less than four years, there had been five new Sales Managers and four different Accountants. Sales personnel came and went with astonishing frequency in many companies, Decker knew, but *four* accountants? An accountant was a different breed of animal and far more difficult to replace.

Briefly from April 1989 to August of the same year a Financial Director had been appointed – and then summarily been dismissed – allegedly for incompetence.

Surely not, thought Decker, *for the man had barely had the time to find his feet.* A bizarre possibility sprang to mind – that he had been taken on for the sole purpose of being used as a scapegoat.

What kind of employer would do that? Decker pondered.

In total, the records showed, there had been twenty-seven staff changes in the one year. For a self-professed *caring* company it was a horrendous industrial relations record

*

Decker also discovered that over a period of two years, the same length of time that the late Maxwell Bull had been its Chief Executive, the Board of Directors of the North Pennine Health Scheme had also changed in its composition. With the exception of two elderly medical practitioners in their seventies the present members were all new faces.

By the middle of the afternoon the policeman had filled several pages of his notebook with information, yet seemed as far away from finding a solution as when he had started. There were so many possible suspects. Too many. Within the space of two years Maxwell Bull had made many enemies and any one of them could be the man or woman with enough hatred in their heart to want to kill him.

*

Mrs Bergen, having left Decker alone to pursue his researches, returned to her office. She offered him a guided tour of the building. He thought it would provide an excellent opportunity to assess the staff without having to ask official questions.

The results were disappointing.

They began on the top floor, a series of sprawling rooms that ran off one another. Because they were tucked up under the roof, low beams were everywhere. Decker ducked under one to avoid cracking his head, straightened up only to receive a painful knock from the architrave of an even lower doorway. The offices were all furnished with cheap reproduction desks and chairs. Filing cabinets and bookcases being carefully chosen to fit against the low outer walls under the steeply angled ceilings.

A century earlier the level would have been used as the servants quarters.

'This floor used to be the Marketing Department.' Rachel Bergen informed Decker, 'After the DTI enquiry we were forced to close it down and make the staff redundant.'

'Any particular reason?' he asked.

'A cost-cutting exercise.' replied Mrs Bergen primly, her lips pressing tightly together in disapproval, 'It was a *very* expensive department to run.'

It was what was left unsaid that was significant. Without putting it into words Rachel Bergen implied unwarranted extravagance. Just two young women worked on the top floor. Mrs Bergen explained that their prime function was to make calls and arrange talks for the Health Schemes' representatives.

'Do you have many reps?' asked the policeman.

'Until last July there were twenty-four, then we were forced to cut back by fifty percent. Two left of their own accord. We are now down to ten.'

'Is that about average?'

'Sales reps tend to come and go rather more than the average employee,' explained the General Manager, 'Some of them only

10

stay for a few months and others have been with the scheme for three to four years.'

The policeman nodded his understanding. He knew from experience that sales people were itinerant by nature. The grass over the sales hill always looked greener.

But an accountant was a different breed. When fraud or embezzlement raised its ugly head the Company Accountant was the first person to be scrutinised. *Four* Accountants in less than *five* years, not forgetting the short-lived Financial Director, now that was suspicious... and needed much closer investigation.

*

He followed the General Manager down to the first floor. Here the rooms had higher ceilings, about eight feet and were less eccentric in shape. One room had been set aside for use as a canteen. It was equipped with an electric cooker, a refrigerator, a microwave oven and an automatic dishwasher. Every modern convenience had been provided without regard to the cost. The employees prepared their own food and on the wall a roster delegated daily responsibility for one of them to load the dishwasher. The organisational talents of the General Manager were plain to see.

Mrs Bergen introduced him to the personal secretary of the late Chief Executive. 'This is Geraldine Manners – Detective Sergeant Decker.'

'Just Sergeant,' corrected the policeman, 'Sergeant Decker.'

She was very nervous, half put out a hand...and then withdrew it not quite knowing what to do or say. Decker gave a friendly nod of the head and tried to set her mind at ease. 'It must have been quite a shock for you,' he sympathised, 'Please sit down and carry on with what you were doing.'

Every office, the policeman noticed, was packed with modern technology. Computer terminals rested on every desk and in every room. The secretary used the very latest in word-processors. In addition there were two expensive photocopiers, one for colour, a neat compact fax machine and up-to-date push button telephones. No expense had been spared. Decker readily admitted his experience of computers was limited but even his untutored eye spotted that there were two distinctly separate systems. Some of the screens displayed their information in colour, mainly green or orange, while other screens were monochrome. When he remarked upon this fact he was surprised to be informed that the monochrome screens were the *latest* technology. The brightly coloured ones were behind the times. At least five years old!

'Why are there two systems?' he asked Rachel Bergen, 'Have you more than one computer?' Her explanation came easily. 'Yes. The original one, a DEC is a dedicated system used for the membership, that's the one with the coloured screens. The IBM computer system, the one with the monochrome screens, stores information such as the company accounts, sale details and word-processing. It is much more flexible.'

'*Mmm! All very extravagant,* mused the policeman, but he kept his thoughts to himself as they moved on through the building. *Didn't one of the new Directors own a computer company?* Decker placed a silent bet with himself as to who the supplier of all the technology would be.

He was shown into the most spacious room of all. The Boardroom looked out across open parkland to distant hills. It was a pleasant airy room with a long highly polished reproduction table and at least twenty matching chairs sporting rich green velvet upholstery. The chairs were new and again looked expensive. Two small chandeliers hung from the high ornate ceiling and over the centre of the table was a large decorative Bahamas style fan. It was finished in brass and had four wooden cooling blades. Decker was reminded of a World War Two Spitfire propeller.

A Boardroom is probably the least used room in a company yet it is always the largest, the most impressively furnished and the most lavishly fitted.

Decker reflected that cost conscious companies, particularly multiple stores, actually calculated how much each square foot of space was deemed to earn. Did they apply the same rule of thumb to their Boardroom? He doubted as much.

The busiest departments were on the ground floor. In one office, the second largest room in the old Mansion House, six young women worked ceaselessly on terminals. Their fingers flittered over the keys with astonishing speed. It seemed to Decker's inexperienced eyes that information was being stored at an incredible rate.

'This is where our membership is entered,' Mrs Bergen explained, 'It's a very busy office, the girls work under a lot of pressure.'

The Sergeant looked at the unsmiling faces grimly concentrating upon their work. They didn't look very happy. For all her quiet demeanour and gentle manner he suspected that the General Manager was a stern disciplinarian.

The final room they visited was the Claims Office. Again computer keys rattled out a tuneless symphony. Again the same serious faces prevailed. When Decker asked if it was possible to speak to the Company Accountant he was informed that the present incumbent of that precarious position had been called away to London. He was urgently involved with the auditors.

'London?' commented the policeman, 'Isn't that inconvenient? I would have expected the scheme to use a local company… being a regional Health Scheme.'

Rachel Bergen's grey eyes looked steadily into his face, 'We used to do,' she answered, and mentioned the name of a well-known accountancy, 'Until two years ago, then the scheme changed to a London based firm. It is all part of Maxwell Bull's plans to re-shape the organisation. "To prepare it for the twenty-first century" were his exact words.'

Her words were accompanied by a casual shrug of the shoulders. Whatever her words, her eyes meant, if Decker was reading them right, *I don't know why… but I have my suspicions!*

So far the results of his investigations were disappointing. It was impossible at such an early stage to rule out anyone as a suspect, but Decker knew, his policeman's intuition told him, that he was unlikely to find his murderer amongst the young people at the Mansion House. To them, Maxwell Bull was just a remote figurehead.

The thought occurred to him that Mrs Bergen knew a great deal more than she was prepared to reveal. Not only was she obviously loyal to the company, but also her job could be on the line if she spoke out openly. However, if she were to point him in the right direction…?

Decker showed her the list of former employees he'd jotted down in his notebook and asked, 'Who would you recommend I ask to get a little more background on the workings of the scheme?'

She didn't hesitate and pointed immediately to a name on the list.

'If I were you,' she said, 'I'd pay Martin Sellaney a visit, talk to him. He has only recently... *retired*.' There was a slight pause before her final word and an inflexion in her voice which completely altered its meaning.

As he drove away from the Mansion House, Decker pondered deeply upon her choice. It was not the name of a former accountant she had given to him. It was that of the Claims and Membership Manager. The records showed that he had taken early retirement due to poor health.

Chapter Three

June 1989

He plotted his revenge very carefully. For a long time now he had realised that one day his turn would come. That was the reason he had kept meticulous notes about everything that had happened over the last few years. All the comings and goings, all the details of each and every venture which had ended in disaster. If *he* was about to end up as a scapegoat for yet another of Maxwell Bull's feckless business deals then he was determined not to be sunk without trace as many of his predecessors had been. His passing would leave waves. Big waves he determined, big enough to rock the boat. And who knows, perhaps waves large enough to swamp the dreadnought - Bull!

*

On Sunday he scoured the newspapers until he found what he was looking for, a vanity advert. For shoes with built in platforms guaranteed to raise a man's height by three to four inches. He cut the advert carefully out of the paper. A postal order, unlike a cheque, would be impossible to trace, he reasoned. It cost a little more but it was commonsense to take every precaution.

In Nottingham there was an excellent theatrical shop. Choosing a busy Saturday afternoon he paid the shop a visit and purchased a wig of thick dark hair. He paid for the item in cash, careful to hand over old and crumpled notes. A tour of the local charity shops; Oxfam, Help the Aged and Cancer Research eventually produced the result he was looking for; a dark blue raincoat with a detachable lining. The coat he selected was several sizes larger than his normal thirty-eight inch chest. Perfect.

After several attempts and a fair amount of wastage, he was able to bulk out the garment with pads of foam. Achieving a natural appearance was tricky but with perseverance and a little invention he was finally able to wear the raincoat with confidence. It made his slender frame look very substantial.

The Chief Executive of the North Pennine Health Scheme had a fondness for memoranda. He signed them in thick black ink with a sprawling flamboyant signature. His first name in full – Maxwell – followed by a large B - the remaining characters deteriorating into an untidy scrawl. He selected a memo bearing the blackest clearest signature he could find. Slipped it into his briefcase and smuggled it home. Once in the sanctuary of his study he flattened out the memo and secured it to the underside of a sheet of glass with sellotape. Then he rested the glass across the well of a writing desk and placed a bright light underneath the glass. The signature was thrown into sharp relief. Now he was ready to start. Every night for two whole weeks he practised the sprawling writing over and over again, slowly and carefully at first, then with increasing speed and confidence until finally he was able to write a perfect facsimile.

*

For the first ten days the elevated shoes were painful to wear. His weight was thrown forward by the height of the heels. The strain upon his leg muscles was unnatural and his cramped toes rapidly became sore as the skin rubbed away. A red chafe mark cut across his Achilles tendon. He gritted his teeth and persisted. Slowly his calf muscles adapted, the chafe mark eased and the cramped sore discomfort in his toes disappeared. Finally he was able to walk reasonably well.

With a little bit of padding to plump out his cheeks, the wig of thick dark hair upon his head and the extra height provided by the elevated shoes he now bore a passing resemblance to the Chief Executive of the North Pennine Health Scheme.

It had never been his intention to be recognised as Maxwell Bull, but rather to create an overall impression, just enough to suggest familiarity. He expected to use the disguise twice or three times at the most when he visited the busy city bank where the North Pennine Health Scheme had its accounts. By using a variety of paying in positions on each visit it was unlikely the same bank clerk would attend to him every time. If his luck held there was the possibility of being served by a different employee on each visit.

*

Beginning in April, whenever he had cashed a cheque at his own bank he had drawn out slightly more money than he needed. He set the cash aside to build up a little fund. The small increase, insufficient to attract attention, quickly mounted to a thousand pounds.

The North Pennine Health Scheme account was serviced by one of the big four banks. When the scheme moved into the Mansion House its accounts were transferred into a branch in Derby. He chose a busy Friday lunchtime to open a new account there. It meant having to wait and join a queue of customers, but that was to his advantage. The female clerk who attended to his needs was hard pressed and scarcely raised her head. He opened the account in the name of Maxwell Bull and deposited the one thousand pounds, signing the form with the sprawling signature he had practised so assiduously.

'Thank you Mr Bull.' said the clerk, reading his name from the slip of paper. Her cursory glance swept past him to the next customer fidgeting impatiently, waiting to be served. Stage one of his plan was complete.

*

So far it had been comparatively easy. Stage two would need careful timing and he needed vital information to ensure it would be fully effective. The membership computer of the North Pennine Health Scheme held the facts he required. First he needed to programme the computer to search through its records and produce a report.

A secret report... for his eyes alone!

Good computer housekeeping requires a daily back up, the copying by a company of its files on a regular basis onto magnetic tape. The alternative is to risk losing vital information. A sudden power surge, a power loss, even a thunderstorm can cause a computer to crash and wipe its memory clean.

Just as likely is the possibility of an inexperienced operator accidentally deleting data, or worse, a vindictive employee, given the opportunity, can create havoc.

The database of the scheme changed rapidly. Volatile is the word that comes to mind to describe it. On average some two hundred new members were recruited daily and half as many benefit claims were made, processed and paid out. With so much vital information at risk he had initiated a regular system of overnight copying of the files. It was his responsibility.

On the last working day of each month progress reports were produced. The practice was to close down all the computer's terminals early, carry out a security *backup* and then leave the system running overnight to produce the reports.

Carefully timed, at the next month's end, it would be a relatively simple matter to set running an additional terminal to search out the details his plan required. One more report amongst the dozen or so he had to produce would pass unnoticed.

*

He chose the last day of June, which by good fortune fell on a Friday. Some computers take hours to produce long reports, especially when they have to search out information from a quarter of a million sources. But two clear days over a weekend allowed more than ample time for the search to be completed. On the following Monday he would make sure and be the first person to arrive at the Mansion House.

A young woman by the name of Molly nearly upset his carefully arranged applecart. She was nineteen years old, pretty in a plump-faced way and had developed an enormous schoolgirl crush of embarrassing proportions.

Oh Lord! He thought when he realised, *I'm as old as her father.*

It happened all too frequently and he had never found a way to handle it. Born with a natural empathy towards the fair sex, always considerate, always polite, exuding an unconscious charm of which he was scarcely aware, it took new female acquaintances time to appreciate that he treated *every* woman with the same thoughtful courtesy.

At 4pm on Friday the 30th June the girls logged out without a second thought as soon as he informed them he wished to run the

18

nightly backup. They spent the final seventy-five minutes of their working week completing menial tasks, tidying up and touching up their makeup. Then with a unanimous sigh of relief that another working week had drawn to a close, slipped on their coats, gathered up their handbags and happily rushed home. The one exception was Molly.

'Can I 'elp?' she asked, leaning over his shoulder in a haze of cheap perfume. Her generously proportioned breasts pressed against his body. He was very conscious of her presence. 'I don't mind staying on a bit… for you.'

'Erm…er…No! It's very kind of you to offer but… thank you Molly. I'll manage.'

'Are you sure?'

'Certain. Thank you all the same. Perhaps another time…?'

'Oh! I really don't mind.' Disappointment was thick in her voice. Her long lashes, heavy with mascara, hung down. Her fleshy shoulders slumped with the weight of dejection. Pure drama. An Oscar winning performance!

'Let me help you with your coat.' He held out her summer-weight jacket, his five foot eight inches stooping over her small dumpy figure. As she wriggled into the garment she leaned back, pressing unnecessarily against him and peeped coquettishly from under long dark lashes. With both hands upon her shoulders he turned her gently but firmly towards the door and guided her on her way.

'Goodbye, Molly. Have a nice weekend.' As the door closed behind her he let out a long sigh of relief. 'Phe-e-ew!'

*

An all-pervading silence descended upon the deserted Mansion House. Without fuss he logged into several terminals and using each one, set off a series of reports to run simultaneously. Multi-tasking was the computer jargon. Each terminal required an identity code and a password to allow him access. He used his own for the regular reports. To run the additional search he first created a new identity and entered a new password. With ironic humour he decided upon the letters – R.O.B.B.E.R.Y.

Then on the master terminal in his office and using the new identity and password he triggered the search for the vital information he required.

Satisfied there was nothing more to do he gave a final glance around his office, locked its door, checked the building was secure, its burglar alarm was set and left.

*

There was an unexpected mist on Monday morning which slowed his drive to work. He fretted at the delay and his driving lacked its customary caution. He pushed his luck to the limit driving faster than commonsense decreed to arrive early. A huge sigh of relief escaped his lips as he unlocked the ornate wrought iron gates of the car park, looked around, and found it empty. He was the first to arrive after all.

Over the weekend each terminal had completed its specific search, passed on the information to a spooler file and when the printer became available, produced its report. Impatiently he leafed through the stack of green-lined listing paper until he came to the extra report. Tearing carefully along the perforations he separated the pages he required, folded them into an A4 size and slipped them into a compartment of his briefcase. Later in the evening, in the sanctuary of his home, he planned to study them carefully. The report highlighted the date upon which the maximum number of members was due to pay their annual contributions to the scheme.

*

Contributory Health Schemes are an anachronism left over from an earlier century. They are a unique kind of business, invariably local in origin, yet they still provide a valuable service to less fortunate members of the community they serve. Without exception they are non-profit-making organisations granted charitable status by the Inland Revenue. The Directors of such schemes are part-timers, unpaid and all too frequently unappreciated. Although worthy, honest well-intentioned men and women, their management of the schemes all too frequently lacks professionalism.

The concept has always been that working people contribute a small amount from their wages each week to create a fund from which, when the need arose, financial help is available towards the cost of medical treatment. Old fashioned though the idea is, even in the nineteen nineties, tens of thousands of ordinary working-class men and women still benefit from their membership.

At the North Pennine Health Scheme Maxwell Bull had gradually changed the emphasis on contributions methods. It had not been easy but slowly and steadily over a period of three years one quarter of the scheme's membership had been persuaded to pay directly into the organisation by Direct Debit rather than by the traditional method of a deduction from their wage or salary. Seventy thousand working people now paid their dues this way.

The additional report showed that a large percentage of these members were due to make a *one-off* annual payment on the last working day of August. It would be the largest single transaction of the year. The amount due for transfer was £250,000.

The time to strike was now, when the fruit was ripe and ready for plucking!

It couldn't have fallen at a better time. With the summer holiday season at its peak, every department would be short of staff – particularly the accounts department. With good fortune on his side it would be late into September, possibly even October, before the shortfall was discovered. By which time he would have moved the money on from Maxwell Bull's fake account. It would vanish without trace!

August was a busy month. Recruitment to the scheme was at an all-time high. A vast backlog of work built up. Molly continued to flutter her long dark lashes and to drop hints about her availability. As the Sales graph soared so her neckline plunged ever lower. Both events set his pulses racing. He was delighted by the former but agitated by the latter. With the pressure of work increasing daily it became even less likely that his deception would be discovered until it was too late.

*

Every bank can be identified by its Sort Code. A Sort Code is made up of three pairs of numbers and they appear on the top right hand corner of cheques. A Sort Code is unique. It is possible by referring to a directory to look up the exact address and postal code of any bank that is listed. The membership computer held the account details of all the contributors who made their payments by cheque or Direct Debit. It also held the same information about the North Pennine Health Scheme's own bank account. This wasn't obvious to the casual operator. Access to such confidential information could only be obtained by entering the Systems Manager file. Entry was restricted to the privileged few given the password.

Once every month an extract programme was run to enable the contributions of its members to be transferred from their private accounts into that of the scheme. The information was transferred onto a twelve-inch magnetic tape, sealed in a special transit bag and sent by Data Post to the Bankers Automated Clearing System. (BACS). A processing date determines the day upon which the actual transfer of money takes place. The normal practice of the N.P.H.S. was to use the last working day of the month as the transfer date.

In August 1989 it fell on a Thursday. Once again it was a fortuitous occurrence.

His plan was to substitute the company's account number in the computer with that of the fake account number he had opened in the name of Maxwell Bull. Because he had deliberately used the company bank for both accounts they carried an identical Sort Code. The official account number of the North Pennine Health Scheme was 90127400 while the new bogus account number opened in the name of its Chief Executive read 90172408.

*

On Tuesday 29th of August he carried out an early security back-up so that overnight he could set the computer to create the debit transfer tape. Logging into the master terminal he selected the Systems Manager file and typed in his password. With access gained to the file it was a simple matter to amend the company's account number to the bogus one. He selected a brand new tape from a row neatly stacked in the computer room, mounted it onto the magnetic tape deck, set the density to 1600 bytes per inch and began the extract sequence. In the morning he would log back into the Systems Manager file, reset the account to its correct number and nobody would be any the wiser. When the tape was returned from the Bankers Automated Clearing System it would be used for the next security backup. Once written over and relabelled the evidence would be wiped clean. Gone forever... just like the money!

Driving home that evening he whistled happily, slightly out of tune with the song playing on his car radio, but who cared?

*

Monday was the critical day for the final stage of his plan. The danger day. The day most risky to himself when, posing as Maxwell Bull, he had to walk into the bank and draw out one quarter of a million pounds *in cash!*

The mere thought made him sweat with apprehension. *Keep calm. Keep calm.* He repeated to himself, *Think like Maxwell Bull. Act like him. Be like him.*

His mind raced in circles, turning over one idea after another. What reason could he give for so massive a cash withdrawal? Suddenly, from nowhere the answer came to him. Of late a fair percentage of the scheme's revenue had been channelled into the purchase of overseas property, investments in Spain and in France. Holiday apartments which would appreciate in value and earn the scheme revenue while doing so. He would intimate that he needed a large cash sum to bid at an auction for a similar place in England.

Tomorrow it would be Wednesday. He still had three clear days left to act. First thing in the morning he planned to telephone the bank and insist on speaking to the manager. The call was a calculated bluff for he was already aware that the man was on holiday. The likelihood was that his call would be transferred to the assistant manager, a man who would be less familiar with the voice of the real Maxwell Bull.

*

Sunrise on the 30th of August was at three minutes past six. He was awake long before that, out of bed, showered, shaved, dressed and on the road to the Mansion House well before seven.

It was yet another beautiful summer's day, a time of year he loved with all his heart. On a normal day his drive to work through the rolling fields of ripening wheat was a pleasure to be savoured, a time for quiet reflective thinking and planning before he plunged into the hurly-burly of his work.

Not so today.

Today his pulses raced as the adrenaline coursed through his body. Today he was walking a tightrope. He felt vibrant and fully alive. Living on the very edge!

His arrival was needlessly early. It took only a minute to log into the computer and reset the account number. Then he unloaded the completed tape, attached a blue gum-backed label with an identifying number, packed it into a protective bag and wrote out an instruction to the mailing clerk for it to be despatched forthwith, most urgent by Data Post.

A full hour passed before anyone else arrived in the office. It was usual for him to be in early. Without exception the rest of the staff regarded him as a workaholic, a loner, a solitary man whose work was his life and his life all work.

*

At nine-thirty he picked up the telephone, dialled the number of the bank and asked to be put through to the manager.

'I'm very sorry sir,' was the polite reply, 'He's on holiday. I can put you through to his deputy, Mr Baker.'

Good, he thought, and kept on repeating in his mind, *Think like Bull. Act like Bull. Be him.*

'Baker here.' a new voice on the phone spoke. *Maxwell Bull* coughed loudly into the mouthpiece, blasting the listener's eardrum. The man winced and held the hand piece away from his ear.

'Bull.' He barked by way of introduction, 'Now listen. I have arranged for a large sum of money to be transferred into my new account on Friday. Got it? Right! It's approximately two hundred and fifty thousand pounds. Did you get that? Two-Fifty Thousand. Right!' He gave another barking cough down the line.

'On Monday I will call in to collect it *personally. In cash.* Right! Cash.'

Baker was allowed little time to think and no time to question him as he hurried on with his instructions. 'The money will be transferred into my account by BACS on Monday morning. Is that clear? Be certain to have it ready on the dot. My account number is 90172408.' He repeated the number a second time, speaking slowly and distinctly so there would be no misunderstanding. '9 – 0 – 1 – 7 – 2 – 4 – 0 – 8 Have you got it?

'Erm... er... er?' The voice on the telephone sounded petrified.

'Baker. You bloody idiot.' He thundered down the phone, 'Are you still bloody there? You *do* understand my instruction … Yes?'

'Oh yes Mr Bull.' Baker hastened to reassure him, 'Most certainly Mr Bull. Eleven o'clock sharp, Monday morning. Two hundred and fifty thousand pounds will be ready… in cash. I fully understand.'

He replaced the receiver firmly and sat back. A long sigh escaped his lips as the tension escaped. That was it then. Everything set up. Just one final stage to go!

Chapter Four

Sergeant Edward Decker planned his day with precision. He spread out his road map on the kitchen table, much to the annoyance of his partner, Helen Argosy who was busily trying to serve breakfast, and plotted out his visits.

Most of the staff of the North Pennine Health Scheme lived within a tight radius of five miles from the Mansion House. But other employees, on the Sales and Managerial side, lived much further away. Martin Sellaney lived south of Nottingham, a journey of twenty-five to thirty miles from the village of Briseley T'ill. The former Claims and Membership Manager was the one he had been recommended to speak to by Rachel Bergen.

Another possible suspect on Decker's list, Harry Radge, one of the luckless accountants, also lived in the vicinity. *With a bit of luck,* the Sergeant mused, *I could combine both visits on the same day.*

'Do you think I could have the table back?' Helen Argosy asked with an edge to her voice, 'I *am* trying to serve breakfast.'

'Sorry! I'm so sorry!' the policeman apologised soothingly to the woman whose life he had shared for the last six months, 'I'm trying to work out the best way to interview all these people. There are so many of them.'

'I thought this case was cut and dried.' commented Helen, 'Didn't the powers that be decide the man committed suicide?'

'That *is* the general opinion, mainly influenced by the media.' Decker replied with cutting irony in his voice.

'But you know better?' she replied wryly. He grinned and parried the comment with a question of his own.

'Well! Personally, do you think Maxwell Bull was the type of man to kill himself?'

'But I barely knew him.' she protested, 'except through the media. There has always been a lot about him in the local press over the last two years.' She paused reflectively, a tiny frown wrinkled the clear smooth skin of her forehead, 'He seems to have a talent for being in the thick of it. Getting onto the front page. Maxwell Bull presenting a cheque to one charity or another. Maxwell Bull speaking on the local radio station or sponsoring the football team, appearing with a celebrity at the Rotary Club…And didn't he offer a job to that ridiculous ski-jumper, the one who always fell over and came a cropper. The salary quoted was quite ludicrous. But…Yes! I have to admit the man is - *was* a positive type of person. Hardly the sort one would expect to commit suicide.'

'Exactly.' Decker exclaimed with satisfaction, 'Your Honour, I rest my case.'

'Never mind your case. Just try resting your bum on that chair and get stuck into this lot.' Her oven-glove clad hands laid a sizzling hot breakfast of bacon, eggs, sausage, tomatoes and fried bread in front of him. 'I also have work to do,' she said, 'and the sooner you are out of my hair the better.'

*

Helen Argosy earned her bread and butter as the creator of a strip cartoon. Five days of every week she produced the on-going saga of "Winnie the White Witch". She used the pseudonym, H.A.G. derived from her own initials and her mother's maiden name: Gardner. Helen Argosy Gardner – HAG. It seemed appropriate.

Her ingenuity and inventiveness never ceased to amaze Edward Decker. He had lived with her for the best six months of his life, loving both her and her young son, Jason. They filled an aching void in his life at a time when he least expected it. Ted Decker was forty-seven yet felt twenty years younger than his age. Jason had recently turned seven while Helen herself was fast approaching thirty-two, an age at which she decreed she would stick (as in the game of Pontoon) and resolutely refuse to become one day older.

Jason's real father had been killed soon after the boy was conceived. The poor man had never even been aware that the young art student he had fallen in love with was pregnant. For six years Helen Argosy struggled alone, proud and independent, to survive and raise her son. Pure chance took her to the little Peak village of Briseley T'ill and fate decreed that she met Edward Decker at the scene of an accident.

'Ja-a- son!' Helen called upstairs to her son, 'It's on the table.'

'Com-ing Mum.' The boy's voice was high and piping like a flute. He suffered from a slight speech impediment, his "R's" came out like "W's" although Helen's repeated attempts to correct him were beginning to bear fruit.

'I don't know what he finds to do in that bathroom.' Helen complained, 'He's forever gazing in the mirror.

Decker was not too old to have forgotten his own childhood. 'He's either practising pulling funny faces or searching for his first whisker. When I was that age I spent hours trying to look like Stewart Granger.'

'Stewart Granger! Who was Stewart Granger?' Helen Argosy's tone implied that Decker's childhood idol pre-dated Methuselah.

'He was a film star. You *must* have heard of Stewart Granger. Why he buckled many a swash. Very dashing. Made a pile of films.'

'Name one.'

'Well! Er... there was er... er... Scara... er... Mooch...or something. And...er...er...'

'Unforgettable.' said Helen.

'Unforgettable? No. I can't remember that one.'

'Oh Ted! I mean *he* must have been unforgettable... all those incredible films you can't remember. Some film star!'

'He was... Honestly. He made lots of films. Costume dramas, that type of thing. With bags of action, leaping from balconies, swinging from chandeliers, lots of cut and thrust.' Decker made fencing movements across his breakfast plate. Defending his pork sausages from an imaginary attacker. Helen rolled her eyes in despair and called again to her son.

'Jason! Are *you* coming? Your breakfast will be stone cold if you don't come soon.' In answer to her plea there was the sudden sound of feet clattering down the steep narrow staircase from Jason's room on the top floor of the building. He burst into the room, bright-eyed, full of energy, intelligent. A dynamo, just seven-years of age.

It was the one time of day when they all ate together, a ritual close to Helen's heart. Whatever else happened, at least, they started every day as a family.

Conversation was always lively. Decker talked about his work, always providing it was not confidential. He treated the boy as an equal and frequently asked for his opinion. It was his way of teaching Jason to think for himself and encourage him to grow up in a responsible manner. Helen listened happily and liked to try out her ideas on the two men. She often based her storylines of Winnie the White Witch on real life events that cropped up in conversation.

From small beginnings the cartoon strip had grown in popularity. It made her financially secure and its success gave her a degree of self-confidence she had never dreamed possible.

*

After breakfast Decker set off on his investigations. Jason left for school, leaving Helen alone to deliberate upon the adventures of her creation. She tried to stay one week ahead of her publishing deadline so that there were always five episodes in the pipeline. A safeguard against misfortune.

Now there was interest from an American publisher. Her years of hard work were paying off. Winnie the White Witch and her magic conjured a promising future.

*

Martin Sellaney lived in a 'Neighbourhood Watch' area. There were signs indicating the fact strapped to every concrete lamp standard and stickers adhered to the front windows of all the houses.

Decker did not actually see any curtains twitch but he was soon made aware that eyes were watching him when, he was challenged by a very stout and fearsome lady. He had rung the bell, hammered on the door and tried to peer into the back windows of the Sellaney household. All to no avail.

'I have telephoned the police.' The large and officious woman warned him.

'I *am* the police.' He countered wearily. Even when he produced his warrant card the woman remained unconvinced and hovered expectantly until a young policeman in uniform drove up in a blue and white car with lights flashing.

'Sorry you've been called out,' Decker apologised to the fledgling officer, 'but I'm looking for a man by the name of Sellaney... Martin Sellaney. Do you know him?'

'Yeah! Know him well.' answered the other cheerily, 'You won't find him in until after lunch. He'll be at the Leisure Centre until noon. Does a bit of cricket coaching - schoolboys. He taught me.'

And not so very long ago, thought the Sergeant. Aloud he said, 'Damn!'

Frustration showed on his face.

'Can't be helped,' consoled the young officer, still being unbearably optimistic, 'Can it wait?' If looks withered, the officer would have curled up and turned black immediately.

*

Decker drove off angrily with a noisy crunching of gears. Henry Radge, former accountant to the North Pennine Health Scheme would have to be the one he interviewed first after all. There was a mental picture fixed in his mind of the route to the accountant's home. He found the house easily. It was located in an established but select area just off the ring road. The plots of land had been privately developed over a period of years. Every house and bungalow had been individually designed and stood proudly in its own grounds. The name of Harry Radge's house had been painted onto a crosscut of timber and mounted on the gatepost. It read, "Audit's End.'

Edward Decker smiled. Someone had an apt sense of humour.

He left his dark green Morris Minor parked on the tree-lined road and walked with scrunching footsteps up the gravelled drive. From a distance the house had looked impressive with its double fronted Mock Tudor gable ends, its bay windows with diamond shaped leaded lights and its inbuilt double garage. As the policeman drew closer to the building he became aware of the signs of neglect. Worn paint, like dead skin, peeling from the woodwork. Loose ridge tiles beginning to slip. Guttering that sagged and allowed water to drip down, staining the walls with unsightly green mould and a gate hanging askew with a twisted hinge. All was not as well as it appeared from a distance.

Decker rattled the heavy brass knocker of the solid oak door. The sound echoed eerily through the house and seemed to bounce back at him… but no one appeared.

Again he knocked and waited… and waited. Somewhere, in the near distance, he picked up the sound of an engine running. The policeman stepped back from the door and gazed searchingly at the upstairs windows. At one of them, obviously a bedroom, the curtains were still drawn. A quick glance at his wristwatch confirmed the time as ten o'clock. The occupant may be sick, he surmised, or just a very late riser.

Again he rattled the knocker, banging loud enough to wake the dead. But there was nothing. No one stirred. Two fresh bottles of milk rested on the doorstep and the empties had been collected. Someone must be up and about or why could he hear the sound of an engine running? The door of the double garage was the up and over type. Painted black in keeping with the mock Tudor style of the house. It had a central locking handle. He listened, head pressed close against the metal. The muffled sound of an engine ticking over came from within.

Madness! He thought, *Only a fool would run a car engine with the doors tight closed. Unless…?*

Frantically he tried the handle. Useless. The key had been turned. Perhaps there was another door? A side entrance? Anxious now he searched around the back of the house. There was a side door to the garage but that also was locked. But the top half of the door had a glass panel. He peered through dust and cobwebs to see a key sticking out on the inside. Decker cast around for something – anything – with which to break the glass. He picked up a lichen-covered boulder from the garden rockery and with a wild swing shattered a large jagged hole in the panel. Gingerly he reached through and turned the key. As he stepped through the door the car's engine coughed and spluttered, misfired twice… and died.

It had run out of petrol.

The air was thick with carbon monoxide fumes. Decker was far too late. The engine must have been running for hours. He flung the door wide to try and clear the air. Searched and found the keys in the ignition. A small Yale key fitted the central locking handle of the main door. The huge black barrier swung up easily and remained in position, held by its counterbalanced springs. With a draught blowing freely through the spacious garage the poisonous fumes soon thinned and cleared.

Decker was able to distinguish the figure of a man slumped in the rear seat of the car. His eyes were closed and he appeared to be sleeping peacefully… except for the colour of his skin. Blue tinged. Cyanosed.

Decker's car did not have a radio transmitter. It was his personal vehicle. There had been times when he blessed the lack of communication, for it afforded him a degree of independence and privacy, but not now.

Telephone wires lead to the house. Another of the keys on the ring from the ignition fitted an internal door which lead directly into the house. He went through and found himself in the hall. A telephone rested upon an elegant semi-circular rosewood table. To Decker's intense annoyance the only sound from the receiver was a continuous drawn out tone.

God damn it! Disconnected.

Random four-letter words formed in his mind. Remained unuttered. It was no time for wasted effort. He thought about the drawn curtains and pounded up the staircase leaving gritty footmarks on the creamy white carpet. The bedroom was at the front of the house and he crashed into the room fearing the worst.

A middle-aged woman lay in the centre of a king-sized bed. Her head was back. Her mouth wide open, the loud sound of stertorous breathing filled the room.

Decker sighed with relief. He had half expected to find another body. The woman was in a very deep sleep. Probably drugged, but undoubtedly still alive. Her skin was a natural colour and her pulse, when the policeman found it, was strong and regular.

His immediate concern was to find a telephone that worked and alert the local police. He drew apart the bedroom curtains and peered out, trying to locate a public telephone box. It was futile for too many trees obscured his view. Then he had a stroke of luck and spotted a postman cycling down the road. Better still the postman slowed down and swung in through the open gates to deliver a letter to Audit's End.

Decker scampered down the stairs and opened the heavy oak door upon an astonished postman as he was in the act of bending down to thrust a brown manila envelope through the low level letterbox.

'Phew! You're keen.' ejaculated the ruddy-faced man, 'Don't know why they 'as ter make cruddy doors wi' letterboxes so close to the cruddy ground do you? Just about breaks my bloody back it do. 'Ello! Oo the 'ell are you?'

'Police.' Decker explained briefly and showed the man his warrant card. 'Quick! I need help. Where's the nearest phone box?'

'Erm...' The astonished postman thought for a moment, 'Up the road, about two 'unnerd yards. Eh! Whatsup?'

'Accident.' The sergeant pressed him into service, 'Stay here. Don't let anyone in. Okay?' He left the man gaping open-mouthed after him as he sprinted up the road to make his call.

B.T. had installed one of its new glass-panelled booths which accepted phone cards. An innovation that was totally new to the policeman. Briseley T'ill, still in a time warp, lagged behind the rest of the nation and, as yet, still managed to cling to its old fashioned red box. Progress was due to reach the tiny Peak village any day.

Carefully and deliberately Decker pressed the 999 to make his emergency call. 'Police.' He answered in reply to the question of which service. He gave his name and brief details of the tragedy before setting off back to the house.

The postman sat slumped on the doorstep, his head bent down between his knees and his bicycle propped against the wall. There was a greenish hue about the gills.

'Is 'e dead?' he asked as he looked up. His head nodded, seeking confirmation, in the direction of the garage.

'As mutton.' Decker replied in a matter of fact voice, 'You didn't touch anything?'

'Me! Not on your cruddy life. Poor bugger. It's 'Arry Radge y'know. Aint surprised... seen it coming I 'ave. Suicide was it?'

'Looks like it.' The postman was an even bigger stroke of luck than Decker had first thought. He asked, 'Radge, did you know him well?'

'Naw! Bin on this round about three years now. Loads of letters at first, tailed off a bit lately. Poor bugger...all them rejection letters. Enough ter grind any bugger down. ''E wor out o' work y'know. Yer gets ter see a lot, being on same round like, gets ter recognise the signs... and the letters turnin' y'down.'

'How's that?' asked the policeman.

'How? S'easy.' he shrugged, 'Second class stamp, plain brown envelope wi' just a single sheet of paper in it. S'orl it takes to shatter a man's dreams.'

*

It was obvious. It's a hard world for the unemployed, especially so for an aging accountant, a man who had enjoyed an affluent lifestyle before sinking into the trough of despair. The recession had hammered even the professions this time around and, oddly, they did not possess the resilience of the working classes who were far more familiar with summary dismissal.

Decker knew from the records faithfully copied into his notebook that Harry Radge had been forty-nine years of age at the time he had been so abruptly sacked. That had been in 1986 and the evidence all around indicated that the man had been unable to secure another position. The neglected paintwork, the gate lacking repair, the dangerously loose ridge tiles and the guttering sagging alarmingly from the once elegant Tudor house. All bore the symptoms of reduced circumstances.

Police Sergeant Decker had never been unemployed, but he *had* seen its effect upon other people. He'd noted the slow erosion of their confidence, the sad disintegration of their character and the debilitating sapping of their energy. He could easily imagine the anger and resentment building up inside a man like Harry Radge.

Enough to commit murder…?

'Can I go?' asked the postman, looking anxiously at his watch, 'I'm getting behind wi' me round.'

'Oh! Sorry. Yes, of course. Thanks for your help.' He watched the man pedal steadily away. His blue and red waterproof flapping in the fresh January breeze.

*

Two suicides was too much of a coincidence, ran Decker's thoughts, *Two suicides?… or one murder and one suicide? Or could it be a case of two murders? Murder made to look like suicide? Mmm… Perhaps not!* He dismissed the thought. Better check on the sleeping woman. The living came before the dead and there was nothing he could do for Harry Radge.

He re-entered the house, this time carefully wiping his feet on the mat. Unable to see anything particularly unusual downstairs he made his way back to the bedroom where the sleeping woman lay. From the window he had a clear view of the drive and would easily see anyone arriving. There was a photograph upon the dressing table, a picture of the late Harry Radge and his wife: a happy picture of a smiling couple. Decker compared the features of the sleeping woman with the face in the photograph. Without a doubt it was the same woman. Across the bottom of the print she had written, "Harry and I – Torquay 1985". Although middle-aged, the face of the woman was round and full, with attractive auburn hair and laughing eyes. Now the fullness of her features had disappeared, they were gaunt and sallow looking. Even in repose worry lines creased her forehead. He guessed she must be some twenty pounds lighter now than when the lens shutter had closed.

On the bedside table stood an empty tumbler with a misty white coating on the inside. Probably milk, decided Decker, a bedtime drink to wash down the Mogodon tablets contained in the bottle alongside the glass. A gritty residue at the bottom of the glass encouraged the policeman to believe that very likely Radge had crushed an extra tablet into his wife's drink. He had wanted her to be sound asleep when he went out into the garage for the very last time.

The poor man, how desperate he must have been and yet he still tried to show consideration for his wife. There are many ways to commit suicide, some incredibly messy, but at least Harry Radge had chosen one of the less unpleasant ways to die.

Reason argued that the late accountant would also have left a note if he really had committed suicide. Such men are trained to be organised and orderly.

It was easy to find. Harry Radge had left the note where his wife was certain to find it, in the top drawer of her dressing table, lying face up on the fresh underclothes she was due to wear. The letter was in an unsealed envelope and addressed to Iona.

Iona?   What a lovely unusual name. thought Decker, *Iona Radge?*

He wondered what her maiden name had been, something a lot more exciting than Radge. Iona, wasn't that an island where Scottish kings were reputed to have been buried? She deserved a better surname, one with a fine ring to it, say MacLaren … or MacDougal. Iona MacDougal? Now that *did* have a fine Scots ring.

No doubt Forensic would want to examine the letter in minute detail. Check its authenticity. Days could go by before he had the opportunity to learn its contents… if ever. Would anyone find out if he looked?

He looked.

Only an accountant could have put together such a letter. Have written it in small neat handwriting. Such tiny script. So clear and so precise, the most explicit document Edward Decker had ever read.

It set out in minute detail all the couples' assets and what they were currently worth. Suggested to his wife, ways and means through which she could realise their full value and the most sensible manner in which she might invest the proceeds to ensure for herself an income. 'Sorry my darling,' Harry Radge had written, 'You deserve so very much better than I have been able to provide. Goodbye my one and only love until we meet again in Heaven.'

Feeling acutely uncomfortable, Decker returned the letter to its envelope and replaced it back on top of the underclothes. Let the local police find it and draw their own conclusions. It wasn't his investigation or the reason he had come to talk to Harry Radge.

*

The response to Decker's emergency call took ten minutes. Pretty fair taking into account the volume of traffic on the city's roads. Two police cars with flashing lights turned into the drive and came to a skidding halt on the loose gravel surface. Thirty seconds later an ambulance followed suit, its doors flying open almost before it ground to a halt. Two yellow-jacketed paramedics leapt out. One headed towards the open garage door and the other made towards the house.

*

'You're the one who discovered the body?' A keen-eyed young Inspector asked Decker. She made the question sound like an accusation, her fierce blue eyes boring into him. *About twenty-eight,* he decided mentally, *Younger than Helen in years, a century older in experience. Tough and uncompromising.*

'Sergeant Decker,' he replied coolly, nodding in the affirmative, 'Yes, for my sins, I *am* the one who discovered the body.' He handed his warrant card to the young Inspector who regarded it with suspicion and handled it as though at any moment it would explode.

'You're not local.' another accusation, 'What are you doing here?'

'I came to see Harry Radge,' explained a bemused Decker. It was a strange feeling being questioned as though he were a criminal, 'I never expected to find him dead – assuming the body in the garage *is* that of Harry Radge. I've never met him before.'

'Is that Harry Radge?' The Inspector looked around at her fellow officers. Her question was met with vacant faces and nonchalant shrugs. No one, it appeared, knew the late Mr Radge. In Briseley T'ill Edward Decker knew just about everyone, as well as a very large percentage of the inhabitants of the surrounding eight or nine villages he was expected to police. Oh well! A city had a population running into millions. Just to be aware of the known villains was all one could expect.

'What were you after him for?' The Inspector turned her attention back to Decker, an underlying resentment at the invasion of her patch. 'What had he done?'

'Done? Nothing. Not as far as I'm aware. I wasn't *after* him, just called for a chat, that's all.'

'What about?' Suspicion still lingered in the fierce blue eyes. Unremitting hostility. *What a way to go through life,* mused Decker, *she could be an attractive woman if only she allowed her face to soften once in a while.*

'Money.' explained the policeman, 'Harry Radge used to be an accountant and I thought he might be able to give me some financial advice.'

'Huh! Accountant eh!' The Inspector's grunt was scornful. Her eyes swept around the neglected house absorbing its dejected state. 'I wouldn't say his opinion is worth much right now. Would you?'

'Erm … No!' replied Decker dryly, 'Not now that he's dead.'

Thinking about the advice Nigel Rowthorne had given him Decker decided to keep the real reason for his visit to himself.

The two yellow-jacketed paramedics carried the unconscious body of Iona Radge down the staircase with practised skill, through the hall and into the waiting ambulance. Only Decker showed concern.

'How is she?' he asked the nearest paramedic.

'She seem alright.' the man replied, nodding as he spoke, 'Probably a few too many sleeping pills… otherwise there doesn't seem much wrong with her. I expect they'll keep her in overnight for observation.'

'Where will that be?'

'The Queen's Med. You know, where they treated Prince Charles.' There was justifiable pride in the young paramedic's voice as he answered Decker's question.

Mrs Iona Radge would be in good caring hands.

A young W.P.C. followed the stretcher into the rear of the ambulance. Its doors closed and the vehicle sped away around the ring road in the direction of the hospital.

'If there's nothing further I'll be on my way.' Sergeant Decker told the Inspector. 'Your sergeant can expect my statement in the post. First thing tomorrow okay?'

'Uh-uh!' She grunted a reply, eyes noncommittal, looking through him as though he was invisible. Decker smiled forgivingly and permitted himself a mild riposte.

'Morning Ma'am,' nodding cheerily, 'Just as well we're all on the same side... Eh!'

Chapter Five.

11:30am. The morning had flown by and it seemed that he had very little to show for it. He wondered how much Iona Radge would be able to tell him. From his observations they had been a close-knit couple, but an awful lot of men refused to discuss their working life with their wives. Give her a couple of days to recover, he told himself, then call around to offer his sympathy and listen to her chatter.

A blue Fiesta was parked in Martin Sellaney's drive. *Good,* thought Decker, *This time his quarry was at home. Mrs Neighbourhood Watch would have nothing to report.* He parked his Morris clear of the drive and rang the bell.

The man who opened the door couldn't possibly be Martin Sellaney was the policeman's first judgement. He was around five feet eight tall, lean built and wiry looking. Even in the middle of January there was a healthy outdoor glow to his cheeks. He had the whippet-taut frame of an athlete.

'Mr Sellaney, Mr Martin Sellaney?'

'Yes. Can I help you?' The response was friendly and relaxed. Not a hint of tension, just an open honest face. The greatest asset a criminal could have...!

'Decker, Sergeant Edward Decker. May I come in?'

'By all means.' The friendly smile did not falter and a welcoming hand waved him towards the kitchen. 'In here, it's warmer. If you will excuse me, I'm just about to have a bite to eat.' The smell of a toasted cheese sandwich filled the kitchen. It was a pleasant room, light and airy with panelled walls in varnished pinewood and a suspended ceiling to conceal the strip lighting.

Martin Sellaney perched his slim bottom on a matching pinewood stool drawn up to the breakfast bar. 'Take a pew.' He waved a casual hand in the direction of a second stool, took it for granted that Decker would accept, then swivelled ninety degrees to reach and plug in an electric kettle. 'Tea or Coffee? Take your pick.'

'Umm... Tea, milk, no sugar.' decided the policeman, 'Thank you.'

' No probs.' replied Sellaney breezily, 'Now what can I do for you?'

'A lady by the name of Rachel Bergen suggested that you would be a good person to talk to,' began Decker, carefully watching his man's face. 'She seemed to think you would know the answers to my questions.'

'Rachel?' Mild surprise showed on Martin Sellaney's face. His eyebrows lifted slightly and a tender look of affection crossed his features. 'Well! It depends upon what your questions are about. Ask away.'

'Rachel Bergen... is she a close friend of yours?'

'No. Just a former working colleague.'

'Nothing more?' pressed Decker, following his instincts.

'Again. No. She was a *working* colleague and a good one. There was a time when I thought we might become more than that... but nothing came of it.'

'Oh! Why was that?'

'Difficult to say really. I'm a fairly shy person when it comes to women, a bit on the slow side. I suppose I missed my chance. No one to blame except myself. And... erm... Well! She's a very private person. I was never quite sure how she felt about me. I didn't want to make a fool of myself. You know what they say, "There's no fool like an old fool." I didn't want to appear an old fool.

Edward Decker sympathised with the man. Until he had come to know Helen Argosy about nine months ago, he had been a lot like that himself. Sellaney's manner struck a familiar chord.

Sudden concern showed on the man's face, 'She's alright... isn't she? Has there been an accident?'

'No! No! Nothing like that.' the Sergeant hastened to reassure him, 'She was fine when I spoke to her yesterday. That isn't what I'm here about at all. It's to do with the late Maxwell Bull, former Chief Executive of the North Pennine Health Scheme.'

A rapid change of expression swept across the man's face. It was as though a cold bleak wind had blown across the surface of a lake, disturbing the surface, turning it into a dark and violent place. One moment it had been calm, still and beautiful, then a moment later its surface turned to a squall of angry chopping waves.

'Him!' Sellaney spat out the word with a wealth of scorn, 'I can tell you a lot about him... and none of it good. Anyway he's dead now. One should not speak ill of the dead, or so they say, but there's a fearful lot of people I can name who would find it hard to think anything else about Mister Maxwell bloody Bull.'

'I take it that you didn't like him?'

'You can say that again.'

'Can I ask why?'

'Why? Huh! How many days have you got to spare?'

'Just a few.' replied Decker casually.

Martin Sellaney's anger went as quickly as it had appeared. The waters of the lake became smooth and calm again. He visibly relaxed and remarked, 'Anyway, why should I worry about him? It's all in the past. Besides, I can only spare you an hour or so. I have another coaching session due at two o'clock. It's at Trent Bridge.'

'Trent Bridge?' the policeman looked surprised, 'I assumed you were a football coach? It being winter.'

'Nah! Cricket's my sport, the indoor variety at this time of year. I coach schoolboys mostly, from about the age of eight or nine. It's the best age to catch them. I love it. Great fun. Keeps me fit and young at heart.'

A wide grin spread across Martin Sellaney's face. He looked very boyish. Very fit. In fact disgustingly healthy for a man supposedly retired on the grounds of ill health.

'In your records, at the Mansion House, it indicates that you took early retirement due to poor health?' Decker's eyes swept the man from head to foot and back again. 'I must say you look remarkably fit to me. In fact a darn sight fitter than I am.'

'Is that how he explained my departure?' remarked Sellaney, an ironic smile playing about his mouth, 'I'm not one bit surprised. It's a typical Bull ploy. Just what I would expect, he wouldn't know the truth if it bit him.'

'If you resented the man so much then why did you stay?' asked the Sergeant, 'I mean, five years, it's a long time to work for a man you despised.'

'Too long! You're right of course. I suppose to an outsider it doesn't make much sense. But, put simply, I loved my job and for the most part I got on well and liked the people I worked with. It *is* a good scheme. Excellent in fact and it benefits so many deserving people. It's hard to explain and perhaps the only answer I can give is, job satisfaction. Does that make sense?'

41

It did to Ted Decker. He knew many to whom it would not; people who worshipped money, those who measured success by the size of their bank account. To them job satisfaction only related to the salary they were able to command.

'I'm a member of the North Pennine Health Scheme myself,' explained the policeman, 'And, from what I read in the local press and the scheme's own magazine, Maxwell Bull was very highly thought of, a very successful Chief Executive. He was always making donations to charity as well as supporting worthy causes. And didn't the organisation make enormous progress under his leadership?'

'On the face of it… Yes.' replied Sellaney, nodding his head in agreement as he spoke, 'that's because Bull made certain that the only facts ever to be published were his successes, or rather those of the scheme. To him it was one and the same thing. Maxwell Bull could do no wrong. *He* said so. And whenever there was a foul-up, he always found a convenient scapegoat. Some other poor sod would pay the penalty. I should know… *I was one of them.*'

'Have there been many mistakes?' asked Decker, probing gently.

'Too right there have,' exploded the former manager, 'You wouldn't believe some of the stupid errors of judgement that man has made, and like I say, every time he laid the blame on some other poor bastard's shoulders. That is why, when I first began to realise what Bull was like, I started to write a list of all the disasters that occurred. His version of them… and what *really* happened.'

Decker thought quietly for a few moments before asking, 'Alright, assuming that what you say is true, then how did he manage to get away with it for so long? After all, he must have been responsible to a Board of Directors… Yes? Didn't *they* want to know what was going on? Surely they must have suspected what he was like?'

Martin Sellaney nibbled on his toasted cheese sandwich while he thought about his answer. He chewed slowly, masticating every bite before washing down his simple meal with sips of hot coffee. 'Quite obviously,' he said with deliberation, 'You never met Maxwell Bull in person. It's hard to convey the power of his personality. It was overpowering. He came at you like a tank. Rolled right over people. Crushed you into the ground. No one, but no one, was allowed to voice an opinion unless it agreed with his own. All he ever wanted around him was "Yes-men". If any one crossed him, that was it, on your way matey. Out! That was the Maxwell Bull his employees saw.' Sellaney shook his head in dismay at the long list of departed souls. 'Then of course there was another Maxwell Bull, the one seen by the Directors. The man was a consummate actor. You wouldn't believe the difference, wouldn't credit that it was the same man. He was charming, attentive and considerate. Ha! He would listen to everything they had to say, appear to agree with them and then turn on the silky charm. Persuasion, you don't know the meaning of the word until you have listened to Maxwell Bull. I have to hand it to him, he is, *was*, a brilliant salesman. Positively brilliant!

He could sell ice cream to Eskimos and sand to an Arab. And, what is more, he'd convince them they were getting something special.'

'Mmm! But surely over a period of years...?' Decker needed to be convinced, 'They must have had their doubts, suspicions?'

Martin Sellaney shook his head emphatically and continued with his explanation.

'What you have to appreciate is that the North Pennine Health Scheme isn't like a normal company. Okay, it has Directors, but they are only part-timers. At the most the Board only meets four times a year. And the only information they heard was what Maxwell Bull *wanted* them to hear... and *that* wasn't much.

'Don't get me wrong,' Sellaney hastened to add, 'The Directors were, *are*, genuine people... but *not* businessmen. For the most part they are retired medical people, a couple of elderly doctors, a retired nurse, a welfare officer from one of the member groups. They are people who look upon the scheme as a good cause. A lot of the time they have no idea *how* it is run. The nitty-gritty so to speak.'

Some doubt still showed on the policeman's face. Seen from the outside the North Pennine Health Scheme appeared as a successful organisation. Its membership continued to grow. Its range of benefits continued to expand. Its outward image became more widely known. A lot of intelligent people were members. Could all of them be mistaken? Surely not!

'Look!' blurted Martin Sellaney, 'you don't have to take *my* word for it. Ask around. Talk to other former employees. Find out for yourself. If you like I can give you a few names to contact. Harry Radge for one, and er… there is a woman by the name of Marianne Ortega, lives in the Lichfield area, she would be a good one to speak to. Maxwell Bull stitched her up good and proper.'

He broke off abruptly and glanced at the kitchen clock, turned back to the Sergeant with an apologetic face. 'I have to go now. Running out of time. Would you mind telling me what this is all about? I mean, Bull's dead isn't he? Suicide.'

'That was the general opinion… but I'm not so sure.' Decker replied speaking slowly, 'Do *you* think Maxwell Bull was the type to commit suicide? Honestly?'

. 'But! … It was in the papers. He…'Sellaney paused, looked pensive, 'No.' he said at length, 'No. You're right. He would not have taken his own life, never in a million years. Not a man with an ego as massive as his. What are you saying then, that it was an accident…?' He stared at Decker waiting for a reply. The Sergeant waited, staring back. Waiting for the penny to drop. Enlightenment came!

'Murder?' whispered Martin Sellaney slowly, 'You think he was murdered? Oh my God! Where does that put me?' Again Decker waited, his eyes watching.

'Me? … You think it was me?' His face suddenly changed, creased into a wide disbelieving smile, 'No! Not me Sergeant, I'm just not the type. Ask anyone.'

'I probably will.' replied the policeman, 'Just for starters, where were you at midnight on New Year's Eve?'

There was no hesitation. The reply came out immediately, without the need for thought. 'In bed. I was sound asleep in bed. I don't go in for all this New Year Celebration stuff. I was fast asleep.'

'Can you prove it?'

'Prove it? No, I don't suppose I can.' Sellaney's attitude showed a lack of serious concern, 'Can you prove I wasn't?' he replied.

*

Sitting in his little green Morris Minor, watching Martin Sellaney speed away to his coaching session, Decker considered the results of his morning's work. One man dead and the second just had to be considered as a prime suspect. He had the motive and possibly the opportunity. On top of that the only alibi he could offer was so feeble that it was hard to believe it was not true. A guilty man would surely think of something better.

From his attitude Martin Sellaney had seemed totally unconcerned. Was that because he was an innocent man... or was he a brilliant actor?

Chapter Six

Monday 4th September was the day of the final stage of his plan. At 10:30 he picked up the telephone and rang the assistant manager of the bank.

Think like Maxwell Bull, he told himself, *Believe who you are. YOU... ARE... HIM.*

'Baker!' he barked sharply into the mouthpiece, 'It's Bull. Just checking to ensure that everything is in order. Right?'

'Oh yes Mr Bull,' came the hasty reply, 'No problems. I have the money ready now. When you arrive at the bank, step into my office. It is to the right of the counter as you come in the door. With that amount of cash I thought it wise to hand it over in person, away from prying eyes. A sensible precaution I'm sure you will agree.'

There was a more confident sound to the assistant manager's voice than on the earlier occasion.

'Hrrrmph! Quite so, quite so.' He allowed just the faintest trace of praise to creep into the tone of his voice, 'Good man. Well done!' At such a crucial stage the last thing he wished to do was to antagonise the man. Most people responded to approval. Sometimes it over-ruled their judgement.

*

How to be in two places at once? That was the critical question. Of course it was impossible, but memories are never as accurate as people suppose. Just to create the impression that he was elsewhere at the time could be sufficient. When questioned at a later date, probably days, perhaps even weeks later, they'd remember he was occupied somewhere else... and that could be sufficient to cause confusion.

He picked up the phone again and dialled an internal number. 'Charles,' he purred in his own quiet persuasive voice, 'I've got a damned annoying rattle developed on my car. Can't track it down. Thought I'd pop it into the garage for an hour or two to see if they can sort it out. Can you spare a body to pick me up? Say at about 11:15... 11:30ish?' He knew only too well that in an organisation as small as the Health Scheme there were few members of staff who could be spared, that in all probability it would be Charles Chapling himself who offered to collect him.

'Erm...erm...' He pictured the accountant casting an eye around his meagre staff, two women and a young man. 'Sorry, 'fraid they're all busy. End of the month you know. Have you asked Rachel? She may have someone free.'

'Already tried. No luck. Most of her staff are on holiday, and the rest can't drive'

'Erm... er... Oh all right then. I'll pick you up myself.'

'You will. Magic! Thank you Charles. I owe you one. See you about 11:30 then.' And with that he rang off, a little smile of satisfaction lurking at the corners of his mouth at the success of his ploy. Now it was all down to timing. To timing, a modicum of good fortune and a lot of nerve.

'Molly.' He called out, 'Have you got a minute?'

She slipped into his office eagerly, leaving behind a trail of raised eyebrows and suggestive expressions on the faces of her colleagues. Of late her eyes had followed him around with a sad resigned expression in them. Now they sparkled with anticipation.

'You wanted me.' She stated the obvious with breathy longing.

'Ah! Yes Molly. I have a job for you. I have to go out for a while to take my car to the garage. Mr Chapling is picking me up so I'll be about three quarters of an hour. What we need to do is sort out some of the old claims files, up until the end of February '89, and transfer them into the archives. If you'll make a start while I'm away I'd appreciate it. When I return we can move them downstairs together. Is that all right? ' He smiled as he asked the favour, opening his eyes wide in a disarming ingenuous look. There was only a moment of hesitation before she agreed.

*

Part of the cellars of the old Mansion House had been converted into a capacious vault, a gloomy claustrophobic place with no windows, thick walls of reinforced concrete, dim lighting and a heavy steel-plated door with a sturdy five-lever lock. Very few members of staff ventured there. It was a depressing place to

47

work, yet dry and secure, ideal for the storage of the mass of documents which the scheme's operation generated.

Inside the massive vault stood the company safe. It had a peculiar old key that split into two halves. For security reasons he kept one half of the key and the other half was retained by the Company accountant, Charles Chapling. What Chapling was unaware of was that he had a duplicate of the key section held by the accountant. He had retained it after finding it by accident tucked away in a remote drawer of the desk he'd inherited when he joined the organisation.

The remainder of the vault was sectioned off by rack upon rack of Dexion shelving. Here were stored thousands upon thousands of membership forms, copies of authority to deduct money from the pay or salary of its members, Direct Debit forms to authorise the transfer of payments, and, in a separate section of its own, sealed in archive bags, the original claim forms dating back over a six year period.

This was the place to which he and Molly would transfer the claim forms when he returned from his trip to the garage. It was a quiet and secretive place and it was here where, unseen and undisturbed, he planned to make a mild pass at the voluptuous young woman. A harmless grapple in the dark. A stolen kiss. A mild flirtation to ensure she remembered his whereabouts at that time and on that particular day.

*

On his way out of the Mansion House he spoke to the girl on the reception desk, brushing aside the need to sign out in the staff book she maintained religiously.

'Just popping my car to the garage Jane.' he said, 'Back in a few minutes. Charles will pick me up. Should anyone want me, take a message. I'll ring them back. OK?'

Jane was tied up on the switchboard and simply nodded in understanding. He peered briefly at the open book and noticed with relief that it showed Maxwell Bull to be out for the day, not expected back until the following morning.

Good. It couldn't be better.

*

A few seconds before 11am he drove into the car park at the rear of the bank. There was no one about, just lines of empty cars parked in the bays. The special shoes with their elevated heels were tucked under the driver's seat. It took only a moment to change into them and tie the laces with trembling fingers. On the rear seat a large suitcase lay containing the wig of dark hair and the padded Oxfam raincoat. He leaned towards the driving mirror, taking care to ensure the wig fitted snugly. With his fingers he coaxed the lock of false hair to fall across his forehead. The general appearance of the wig had a vaguely *Beetles* look, but lacking the distinctive fringe. The style was almost identical to the one affected by the Chief Executive.

He eased himself out of the car, took the raincoat from the suitcase and slipped it on, wriggling his shoulders into the garment and smoothing out any bulges caused by the additional padding between the inner removable lining and the waterproof outer layer of the raincoat. A glance at his reflection in the side window confirmed the natural look of his disguise. He added one final touch, a pair of square-framed glasses although neither Bull nor himself needed to wear spectacles. The assistant manager of the bank was not to know and later, when he came to describe the man he believed to be Maxwell Bull, it would add to the confusion.

Calmly he walked into the building and through the swing doors. There was the office door to the right of the counter. A name on the wooden placard read; David Baker – Assistant Manager. He nodded towards the girl on the reception desk. Mouthed the words, 'Appointment, eleven o'clock.' His knuckles rapped sharply on the woodwork. *Think Maxwell Bull,* whispered his brain, *be him. Now!*

He burst into the office with the subtlety of a Sherman tank.

'Baker!' he barked, 'Bull. No time to delay. Vital appointment to keep. Everything ready? Yes!'

The man behind the desk sprang to his feet. A nervous stammer impeded his speech. 'C-c-certainly Mr B-B-Bull. If y-y-you will just s-s-sign the receipt.' He pushed a ballpoint pen towards him, 'Here and h-here.' Indicating places upon the acknowledgement form where a signature was required.

Maxwell Bull ignored the offered pen. Without fail he always signed his name in black ink using an expensive fountain pen with a broad gold-plated nib. It was as much the man's trademark as were the flamboyant strokes with which he signed the document. The down strokes thick and strong, the rising ones lighter, finer and extravagant. The pen glided across the paper without a trace of hesitation… or error. It was as good a forgery as one could hope to achieve.

Two hundred and fifty thousand pounds in crisp new notes lay before him. It was the largest single sum of money he'd ever seen in his entire life. For a brief moment he hesitated. Then Baker snapped the case shut, secured its catches and slid it across the desk. 'There you are sir. I hope your transaction goes well.'

'Transaction? … Ah! Yes. The transaction. Yes indeed. Thank you. Thank you.' Maxwell Bull gave a curt nod that passed as appreciation and turned to leave. The case was unexpectedly heavy and pulled him off balance. He stumbled slightly because of the elevated shoes. Pulled up sharply, recovered his poise and adjusting his balance made towards the door.

There was a sudden rush of feet as David Baker charged past him towards the door. A cold hand seemed to grip at his heart. Had his deception been discovered? But all Baker did was to fling the door wide and give a little bob of acknowledgement as he bid his visitor a courteous farewell.

'Good day sir.' He ushered the bank's client and a quarter of a million pounds on their way with an inward sigh of relief, thankful that all had proceeded so well.

If only he had guessed the truth.

*

11:05am. Was that really the time? The minutes he'd spent in the bank had seemed like eternity. As though time itself had deliberately slowed to taunt him and stretch his nerves to breaking point. He was back in the car park moving towards his car. Another customer edged his way out, reversing cautiously into the main road. There was no one else about. Excellent. He unlocked his vehicle and transferred the large suitcase from the rear seat into the boot. Screened by its upraised lid he quickly removed the padded raincoat, folded it neatly and packed it away with the thick dark wig at one end of the case. There was sufficient space left for the case of money to fit, crosswise, in with the wig and raincoat. He slid the elevated shoes back under the driver's seat, sighing with relief to feel the comfort of his size eight casuals again.

Just five minutes later he turned the nose of his car into the forecourt of Bladen's garage and sought out the receptionist. Charles Chapling arrived as he was in the middle of describing the imaginary rattle.

'Don't 'e worry sir,' the grizzled elderly mechanic assured him, 'We'll soon 'ave 'er fixed. Sounds ter me like a loose engine mounting.' He noticed the new arrival, 'Mornin' Mr Chapling.'

'Good morning Bert.' The accountant greeted him, 'About ready?'

'Yes. Thanks for coming. Very good of you Charles.' He turned towards the grizzled grease-smudged Bert. 'Ready about five? Ok, I'll just transfer my suitcase into Mr Chapling's car then it's all yours. See you later Bert.'

*

They were back at the Mansion House by 11:20am. Jane was still on the telephone brightly projecting a caring image to all who called. She nodded acknowledgement of their return, signalled that there had been no special messages, murmured soothing platitudes into the ear of a distraught member and transferred calls briskly and calmly, all with an air of smooth untroubled efficiency.

He waited by the desk, watching as the accountant bounded up the wide sweeping staircase to his office on the first floor. *He's a good and decent man, Charles Chapling,* he decided, *but weak, lacking the strength of character to stand up to a bully as powerful as Maxwell Bull.* Chapling was one who would put his wife and children first, who thought about his home, the size of his mortgage... and diplomatically agreed with every decision the Chief Executive made.

'Back again Jane.' He commented needlessly when the receptionist was finally free, 'Should I be needed in the next hour I'll be downstairs in the vault. Molly and I have work to do sorting out files and moving them into the archives. I'll let you know when we are finished.'

'Ugh! Sooner you than me,' the girl remarked with a shudder, 'It's like a morgue down there.' There was respect in her voice. They had worked together for the last five years, ever since she

51

had joined the company on a YTS placement at the age of sixteen. Jane had been his first recruit, developing from a shy and awkward teenager into a mature and competent young woman. In part, her growing confidence had been his doing, the seeds of his trust ripening into fruition.

*

The décolletage of Molly's summer dress seemed to have slipped lower than he remembered. Her full round figure leapt out to greet his started gaze. *Surely,* he thought, *there had been many more buttons down the front of her frock earlier in the day... hadn't there?* Doubts about the wisdom of his strategy began to grow.

Behind his back the other three young women who worked in his department exchanged knowing looks. They winked encouragement at the nineteen year-old and jerk their thumbs heavenwards in gleeful support. *Good for Molly. She would enlighten the old prude with more than he'd bargained for, wouldn't she?*

It wasn't that they bore him any ill will. Quite the contrary, over the years each one in turn had been attracted to him. It was just that he was so prudish. So correct. So aloof and *always* so polite. He was never anything but courteous. It was like he was trapped in a strait jacket of political correctness. And what kind of girl, they asked themselves, wanted that. Just what *did* a girl have to do?

*

In the Claims and Membership office it was warm and pleasant. The sun shone through its south-facing windows from mid-morning onwards so that even in early September, summer dresses were the order of the day. In sharp contrast a penetrating chill persisted in the gloomy recesses of the vault. Heating had never been installed in the windowless room. A triangular wedge of wood held ajar the massive steel-plated door. It could only be locked or opened from the outside, a fact that caused him no little concern. From early childhood a morbid fear of being trapped in confined spaces had haunted him.

Side by side they worked steadily. Molly, neatly packing each day's claim forms, doctor's notes and receipted accounts into the stiff brown archive bags. She secured the mouth of each one with a drawstring and tied the knot with a double bow, then passed it on to be labelled with a black marker pen: the day, the month and the year.

The chill air struck through the thin material of Molly's summer dress. With grim determination she gritted her teeth and suppressed a shiver as she stored the bags in strict chronological order along the racks of Dexion shelving.

The space between the rows of shelving was limited and Molly took full advantage of the fact, squeezing past him time and time again in the confined area. With each pass she pressed closer than was necessary, brushing the softness of her body against his back, his bare arms and his chest. Despite his self-control feelings of desire began to grow. His pulse raced as his heartbeats increased. There was a catch in his breathing and his concentration faltered. It was with a sigh of relief that he labelled the last of the archive bags, inking in the letters with the thick black marker pen. He turned to pass the final bag, stopped and gazed with an open mouth. It couldn't be his imagination working overtime. It was for real; the front of Molly's dress gaped open almost to her waist. Buttons popping like Champagne corks. Her face was strangely pale, as white and ethereal as a ghost in the dim lighting of the vault. A determined ghost, one not to be denied…

'Molly…?' he asked uncertainly, 'Are you alright?'

'C-cold.' she replied through chattering teeth, 'F-f-frozen!'

'Oh my dear.' A sudden rush of sympathy overwhelmed his commonsense, 'Here, let me warm you.' He opened his arms and enveloped her against the warmth of his body. Pressed his mouth down upon the top of her head in a kiss of contrition.

Too late he realised his mistake.

Now his body was trembling… and it wasn't from the chill in the air. Molly's arms slipped around his waist, gripped him with a strength he found hard to believe. He tried to slip away, edging sideways with his back pressed against the shelving. A space between the rows of Dexion caused him to stagger and fall backwards. Now he was really trapped. His back pressed hard against the wall, racks of shelving on either side like prison bars. The only way out was forward… and Molly's soft warm body blocked his escape route.

'O-o-oo! You crafty old devil,' she murmured in admiration, pressing her full generous breasts hard against his chest. Her lips fluttered across his face, teasing, nibbling at his neck and earlobes, triggering off urgent erotic messages to his brain. Despite himself he could feel his body beginning to respond.

Nimble fingers flipped undone the buttons of his shirt. Eager hands pushed aside the garment. All the Champagne corks must finally have popped for the front of Molly's dress flared wide and underneath... not a single stitch of clothing. There was nothing to separate their bodies. It was flesh on warm quivering flesh. Her full round breasts with the soft consistency of pink blancmange pressed against his trembling body. The nipples, hard as shotgun pellets, tormented him until his senses reeled. His hands, free from the command of his reeling mind, had developed a desire of their own. They flew to caress and touch her soft white creamy skin.

Flying fingers unbuckled his belt, slipped the catch on his waistband and worked their way down, hauling down the zip fastener of his trousers.

'Oh God Molly!' he managed to gasp out as finally his lips escaped from the vacuum suction of her mouth, 'W-What are you d-doing? ...What d-do you w-want?'

Her hands moved around his waist, slipped down inside his underpants, eased the waistband smoothly down over his slender buttocks. Darted to the front to complete their task.

'Oh my darling!' she murmured, her eyes enflamed with desire, 'Don't worry. Keep still. I know just what to do... and *exactly* what I want...'

Her hands found their objective... and his eyes bulged until they threatened to pop from their sockets!

Trapped. Oh God! He thought, *Now what? One thing at least was certain. Molly would not forget today.* And nor for that matter would he.

*

Secure once more in the sanctuary of his office he nibbled sandwiches. Head down. Newspaper up. The print a jumbled blur before his eyes. Even the headlines left little impression on his memory.

54

Oh Lord! ... That Molly... Je-esus but she was some go-er. She knew more at nineteen than he had learned in a lifetime. How his calculations had come unstuck. Never again, he vowed, never again. What would she do next? Anything? Today's generation didn't look at morality the way he had been taught it. Perhaps she would simply notch him up on her bedpost and forget him. Move on to someone else. He didn't like the idea of that.

It bruised his ego.

*

'C'mon Molly! Be a sport. Tell us what happened.' pleaded Sharon. Four young heads huddled together in a corner of the ladies toilet. Three pairs of eyes glistened with curiosity, eagerly demanding the details of Molly's romantic adventure. She played them like an angler plays a fish, luring them into her net of fantasy. Dropping bait-like crumbs of information to tease and titillate their flights of fancy.

'Ple-e-ease Molly... Tell us... He did do *it*... didn't he?'

'Of course he did.' she claimed with pride, 'How could he resist me?'

'Cor! Honest to God... he really *really* did it? A proper all-the-way shag?' Eager ears waited. Three moist pink tongues delicately encircled dry parted lips. Breathing was suspended. Time hung in abeyance.

Molly's long dark lashes fluttered coyly down in affected modesty. She did not exactly *tell* a lie... merely implied it.

'Holy shit! Who would have thought it with him? Was it... was it fantastic? Was it like being transported to Heaven? Did it hurt? Was he the best you've ever had?'

Question after question flew at her, bombarded her ears, paid succour to her vanity. Her self-esteem soared to unimaginable heights. She, Molly, small dumpy Molly had beaten them all. She had scored where all the others had failed. She had achieved the unattainable. Reached the heights. Hit the Bulls eye. If only it were true.

Inwardly she cursed. The silly stupid prude. All that guff he'd given her about respecting her body. Didn't he appreciate what was on offer? God in Heaven! *He* hadn't given it to her merely to be respected... had He?

Chapter Seven.

Marianne Ortega, Sergeant Decker quickly discovered, was a tough cookie. She regarded him with hard suspicious eyes through the narrow gap of her front door. The safety chain was on and she seemed very reluctant to remove it. It required all his powers of persuasion to convince her that he was who he said he was.

'Police?' she queried yet again, 'How do *I* know that you're the genuine article?' Her letterbox had a spring like a bear-trap. He squeezed his fingers through the gap and waved his warrant card around in awkward circles. *Damn the woman! Couldn't she believe the evidence before her eyes?*

'Decker.' he said again, 'Sergeant Edward Decker. A former colleague of yours suggested that I call and talk to you. A chap by the name of Martin Sellaney... you remember him? You worked with him about three years ago for the North Pennine Health Scheme?'

'Just a minute.' She pushed the door shut to remove the tension on the security chain, slid it free, re-opened the door and bid him enter. 'You'd best come in.' Faint traces of a Birmingham accent lingered in her voice.

'Thank you.' Decker eased his fingers gingerly from the bear-trap. *Postmen,* he inwardly sympathised, *have a lot to put up with.'* He was careful to wipe his feet on the welcome mat before stepping into the hall.

'I'm sorry to trouble you Mrs Ortega.' he began.

'Miz!' she corrected him abruptly, 'It's Ms Ortega if you don't mind. I'm divorced, ten years now so don't apologise. Don't even begin to say you're sorry. I'm not. Glad to be rid of the bum.'

Her brusque manner threw him off balance. Despite himself he was on the verge of expressing regret at the departure of the absent bum. Just bit off the words in time. He turned on his friendliest expression. Decker's greatest asset was his solid dependable look. It was said that his frank and honest face would have won the trust of Doubting Thomas within seconds. Marianne Ortega, he judged, would be about forty, give or take a year. A handsome woman who must have been very striking in her salad days, latterly the lettuce had gone limp! *But when it had been crisp! Mmm.*

He sensed a restless air of untapped energy, a determination to succeed in her every enterprise. It reflected in the house around him, in the smart businesslike clothes she wore and the pristine motorcar in her drive. Also she could have given St Thomas a few lessons in the art of disbelief.

'Who did you say you were?' she asked again, 'And how do you know about me?'

'A former colleague by the name of Sellaney, Martin Sellaney put me onto you, gave me your name and address. I understand you both worked for the North Pennine Health Scheme. Am I right?'

'Oh! And my name *is* Edward Decker, Police Sergeant Edward Decker.' He placed additional emphasis on his rank in the vain hope she would be suitably impressed.

'Used to work?' she queried, 'Has Martin Sellaney left? I always thought of him as a permanent fixture there. What happened?'

'It seems he was... erm... *retired*... due to poor health.' Decker placed the same sort of inflexion upon the word that Rachel Bergen had used.

'Retired! Ill health! Bollocks!' Incredulity oozed with every word. 'The man was a workaholic. One of the fittest men for his age I know. Martin never had a day off work in his life. Who are you kidding?'

Why was Martin Sellaney given the boot? It suddenly dawned on Decker that as yet he had no idea of the facts behind the man's abrupt departure. 'That's the official line,' he replied, 'from the General Manager. I haven't yet had the opportunity to discover *all* the facts. May I ask why you left? Martin thought it significant I talk to you face to face to find out for myself what happened.'

She didn't mince words. Came straight to the point and even after three years the bitterness of what had happened was powerfully evident in her voice.

'I was sacked! Kicked out! Thrown onto the scrap heap by that sick vindictive bastard Maxwell Bull. Wrongfully, as it happened, I was wrongfully dismissed.'

'You were wrongfully dismissed?' queried the policeman, putting disbelief into his voice. 'Isn't that a bit strong? I mean… do you have proof?'

'Proof!' raged Marianne Ortega looking at him with withering scorn, 'I don't have to frigging prove it. It's a matter of record, legal record, one hundred percent bloody legal. And that's something Mister Bastard Bull can't cover up.'

'Legal?' Decker's expression clearly demanded further explanation.

'Legal! As in *Courts.*' she answered brusquely, but with satisfaction riding in her voice, 'As in an Industrial Tribunal, if you get my drift?'

He caught her drift but wasn't sure he fully understood and the doubt obviously showed in his face for Marianne Ortega launched into a long and bitter explanation.

'It wasn't the fact that he sacked me,' she hissed through tightened lips, 'it was the way he did it. He impugned my reputation. Made out I was dishonest, a petty crook, said that I fiddled my expenses amongst other things. Why he even had me followed by a private detective. What a fiasco that turned out to be. It was hilarious, if it hadn't been so serious I'd have pissed my knickers laughing.' She stopped short, regarded the policeman with curiosity, 'Look!' she continued slightly puzzled at her own revelations, 'Why am I telling you all this?'

Why indeed? It was a phenomenon that Edward Decker himself didn't understand. Perhaps it was his sympathetic understanding face that caused all manner of people to unburden their souls to his attentive ears, his ability to listen rather than to question them. He was big and solid and rocklike, yet his presence seldom threatened.

'Are you married?' asked Ms Ortega unexpectedly.

'Erm… No! A widower,' he explained, 'but I do have a regular partner.'

'Huh! Just my luck!' retorted Marianne Ortega, then for the first time an impish smile crossed her face, 'I er… I take it she's female?'

He nodded emphatically.

'Thought so, didn't figure you for a gay. She's a lucky woman. Some are and some of us aren't.' she stated bluntly. By which Decker was lead to believe that life had been far from kind to the outwardly aggressive Ms Ortega. He sensed a deep hurt inside, hidden under her hard protective shell. He copied her blunt frankness.

'You're nowhere near as tough as you like to make out.'

'And you, I suspect, are a damn sight shrewder than you look.' she countered, 'Coffee?'

Her sudden change of attitude took him by surprise. 'Oh!... er... Yes please, fairly weak, milk and one sugar.'

She pointed at a door that led through to the lounge. An obsessively neat and tidy room which looked as though it was rarely used. It had a west facing bay window. Weak January sunshine struggled to lighten the room. It revealed half a dozen moderately skilful watercolours adorning the walls. They were all by the same artist, signed *M Warren* in the bottom right hand corner. He had just reached the last one and was admiring it when she returned carrying two cups of coffee.

'Do you like paintings?' she enquired, waving him towards two leather-bound seats and indicating that he be seated.

'Mmm. So-so. I'm beginning to learn a bit more about art since I met Helen, my partner, she's a professional artist so one can't help but learn something.' A flash of insight caused him to ask, 'Are these yours? I quite like them.'

'You do?' She seemed amazed, responding with childlike pleasure to his praise. 'I painted them years ago, long before I was married. After I met the *bum* pleasures like painting went out of the window.'

Idly Decker wondered about the *'Bum'*. What had he really been like? He knew there were two sides to every story. Could he have been as black as she portrayed him? She had retained his name when frequently divorced women reverted to their maiden surname.

He remarked upon the fact.

'Ortega,' she replied, 'I suppose I could have gone back to the family name, Warren, but I found it useful. People remember it because it's foreign and has a touch of the exotic... and it's easy to recall. When you work in "Sales" it's handy to have a name that people remember.'

'Spanish was he?'

'No, South American, the flashy bastard! He was about as shallow as frying pan with no sense of responsibility. Took off when I became pregnant and I haven't seen hair or hide of him since.'

'Aah!' *It was easier, thought* Decker, *to make sympathetic noises than to pass comments, which may prove unwise.*

'Anyway, you're a sly one, letting me rabbit on. Why *did* you come to see me?

The policeman sipped at his coffee thoughtfully, playing for time, deciding on his best approach. Frank and upfront, was his verdict. Marianne Ortega would spot deviousness a mile away. The *Bum* may have fooled her... but that was a lifetime ago.

'I'm looking into the affairs of the North Pennine Health Scheme and particularly into the death of the late Maxwell Bull. No doubt you read about it. There is a lot of money missing and I am not altogether convinced that his death was suicide.'

'Good!' she commented, 'It's about time the truth about that man came out. I suppose there is no doubt that it was Bull who died?'

'What do you mean? Of course it was Bull. Who else could it be?'

She gave him a long look that spoke volumes and suggested, 'It wouldn't be the first time a man disappeared with a pile of money and supposedly died... Now would it? Remember that politician chap who faked his own death, then turned up in Australia?'

'Oh no. It was Maxwell Bull all right,' said Decker with conviction, 'I saw his body myself. I was right there only twelve minutes after it happened. What I am not convinced about is that he committed suicide. If someone did kill him then I intend to find out who it was.'

Marianne looked at him with her head cocked to one side, regarding him as a rare specimen, a dedicated man, intent upon a job well done. 'If *I* knew who killed Maxwell Bull,' she observed. 'I would pin a medal on his chest... the biggest one I could find.'

Sergeant Decker could see from her eyes that she really meant it. Her shapely mouth was tight with loathing. Stark hatred shone from her face. He watched her with his quiet steady rocklike face, saying nothing, oozing empathy, waiting for her anger to subside.

'What I am trying to do,' he continued, 'is build up a feeling for the organisation... what it was like. Fill in the background, so to speak, and the only way I can do that is by talking to former employees. People like yourself...?' He allowed his voice to fall away, a silent invitation for her to explain her point of view.

Indecision lingered in her eyes. Could she trust him? How far should she go? Was he likely to finger her for murder? If, on the other hand she said nothing, then that too would arouse his suspicions!

'I can only tell you what happened from my side,' she began a little warily, 'I have no idea what it was like at Head Office because I was seldom there.'

'As one would expect.' encouraged Decker.

'When first I joined the North Pennine Health Scheme it was like being in Heaven, I loved it. Considered it the greatest job in all the world and that Maxwell Bull was the Angel Gabriel... the best boss a girl could have.' Marianne Ortega sighed heavily and shook her head. 'How wrong I was, if only I had known. I joined the scheme in 1984 – about one year after Maxwell Bull was appointed as Chief Executive. I don't know how *he* got the job but he must have impressed the Directors, which is *not* surprising as he *is* a brilliant salesman. They are old, a doddery lot, lovely people, so well meaning but, sort of unworldly, if you understand what I mean. That is why the scheme was in such a bad way. They lacked business sense and it was dying on its feet. I don't know whether you know, but a medical health scheme, a non-profit making one like the NPHS is responsible to the Department of Trade and Industry. It acts as a watchdog. Apparently they seriously considered winding up the organisation, that's how bad things were.'

'No. I didn't know that.' commented Decker, 'What do you mean by "non-profit making"; surely to be successful a business needs to make a profit, even if it's only a small one?'

'Well! As I understand it,' explained Marianne Ortega, 'nearly all the area health schemes are non-profit making organisations and nationally there are around thirty of them. What it means is that there are *no* paid directors and *no* shareholders. If the scheme makes a surplus then the money goes into a reserve fund or is used for charitable purposes. That's the theory of it, and that's why it is such a dream to sell.'

'A dream to sell?' questioned Decker, a small frown of puzzlement creasing the centre of his forehead, 'You mean it's an easy living?'

Marianne Ortega pulled a face, exasperation curling her mouth at the corners.

'Selling is *never* easy,' she replied with weary patience, 'Especially something like a service, something which the punter cannot see. It's far easier to sell a visible object, say a pair of shoes or a motorcar. That's something the eye can fix upon and evaluate. No, it's totally different trying to sell a concept, an idea.

'With a Health Scheme what one is offering is security, peace of mind. Everyone wants that... *needs* it, but at the same time everyone *hopes* that they never require it. That's where the charity bit comes in, being able to tell prospective members that *all* the money the scheme raises is used for the benefit of those in need. That really impresses them, makes them feel good. People like to feel good about themselves.

'I always made a point of emphasising that as well as protecting their families, they were, at the same time, helping other less fortunate people. It worked. I achieved record membership sales, and earned a very good living.'

'If that is the case,' commented Decker, 'why on earth were you dismissed? It doesn't make any sort of sense.'

Marianne Ortega spread her hands outwards in a Gallic gesture of despair. Her gaze lifted Heavenwards seeking a Divine answer. None came.

'You tell me. I never really understood how Bull's mind worked, it's beyond my comprehension.' She propped her chin upon her knuckles, sitting in the classic pose, a modern flesh and blood equivalent of The Thinker recalling past events and weighing up just how much she could reveal. A flash of anger flared. Tense with frustration she pounded her knee with a tightly clenched fist. 'It was the injustice of it all,' she cried out, 'that's what made me so angry, made me take the bastard to court. Do you know how many members the scheme recruited in the two years *before* I joined? Do you know?'

Her eyes widened with rage as she asked the rhetorical question. 'Around three thousand per year.' She repeated the words again, pounding her knee rhythmically with each word, 'Three... thousand... per... year! That's all. In *my* first year with the company I alone... *Me!*' She tapped her firm left breast with a rigid forefinger, 'I recruited over thirteen thousand, thirteen bloody thousand. More than the entire sales force had done in the previous ten years.'

Marianne Ortega sank back into her leather-bound chair. Head up. Eyes bright. Pride shining out of her face at the memory of her achievement.

'At the start of the new financial year Maxwell Bull organised a sales conference. All very extravagant with around three hundred guests invited. Do you know what he did? No! I'll tell you. He stood up on stage in front of all those people, put his arm around my shoulders and told them, 'This young woman, this *brilliant* young sales woman has single handed saved the North Pennine Health Scheme from extinction. The fact that we are here today, enjoying this celebration, is all down to her.

'Give her a big hand ladies and gentlemen… Marianne Ortega, our top sales lady.'

That is what he said, those were his very words, I can remember them like it was yesterday. I was *so proud*… so proud. I would have done anything for the scheme.'

'I suppose it was difficult to follow a successful year like that?' sympathised the policeman, folding his arms across his broad chest and shaking his head slowly from side to side.

'Oh no! Quite the opposite, the following year we did even better. I had a little team of two part-timers and myself. We worked on a commission-only basis and we increased recruitment by another thirty percent.'

'Thirty percent! What does that work out in numbers?' asked Decker, amazed by her reply. It was the last answer he'd expected.

'I think it worked out at something like twenty-one thousand in all. In the entire history of the North Pennine Health Scheme there had never been a year like it. I was over the moon. Thought I was made. When I was called into Head Office the last thing I expected was to be sacked. I was stunned. Shattered. They escorted me out of the building as though I were some kind of criminal. That really hurt. I couldn't believe how vindictive Maxwell Bull could be. He was vicious. Seemed to enjoy heaping humiliation on me. He just revelled in his power and authority. Would you believe he made out I had been cheating the scheme and fiddling my expenses.'

'And had you?' in a soft voice Decker asked the question very gently.

Of course not.' retorted Marianne hotly, 'why would I cheat? It was a ridiculous suggestion. I had no need. Then I found out about the private detective. That made me furious. It was then that I decided to go to an Industrial Tribunal and sue for wrongful dismissal, even though I could barely afford the money. I was *so* angry.' She paused, breathing deeply, the hot blood running beneath her skin bringing a scarlet flush to her pale winter cheeks.

'How did that work out?' continued the Sergeant in his gentle vein, allowing the anger and information to flow.

'I won.' she stated bluntly, 'The Tribunal found on my behalf. They saw through his lies and false evidence and awarded me damages of six thousand pounds. The tribunal declared the North Pennine Health Scheme to be a completely unreasonable employer, by which they meant that Maxwell Bull was unreasonable and had behaved in an improper manner towards me.'

'You were lucky then?' suggested Edward Decker.

She pulled a wry face and gave a nonchalant shrug, 'Lucky? Perhaps. Fortunately I had friends within the company who believed in me, they helped. Secretly you understand. The other factor was that the private detective hired by Bull was an absolute imbecile. He was hired to keep track of me, to check upon what I was doing. The idiot didn't do his homework. He followed the wrong person. When Bull tried to prove to the tribunal that I hadn't been working when in fact I had, it all came out. His stupid detective followed my housekeeper instead of me, she's about the same height and build, also I passed on one of my coats to her so that could have mislead him. When the details came out before the Industrial Tribunal, Maxwell Bull was furious, lost his temper at being made to look a complete fool in public.'

'Who was it who helped you at the company? Was it Martin Sellaney?'

'Mmm! Ye-e-es.' she replied warily, 'He was one. I'd rather not mention anyone else as they may still work there and I would *not* wish to land them in trouble.'

'No. Of course not.' Decker respected her loyalty and did not push the issue. 'So what do you really think was at the back of it? Why *did* Bull want you out?'

'Do you know,' she replied, 'I've thought about it time and time again and I can come to only one conclusion – Ego! The man had this great massive ego. He couldn't bear anyone to contradict him. He just *had* to be right all the time. And everyone else *had* to be in the wrong.

'My problem is that *I* have a mind of my own. I work things out for myself and draw my own conclusions. I suppose I was tactless enough to make my views known. That, and the fact that I was successful, perhaps he resented my success.'

Decker looked down at his notebook. He had scribbled a few key words to jog his memory and would fill in the blank spaces at a later time. There was just one more vital question to which he required an answer.

'Ms Ortega can I ask where you were at midnight on New Year's Eve?'

She had obviously been waiting for the question. Gave him a little laugh and an enigmatic answer. 'I was alone,' she said, 'in the middle of a crowd. At a public house called "The Crown". Couldn't bear to see in another year on my own... and yet, I was more lonely there than I would have been in my own house.'

He didn't need to ask further, Decker had lived on *his* own for the best part of twenty years until he met Helen Argosy. There were no words sufficiently adequate. Loneliness was a modern social disease. A disease to which there was no antidote except the companionship of good friends or that of a close loving family.

'Thank you Ms Ortega, you've been most helpful.' He levered himself out of the leather-bound chair which had proved to be far more comfortable than it looked and stretched to his full height.

Marianne Ortega also rose and as she guided him towards the door she picked up a business card from the hall table and held it out with the words, 'My business card Sergeant. Should you wish to contact me again it has my telephone number on it. You won't find me in the book... I'm ex-directory.'

Decker took the small oblong of white card and tucked it into the plastic sleeve of his notebook. He held out his hand for a brief and formal handshake. Her fingers lingered slightly longer than was necessary, letting his hand slip away reluctantly. She made a final light-hearted comment as he left. 'Bye Sergeant. If that partner of yours should ever kick you out... Well! You know where to come!'

*

It was 3:30pm and already the daylight was going. January's days are short on sunshine. He peered through the gloom at his notebook, expanding upon his notes before the passing of time jumbled them in his memory. The interior light of his Morris Minor cast a meagre glow, barely sufficient to read the card tucked into his notebook sleeve. **Marianne Ortega – Debt Collector,** he read. Phe-e-ew! A low whistle escaped his lips. A Debt Collector! What a tough unsavoury job for anyone. It was hardly a suitable occupation for an attractive woman. Now Decker understood the chain across the door, the careful checking of his identity and the reluctance to admit him into the house and the absence of her name from the telephone directory.

In the popularity scales her rating was well down the list, along with double-glazing salesmen, traffic wardens, a Jehovah's Witness or, worst of all, a tax inspector.

But a murderess!

Edward Decker hoped not. She was certainly tough enough, driven by the deep abiding loathing she undoubtedly felt towards Maxwell Bull. Marianne Ortega certainly had sufficient motive. She made no secret of the fact that she welcomed his demise. As for her alibi, it was every bit as weak as the one Martin Sellaney had given him.

Decker groaned despairingly. On his list there were over sixty names and as yet there wasn't a single one he felt able to eliminate. If each one had as strong a motive as those he had already interviewed then it would be easier to find the guilty party by drawing numbers out of a hat!

.

Chapter Eight.

Halfway back to Briseley T'ill Decker happened to glance at the petrol gauge and gasped in horror. The needle was flickering close to the empty mark. Belting up the A38 from Lichfield he'd sailed past a number of brightly lit filling stations, never once thinking about petrol. Now he was on minor roads and for the life of him he couldn't remember where there was a garage until he reached John Shackleton's place in the village.

Wait a minute, he asked himself, *isn't there an all night filling station on the outskirts of Rowell?* It would only be a minor diversion to call there and he would feel foolish if he ran out of fuel along the dark country lanes.

Better safe than sorry, Decker comforted himself as he drove steadily, conserving petrol, one eye on the gauge and the other cocked for a signpost to the village.

Another point he reflected upon was the miles clocking up on the odometer of his little green Morris Minor at an alarming rate. It was all down to the additional territory he was forced to cover. Once, it had seemed, there had been a policeman located in every village. With a police house or small station from which the local bobby patrolled on foot or on a regulation bicycle, keeping an eye on the district and in touch with the population.

Not so today. One by one the rural officers had been withdrawn, called to serve in the city centres where the ever-increasing tide of crime threatened to overwhelm the forces of law and order. Even the police station at Briseley T'ill had gone, sold off for the site to be developed as the County Council tightened the financial screw.

It was as well I moved in with Helen Argosy when I did, the dark thoughts ran in the Sergeant's mind, *otherwise who knows where I'd be!*

At last the lights of the all night filling station appeared, as bright and as garish as a Christmas tree. They were completely out of character with the tiny Pennine village with its dim rural iron lampposts, its narrow streets and its dark stone buildings with slated roofs.

Decker swung in alongside the pumps, topped up his tank with leaded petrol and went to push open the door of the shop. It was locked. His forward momentum came to an abrupt halt as his nose flattened against the thick plate glass. It was a symptom of the times that attendants needed to lock themselves in after the hours of darkness.

The young woman inside gesticulated to a side window that had a circular plastic grill he could speak through and a pivoting metal drawer to take his money.

A second motorist drew in at the pumps and was in the act of filling his tank when the crashing sound of breaking glass assailed their ears. The man's head jerked towards the village.

'Bloody vandals!' he swore fervently, 'The little buggers are at it again. Regular as bloody clockwork.' The man shook his head in resigned disgust.

'Where's the bloody law? That's what I want to know.'

The, as yet, un-bloodied law, sprang into action.

'Quick! Where did it come from?' Decker shouted at the startled motorist. He leapt into the driver's seat. The engine roared into life. Rammed the clutch hard down as he slammed the car into gear. His little Morris had never been handled so violently. Its tyres squealed a noisy protest as he sped away following the direction of the motorist's pointing arm. Faintly he caught the frantic words called after him.

'Bull's place… sounds like the stable windows.'

It was seventy yards along the road. A wide five-barred gate, painted white, swung half open bearing mute testament to the sudden departure of the intruders. The Sergeant turned off the engine of his vehicle and listened. Nothing. Whoever had been there seemed to have vanished without trace. He could hear no sound of running footsteps or the noise of a departing engine.

It's just possible, Decker thought, *they are still here, hidden in the shadows or crouching out of sight behind the shrubbery.* He fumbled in the glove box, took out a long rubber-covered black torch with a powerful beam. Slowly, methodically, he swung the beam into every corner of the garden. Its probing light revealed nothing except the shattered panes of the outer stable door. About one third of a broken house brick had damaged the framework of the door leaving jagged splinters of glass and a white scar in the woodwork where it had struck home.

The Sergeant tried the door. Secure, the lock undamaged. He headed for the house. There had been no sign of any response, but then that was only to be expected with just two women in the house, one being an elderly housekeeper and the other only recently having lost her brother. *Very likely,* he thought, *they are both terrified out of their skins.*

A pale light glowed through the curtains of one of the upstairs rooms and a stronger light glared from the window of a ground floor room. Decker rang the doorbell. Waited patiently. Rang a second time. Finally a timid voice asked through the door.

'Who is there?'

'Police! Sergeant Decker of Briseley T'ill.'

'Sergeant Decker...?' Doubt still lingered in the voice, 'What's your first name?'

'Ted.' he called back, Well, Edward really... Sergeant Edward Decker. Is that Mrs McLean? It is isn't it? You must remember me, I'm the one who came in answer to your call... New Year's Eve, remember?'

'Just a minute.' He could sense the relief in the housekeeper. There was the dragging sound of bolts being withdrawn, followed by the heavy click of the lock. She peered out at him through the gloom, a tall woman whose steel-framed spectacles and straight hair drawn back into a bun made her look unnecessarily severe. Having confirmed his identity the door was thrown wide and the policeman invited inside.

'I was in the vicinity, heard the sound of breaking glass, disturbed a would-be intruder. Failed to catch him I'm afraid.' explained Decker breathlessly, 'Are you both alright?'

'It's not the first time,' she complained, 'Ever since Maxwell... that is Mr Bull hanged himself... died, we seem to have been the target of morbid curiosity. Vandals, reporters, sightseers, all trying to get into the stable, trying to see the place where it happened. Some people are so sick!' A little flash of anger broke through her fear and concern.

It's universal, thought Decker, the morbid fascination that violent death held for mankind. Despite a million years of evolution human nature remained unchanged. When the first primate battered and clubbed his first victim to death in all probability a circle of slack-jawed apes gathered to share in the vicarious pleasure.

'I'm very sorry,' he apologised, feeling helpless and inadequate, 'I'll see what I can do, try to keep an eye on the place until things quieten down a bit.'

'Will you? That's very kind.' She sounded inordinately grateful for what after all was his duty. There had to be something further he could do.

'Look!' he said as an idea came to him, 'Perhaps I can secure the damaged window. If you have a hammer, some nails and a sheet of hardboard?'

'There should be materials in one of the horse boxes.' answered Mrs McLean, accepting his suggestion gratefully, 'I'll get the keys and come with you. You may have trouble finding the light switch, it's located in a very awkward place.' She hesitated, raising anxious eyes towards the staircase, listening intently.

'Miss Bull, is she ill?' asked the policeman. Mrs McLean gave a tight little shake of her head. 'Sedated.' she explained, 'She'll be fine for a few minutes.'

An assortment of keys hung from a row of hooks secured to one end of the wall-mounted kitchen cabinets. Her fingers searched along the row, paused beneath a hook labelled *Stables* and lifted down two long shafted metal keys on a split ring. She led the way across the gravelled yard after first shutting the door quietly and gently behind her. Decker would never have found the light switch for himself. For some peculiar reason known only to him the electrician charged with modernising the lighting had chosen to mount the stable switch *behind* the hinged side of the door. It was tucked away between two vertical joists of timber, set flush against the brickwork. The normal position to mount a switch is on the opening side about one and a half metres from the ground, a comfortable and natural height that allows the hand to fall easily onto it.

There was a door at either end of the central passageway that was roughly half a metre wide. The lower half of each door had been constructed in solid timber and the upper half featured four quarter-lights of glass. It was a pane in the door nearest to the road that had been shattered by the house brick.

On both sides of the central passage were stalls for the non-existent horses. Mrs McLean rummaged about in the first of the boxes and finally re-emerged with a hammer, a dozen assorted nails and a section of hardboard. Decker offered up the hardboard against the outer door. It was more than large enough to cover all four panes of glass. He considered the problem for a moment and made a suggestion.

'I can nail this to the outside of the door, covering all four panes of glass. It should be solid enough until you can contact a glazier to replace the broken pane. OK?'

'Fine. Go ahead.' Mrs McLean held the torch with one hand and helped to support the hardboard with the other while the Sergeant hammered home the nails. He tested the finished product for security. It wouldn't win prizes for carpentry but it should serve to deter an intruder.

'There, that should do the trick.' He handed back the unused nails and hammer to Mrs McLean and while she returned them to the box looked curiously around the interior of the stables.

'Is there something wrong Sergeant?' asked the housekeeper.

'Odd don't you think,' he replied, 'for a man to buy an expensive house with stables when he doesn't keep horses? Did he intend to buy some?'

'No-o-o. Shouldn't think so... he was never over fond of animals, which is curious considering his hobby.'

'Hobby? What was it?'

'More of an obsession really, he was fascinated by the old West.'

'The old west?' asked Decker, misunderstanding, 'The old west what?'

'The *Wild* West... You must know; Cowboys, Red Indians, Buffalo Bill and all that rubbish.' The housekeeper's tone was sceptical, 'And him a grown man. T'was a load of old tripe if you ask me. What do they call it? *Memorabilia*! Just a load of old junk is what I call it. Junk! Totally useless... *and* it gathers dust!'

Gathering dust appeared to be the *great* evil in Mrs McLean's world.

'Exactly what kind of souvenirs did he collect?' asked Decker, curious to learn more about the useless dust-gathering junk.

'Oh! Y'know... all sorts.' Mrs McLean snapped waspishly, 'Replica guns, some of them quite weighty, and those funny big knives. What are they called?'

'Bowie.' suggested the fascinated policeman.

'Bowie... that's it, Bowie knives, horrible vicious looking things they are too. Then he had those fancy leather jackets with the frills all along the sleeves and across the front and back. Some

71

funny leather objects to wrap around his legs and two hats, one black and the other white with wide curly brims and an enormous crown to them.'

'Stetsons.'

'Yeah! Stetsons,' agreed Mrs McLean, 'and that's not the least of it. Upstairs in a special room he's got a mechanical horse type thing. With a projector and screen and lots and lots of old black and white movies, all Westerns. He used to dress himself up in his fancy gear, set the film running, jump on that... that daft gadget, and join in. Acted as though he were part of the film he did. Crackers if you ask me. Absolutely crackers!'

Decker was astounded. This man, he reminded himself, is... had been, the Chief Executive of a widely respected health scheme. A man who had held considerable power and authority over the lives and fortunes of hundreds – No! - tens of thousands of people. Yet it appeared he acted with the carefree abandon of an immature child.

'It must have been quite a shock to you discovering his body.' said the policeman, switching the conversation suddenly. 'I believe it *was* you who found him, wasn't it?'

Mrs McLean's eyes travelled up towards the bell tower, recalling the scene with appalling clarity in her mind again.

'Oh yes!' she whispered, 'It was. I was expecting the bell to ring out in keeping with the tradition of the village. The church clock finished chiming and I listened for the bell. There was this one discordant clang... and then silence. I waited about two or three minutes in all, expecting the bell to ring again. Then when nothing happened I began to suspect that something had gone wrong. But I never thought... I never thought...' She paused a moment to regain her composure, her face pale and drained of blood and her wide open eyes glittering in the artificial light of the un-shaded stable lamps.

'I opened the door,' she continued, 'switched on the light, and there he was... hanging there... with his tongue poking out and the rope cutting into the flesh of his neck... and... and... it was obvious he must be dead because... because... his neck was all elongated and unnatural like. Oh God! I'm so sorry Sergeant Decker but... but it still upsets me to think about the way he died.'

'Of course it does.' sympathised the policeman, patting her comfortingly on the shoulder, 'It's only to be expected. If you want to return to the house I can lock up here and return the keys.

I would just like to have a little look around before I go. That is if you don't mind?' He ushered her back towards the house. Watched until she reached the safety of the door and then turned back into the stable.

Looking up into the bell-tower Decker could see the solitary time-blackened brass bell. It hung there, silent and still, its rope missing, removed and taken by the Forensic Department for examination. It was guesswork on his part but he reasoned that when the stable had originally been designed and built a bell-tower had not been a part of the structure. It had been added at a later date. By the same reasoning, Decker figured, the loft had also covered the whole of the roof space. The joists of the loft ran from the front to the rear of the building, in the same direction as the passageway. When the bell-tower had been added on, the centre section of the loft had been cut away to allow access to the bell and to leave a space for the rope to hang down and the bell rung.

Whoever had carried out the alterations hadn't cut along the edge of the joists when removing the centre section of the loft, but had cut the floorboards in such a way as to leave them overhanging the joists by a least a foot. His curiosity aroused, Decker examined the walls at both end of the passage. High up on the walls, exactly over the centre of each door, was the remains of a central joist. It had been sawn off at both ends flush with the brickwork.

He climbed the rickety wooden ladder to the loft choosing first to mount the side where the riding tack was stored. The top of his head was level with the bottom edge of the bell. By standing on the extreme edge of the hole he was just able to reach out and touch the black metal of its rim. The floorboards creaked ominously. Decker moved hastily backwards. Something caught his eye and he bent to examine the boards. Scuffmarks had been scored into the wood running inwards from the edge of the loft. Puzzled, he backed down the ladder, moved it across the passageway and climbed up to the other half of the loft. Similar marks were also scored in the flooring on this side of the passageway. Why? What had caused them? Objects dragged across the planking? He searched, and found nothing obvious to make such marks.

A possibility occurred to him. Perhaps someone, rather than keep using the ladder, had chosen to risk leaping from one side of the loft to the other.

In fact, thought Decker, *they made a regular habit of risking their necks!*

*

'I took the liberty of making you a cup of tea.' said Mrs McLean when he went to return the key, 'You've been most kind and it was the least I could do.'

He was really in a hurry and would have welcomed the use of a toilet rather than drink one more cup of unsolicited liquid. 'Well, just a sip then.' He tried to sound grateful. 'How is Miss Bull? You said she was sedated, still in a state of shock?'

'Marie has always been very highly strung. She's taken her brother's death badly. I'm afraid she doesn't cope with life's problems very well.'

Unlike you, Mrs McLean, thought Decker. A level-headed practical woman, without any sign of lingering grief or prolonged mourning on display.

'Have you been with the family long?' he asked.

'Practically all of my working life. I was their Nanny when the children were little. Imps of mischief they were, all three of them. Now there is only Marie left.' She shook her head sadly, reflecting on the tragedies of life.

'Three?' exclaimed Decker, 'I didn't realise. What happened?'

Mrs McLean pointed to the sideboard covered with an array of family photographs. The sunlight had faded many of the older prints over the years but there was one in particular to which the housekeeper pointed that showed three young children playing together. 'That one is Marie,' said the former Nanny, 'There's Maxwell and the little one is Malcolm. Poor lamb. He was only four years old when he died, a tragic accident, tragic!'

The girl looked to be about ten years old in the photograph. She was tall for her age with long skinny arms and legs, a gangling child. Maxwell Bull was easily spotted. He looked about nine years of age with a shock of black hair, puffy overweight features and even in one so young there were already signs of the aggressive and overpowering personality to come.

The remaining child, who had to be the tragic Malcolm, was five years younger, and at four had the fresh eagerness of a little one trying to keep pace with his older siblings.

Maxwell was dressed in cowboy clothes, a miniature felt Stetson on his head, a chequered shirt, baggy sackcloth trousers, a gun-belt with a tied-down holster around his waist and a shiny tin star pinned to his chest. Marie wore a simple straight brown shift with frills, a band around her head and a solitary feather to play her part as a Red Indian maiden. Malcolm shared the fate of every younger brother, he was doomed to be the outlaw.

'I see what you mean about his obsession with the Wild West,' the Sergeant said to Mrs McLean, 'It's strange how people cling on to their childhood dreams.'

'Nightmares!'

'Eh?'

'Nightmares Sergeant Decker,' There was a far-off brooding look on the woman's face, 'Nightmares... some dreams turn into nightmares. Didn't you know?'

'Umm! Yes.' He replied, and decided to leave it at that.

*

.

She showed him to the door. He heard the lock click shut behind him and the bolts sliding home. Of the sedated Marie Bull he had caught not a glimpse. Losing a close relative such as a brother or a sister was tragic. But to lose two, it would shatter the morale of the strongest person. Like splitting their world into fragments... but *ten* days? Surely it was an excessively long time to be sedated. By now time would have set in motion the healing process.

On the drive back to Briseley T'ill he thought about his unplanned visit to the Bull home. Fate, reflected Decker, had dealt him an ace. A small chance remark now convinced him that Maxwell Bull could not possibly have committed suicide. It was a small thing. Something Mrs McLean had said about finding the body.

I opened the door, switched on the light, and there he was... hanging there...!

Switched on the light!

Maxwell Bull may have been a clever man, thought the Sergeant, but even he would have been hard pressed to find his

75

way around the pitch-black interior of the stables at midnight on New Year's Eve. He would have switched on the light to find his way up the ladder to the loft. Then, having hung himself, Maxwell Bull had performed the incredible trick of plunging the building into darkness once again.

Impossible! There had to have been a second person.

But who?

Chapter Nine.

'How did your day go?' asked Helen Argosy over the dinner table.

'Don't ask!' groaned Decker.

'As bad as that?'

'We-e-ell! Perhaps it wasn't a total disaster. At least I'm now certain of one thing… Maxwell Bull didn't take his own life. As to who did kill him… that's another matter. I wasn't able to eliminate a single suspect, they've *all* got a motive and I've barely started looking. There are at least another sixty on my list to have a go at. It's hopeless. They're all over the place.' His hands swung outwards in two wide circular movements as though to encompass the entire nation.

'Are you absolutely sure that it *is* a former employee?' asked Helen, 'Haven't you always said that the majority of murders are domestic, committed by a relative.'

'Yes, that *is* true, but it's unlikely. Maxwell Bull only has *one* living relative, his sister. She is a year older and something of a recluse. The housekeeper told me she has difficulty coping with life. A nervous type. On tranquillisers is my guess. She wouldn't have the steel to commit murder… surely?'

'Oo-er! A dwuggy.' interrupted Jason, 'Betcha ten pee she done it. Wotten! That's what sisters are. Wotten! Wotton! Wotton! My fwiend at school, Philip Muldoon has got a sister and she beats 'im up evewy day.'

'Jason! That's enough.' Helen scolded her son, 'Tell the truth now.'

'I am. 'onest Mum, 'onest. She's always playing wotten twicks on 'im… just 'cos 'e's little. Gu-u-rls are like that.' His piping voice dropped several tones as he expressed his disgust at the younger members of the opposite sex. 'I'm *never* going to go out with gu-u-rls.'

'Oh! Well! That's another crime solved.' exclaimed Ted Decker, shaking with suppressed laughter, 'Now what am I going to do tomorrow?' He leaned across the table, ruffled the boy's hair with affection, pushed his chair backwards and eased his bulk into a standing position. 'That reminds me, I need to make a phone call before it's too late.' He glanced apologetically at Helen, 'If you'll excuse me.'

Despite the lateness of the hour the telephone in the Forensic department at County Police Headquarters was answered promptly. 'Sergeant Decker here, from Briseley T'ill.' he announced, 'Who am I speaking to?'

A disrespectful and disembodied voice answered breezily, 'Hi Decker, you old bumpkin. How's life down amid the turnips?'

'Maddy Gunn! Good grief! Are you *still* there? I thought they'd have pensioned you off years ago.' He was delighted to recognise an old friend and acquaintance. Maddy had proved to be a good friend at a time he needed the support of his colleagues and friends some twenty years ago. It had been a painful and cruelly shattering time when, as a young and inexperienced constable, his wife had been brutally raped and murdered. Maddy Gunn had been a shoulder to cry on, a ready listener to his rambling unhappy despair, like an older sister in his time of need.

'What can I do for you? Oh yes! By the way, what's this I hear about a *new* woman in your life? All sorts of rumours are flying about at HQ. How about letting me in on the secret?'

'It's about time you got yourself out of that gossip-shop.' Decker snorted, '… and found yourself a place in the countryside, where decent people live.'

Her deep throaty laughter bubbled down the line. 'Seriously though, what can I do for you?'

'It's about the Bull case, you know the one I mean?'

'The man who hanged himself? Yes, I know the one. What about it?'

'Do you still have the rope in forensics?'

'Yes. What about it?' asked a puzzled Maddy Gunn.

'Well! Is it *all* there?' asked Decker.

'All there?' Maddy's puzzlement increased, 'Isn't that a bit like asking "How long is a piece of string?" It's all there that *was* there.'

'Ah! Sorry Maddy,' apologised the Sergeant, 'I'm not making myself clear. Forget about the length… what I want to know is, are *all* the strands intact? Could you just check the bottom end of the rope. The opposite end to the one fastened onto the bell arm and check if some of the strands are missing?'

'Just a minute.' The hand-piece clumped down and he heard the sound of her footsteps fading on the tiled floor. He waited patiently, picturing the scene, hearing giveaway sounds over the telephone, the scraping noise of a filing cabinet drawer being opened and then closed, the rustle of documents and then the sound of returning feet. There was a minute of silence as the forensic scientist examined the rope. Then Maddy Gunn's voice came back on the phone.

'How the devil did you know?'

. 'What is it Maddy?'

'There *is* something.' A trace of anxiety was distinguishable in her voice, 'Right at the very end... about eight or nine inches from the bottom, just a few thin strands are missing. Oh Lord! Have I missed something important Ted?'

'To be honest Maddy I don't really know.' admitted Decker, 'It may be nothing. It's just an idea I had, a possibility, nothing more. I promise, should anything come of it you will be the first to know.'

Her pride was injured. Maddy Gunn was a conscientious officer who paid meticulous attention to detail. Missing the slightest detail that was out of the ordinary would chafe at her like an open sore.

'One more favour; when you have finished with the rope will you let me know. I'd like to return it personally, it will give me an excuse to call at the house again.'

'Sure.' answered Maddy, the concern still obvious in her voice, 'Is there anything else I should know?'

Decker looked over the telephone towards Helen Argosy. He squeezed a broad wink in her direction and whispered conspiratorially into the receiver.

'Straight from the horse's mouth, just to give you the edge, the new lady in my life is Helen Argosy, the artist, creator of "Winnie the White Witch". She's famous!'

'Wow! Good for you Ted... and the very best of luck.'

'Thank you. I'll keep in touch. Bye.' He set the phone down, a broad beam of self- satisfaction on his face.

'What are you smirking at Ted Decker?' asked Helen suspiciously, 'and who is Maddy Gunn? One of your old flames?'

'Me! Smirk? I'm just pleased with myself because I've spotted something that the so-called experts missed. Whether it means anything I don't know yet. Time will tell. As for Maddy Gunn, she's a very mature lady who works in the police forensic laboratory. She's a grandmother, I believe, and a very good friend.'

'That doesn't mean a thing,' chided Helen, winding him up, 'Lots of mature women go for younger men. Toy-boys are *in* you know.'

'Damn!' replied Decker, joining in the mind game, 'That's always been one of my ambitions. The problem is when I was young enough it wasn't done. Now it's commonplace... I'm too old. But I've still got you.' He added, bounding across the kitchen and sweeping her off the ground in a joyous hug.

'Put me down you great bear,' she squealed, 'You don't know where I've been.'

'No-o-o.' he murmured, nuzzling against the soft flesh of her neck. He glanced suggestively up at the ceiling, 'But I certainly know where you and I are going...'

Chapter Ten.

On Friday 8th December he took a day off, legitimate holiday to visit a sick relative in the West Country.

'Take one of the company cars,' Maxwell Bull had suggested when he asked for permission and explained where he was going, 'You can call at the Area Manager's house and drop off some of the new Sales literature.'

He was surprised by the Chief Executive's unexpected generosity. Suspicion never entered his head. Being a man with a trusting nature he accepted the offer at face value. He attached no significance to the fact that the Board of Directors were to meet at the Mansion House that very day. Had he been in the building then there may have been an opportunity to present a case in his defence: a chance to turn aside the blade being surreptitiously inserted between his unsuspecting shoulder blades.

Instead he drove to Weston-super-Mare.

On the Thursday afternoon he exchanged vehicles, leaving his own small Fiesta locked and parked in the safety of the high, stone walls of the Mansion House car-park. When he collected the keys of the company Space Wagon from Rachel Bergen she assured him it was in good condition. It had been recently serviced.

Rachel, with her customary efficiency, had everything ready for him to load. There were boxes of membership application forms, all the latest promotional leaflets associated with the scheme, posters, a sectional display stand, an overhead projector with slides, packs of registration forms to enable new practices to be added to the computerised lists of services available, spare copies of the scheme's promotional magazine and finally boxes of holiday vouchers used as an incentive to encourage punters to join immediately.

Despite the December cold, intensified by a biting wind from the north, he was perspiring freely by the time everything was loaded. The Space Wagon had three rows of seats and the two rear rows, designed to be laid flat created an enormous capacity for luggage. He only needed to adjust the back row still leaving room for his own travel bag and three passengers.

'Thanks Rachel,' he said with genuine feeling in his voice, 'See you Monday. Bye.'

'Bye.' Rachel Bergen replied briefly. She was a very private person. Self-controlled. Her feelings always hidden behind calm grey eyes and words unspoken. And yet... and yet... he *knew* there was more. It was written into her body language, into the moments when she lingered just an extra few seconds before parting. He sensed loneliness there and an inexplicable reticence to reveal her true self. Why? He'd never been able to understand.

*

He drove home. Went to bed early. Rose at six-thirty in the morning and was on the road an hour later heading for the M42, then onto the M5 towards Bristol and the South West of England. The traffic was light, visibility good and the Space Wagon fairly raced along with barely a sound from its powerful engine. He slipped into the overdrive gear and relaxed comfortably, unaware of the fact that his speed was creeping into the seventies... the eighties... touching ninety as the robust machine cruised effortlessly, its engine working well within its limits.

Had he needed to use his brakes he may have noticed a slight sponginess to the pedal. A lack of positive response which at a lower speed would cause him no problems. But in an emergency...

*

Janice Holly greeted him with open arms. A comfortable looking woman in her middle years with teenage sons, a successful husband, the desire to progress in her *own* right and mutual affinity towards a man she recognised as a supportive colleague.

'Janice.' he said, placing a dutiful peck upon her cheek, 'you *do* look well. How are you?'

'Fine! All the better for seeing you.' replied the Area Manager for the South-West Region. 'You don't come to see us often enough, mouldering away in that stuffy old office.' She squeezed him to her generous bosom with such uninhibited vigour that he almost wished himself back in the security of his tiny claustrophobic room at the Mansion House. He wasn't given to unrestrained displays of emotion.

'How are the Sales figures?' asked Janice eagerly, 'Are we on target?'

'Well on top. In fact heading towards our best ever, something like thirty thousand at the last count. And there are still more to arrive. You've done superbly.'

Janice Holly beamed with satisfaction. All the hard work she had put in was about to bear fruit for the top sales representative had been promised a *free* holiday to Majorca. She was on target to win!

'Are you staying to lunch?' asked Janice. He looked at her ample curves and considered the offer well worthwhile. The lady was renowned for her culinary skills.

'Yes please.' he replied eagerly, 'I'll unload first and then, if you don't mind, I'd like to wash and freshen up before eating. OK?'

Janice was eager for information. Only rarely did the Sales Representatives or the Area Managers get to visit the Head Office in Rowell. The internal politics of the company passed them by and it was only on such occasions as these that an opportunity occurred to catch up on the gossip. They ate casually in the kitchen and chatted solidly for over an hour. Eighty percent of the representatives were female, the mature ones being by far the most successful in terms of recruiting new members to the scheme. Exactly why was difficult to quantify.

The time passed all too quickly. He had always been a good listener, particularly to women. They respected his integrity, confided in him with complete trust and liked to express their gratitude for his unfailing support.

As district reps they ploughed a long and lonely furrow. All too frequently their only contact with the health scheme was the sound of his voice on the phone. When their confidence sagged, he encouraged and cheered them on and when they scored a big success, he was the one ready to share their joy.

*

Leaving Weston-super-Mare he headed southeast, cutting across country, avoiding the motorways, heading for the tiny village in the Mendip Hills where his elderly aunt and uncle lived. He drove slowly, stopping on occasions to check his route. There were some steep hills and winding roads and time and again he was forced to shift into a low gear to control his descent into the valleys. Almost imperceptibly the spongy feeling of the brake pedal increased. Each and every time the brake pedal was depressed a tiny amount of brake fluid was squeezed out and lost. It was whipped away by the flow of air as the vehicle sped along. The vital fluid in the hydraulic system gradually became replaced by air. Unlike fluid, air compresses whenever the brakes are applied. Slowly but surely they lost their efficiency. The feeling of sponginess creeping up un-noticed upon the unsuspecting driver…

*

He arrived at the house in mid-afternoon. Already the sun was low in the clear December sky, its light beginning to fade. The next two hours, he thought, will be interminable. It was a long way to travel for so short a visit but two hours would be as much as he could bear.

'How is she?' were his first words to the frail old man who answered the door. Even before his uncle answered he knew. He could see it in the resigned acceptance of the old man's bearing. Heard it in the utter despondency of his voice.

'Bad!' his uncle replied, 'Very bad. I doubt she will last more than a few days, a week perhaps. Only God knows.'

'Oh Uncle Ben,' he cried out in sympathy, 'I'm so very sorry.'

'I know my boy, I know… but it's God's will. He knows best and we have had a good life together, your aunt and I. A *very* good life.'

He put his arm around the old man's shoulders and escorted him into the house. Through the worn woollen cardigan he could feel the frail bones, the skeletal flesh, the shrunken muscles of the man who had been so dear to him in boyhood. So many happy hours had been spent here as a child; sharing their simple life; safe, secure and greatly loved.

Tears filled his eyes and blurred his vision. In his heart he knew that after his aunt died the old man would not last much longer. And then, when they had gone, he would be alone. No parents, no wife, no children. No one.

'Will you be staying the night?' asked Uncle Ben. He shook his head, hating to disappoint the old man.

'No uncle,' he murmured guiltily, 'I need to return home tonight. I don't wish to put an unnecessary burden on you. You have more than enough to cope with as it is.' He knew in his heart that his words were not strictly true. Had he wished he could have stayed overnight but for two hours they had sat beside the bed and conversation had been sparse.

It was hard to tell that his aunt was still alive. She lay back, propped against snow-white pillows, her eyes staring vacantly ahead. A tiny frail figure without pretence to humanity. Already she had assumed the appearance of a skeleton, a thin layer of parchment-like skin stretched tight across white bone, lacking the colour of flesh and blood. A gaunt shadow of a living being.

Duty had compelled him to come and his love and affection for the old couple. Far rather would he have preferred to remember them as they had been in his childhood, alive and vibrant. Bursting with vitality as they took him for long rambling walks across the open countryside. Playing games with him as a child and encouraging his studies as a young man. They had been surrogate parents for the father and mother he had barely known.

*

It was dark when he departed: too dark for him to notice the pool of brake fluid that had accumulated beneath the car. Had it still been light it is doubtful whether he would have seen it for his eyes were blurred by un-spilled tears and his perception deadened by emotion.

Stars glittered in the cold clear sky. There was no moon. The road from the village possessed little by way of lighting. It unwound before him in a thin black ribbon of tarmac. He drove slowly and carefully for even the brilliant halogen headlights of the Space Wagon could not penetrate the twisting winding way.

From the brow of a hill he saw a major road ahead. A string of bright orange lights like beads upon a necklace danced into the distance. Soon be there, he told himself, and then I can pick up speed, make better time and relax a little on the broad expanse of the motorway.

The road dipped sharply and the Space Wagon began to gather speed of its own accord. He eased off on the accelerator but still the car's momentum increased. He dropped down a gear, into fourth, then into third as the needle of the rev counter flickered towards the red zone. His foot eased onto the brake pedal, gradually increasing the pressure. Nothing! It was as though the pedal had been disconnected. There was no resistance to his stabbing foot. Without fluid in the hydraulic system he was just pumping air.

Air alone will not stop a speeding car!

He crashed down another gear. The engine howled as if in pain and the needle of the rev counter flicked sharply into the red. Still the car gathered speed as the gradient grew steeper. A warning sign flashed by his startled eyes. **Danger – Accident Zone -** he read. Only too true!

He remembered the handbrake. Hauled back hard on the lever with his left hand, but the handbrake on a modern car operates only on the rear wheels and is intended purely and simply for parking. As the rear wheels locked and skidded on the surface of the road the Space Wagon slewed violently to one side. Dare he risk trying to change down into first gear? If he failed, and the car became stuck in neutral then he'd lost the braking effect of the engine altogether and his speed would increase. He eased off on the handbrake, leaving it rubbing with just enough friction to control its speed but not sufficiently to lock the wheels.

Concentrate! Concentrate on holding the vehicle on the road, he told himself, *and pray. Pray, pray, pray to God that the road stayed clear and straight.*

It didn't. It curved sharply to the right. A grassy bank rose up on his left hand side. He wrestled with the wheel, trying frantically to hold the line of the bend but his speed was too great. Centrifugal force flung his body to the left. Control slipped from his grasp. The Space Wagon bounced off the road. Its tyres lost traction on the wet grassy surface. It lurched violently to the left and then to the right, slithering and spinning like a top until finally it crashed to a shuddering halt against the trunk of a mature and solid elm.

The angle of the impact threw him sideways and forward so that the top half of his body slipped from under his safety belt. His lap belt held but his head was thrown forward and caught the edge of the steering wheel a glancing blow.

A dark steel shutter of unconsciousness slammed down.

Chapter Eleven.

The telephone rang twice before breakfast. Helen Argosy, who was in the middle of preparing the meal, growled with exasperation and called up the staircase.

'Ted. Phone. Can you take it? I'm cooking.'

'I'm shaving.' he shouted back.

'Te-e-ed!' pleaded Helen.

'Oh! Alright then.' He clattered down the bare wood of the staircase muttering vague obscenities under his breath and picked up the receiver. A bath towel wrapped around his waist covered his nakedness, one half of his face was scraped clean and smooth and the other still covered by a layer of creamy shaving foam. 'Hello!' he said, professionally removing all trace of frustration from his voice, 'Sergeant Decker here. Can I help you?'

'Decker. Maddy Gunn. Hi there!' The forensic scientist's breezy voice came over the wires, bright and alert, full of enthusiasm at so early an hour. 'I had another look at the bell rope, checked it again under the microscope... *Cannabis cannabum.*'

'Cannabis what?'

'Hemp, to you young man. Hemp... it's made from ordinary hemp from the plant *cannabis cannabum.* Sorry Ted but I couldn't find out anything else about it. It's just an ordinary length of rope. If you want to collect it today you can.'

'Thank you very much Maddy.' he replied dryly, 'Did you have to ring so early?'

'Early? I've been up since five. I thought you country folk were the early birds, not we townies.'

'Worms Maddy, it's all to do with worms. We only rise early if there is a particular worm to catch. My problem at the moment is to know which worm is which. On this case they *all* look alike.'

'Tough!' came the unsympathetic reply, 'See you again. Bye.'

He replaced the phone, returned to the bathroom, rinsed the dried shaving foam from his face and was about to re-lather his unshaven cheek when the instrument rang again.

Damnation! Decker cursed under his breath. He dabbed his face dry and went to pick up the receiver. Unexpectedly the voice of Martin Sellaney came over the line.

'Sergeant Decker? It's Martin Sellaney speaking, sorry to ring so early in the day but I wanted to catch you before you went out. I've been thinking about Maxwell Bull and what you said to me yesterday.'

'Yes. What about it Mr Sellaney?' The Sergeant kept his voice noncommittal.

'I wondered…Well! Erm… could we… could we meet again? I.. erm… there's a lot more I have to tell you.' Waves of uncertainty wafted over the wires. Decker took control of the conversation.

'Certainly, Mr Sellaney. When?'

'Oh! Hmm! Yes. What about this afternoon, say about three. I have a coaching session at the Leisure Centre from two o'clock until then.'

'I'll meet you there,' said Decker, 'Perhaps I could drop in early and watch?'

'Are you a cricketer?' asked Sellaney.

'I certainly am.'

'Then by all means come. You'll enjoy it.'

'Thank you. What exactly did you want to talk about?' asked Decker. There was a brief silence as though Sellaney was reconsidering his offer.

'The possibility that Bull was murdered, it bothers me. I loathed the man… but murder… nothing condones murder does it? I think, quite possibly, I'm in a position to help you. Save you a lot of time and… erm… trouble.' His voice faded towards uncertainty again. The policeman wound up their dialogue briskly.

'He *was* murdered. I have no doubt about it. See you at two.' And with that he replaced the handset firmly, a thoughtful expression creasing the skin between his eyebrows.

Now why was Martin Sellaney suddenly so eager to help? Decker asked himself. There was little doubt that the man had a lot of useful knowledge that may save him time and trouble. On the other hand, suppose he intended to use his knowledge to misdirect the investigation. To send Decker off on a wild goose-chase!

Oh well! The indoor coaching school would be a welcome break. He looked forward to the experience. The Sergeant pulled on a clean shirt, stepped into casual slacks and skipped down the narrow wooden staircase to breakfast.

Helen and Jason had already battered their hard-boiled eggs into submission. Broken eggshell lay around the rim of each of their breakfast plates. The toast and marmalade stage had been reached. Decker pulled a rueful face and apologised for the delay in joining them. He sliced the top off his egg and plunged a toasted finger of bread into the bright yellow yoke. Between mouthfuls he asked,

'What are your plans for today? It's likely I'll be out until late afternoon.'

'Oh! The usual,' Helen replied, 'I've got a new idea for Winnie that I'm working on so I expect to be in all day.'

'What's it this time?' asked Ted, who liked to keep track of Helen's storylines. She frequently used everyday events as the basis for her ideas.

'Winnie decides that it's time to decorate her witches cottage but during the night the evil genie casts a spell that makes all the wallpaper come unstuck. Poor Winnie can't get it to stay in place so she has to cast a spell of her own. Do you want to hear it?' Decker nodded, knowing all too well that he wouldn't escape a combined rendition from both Helen and her young son, Jason. They looked at one another, grinned sheepishly and chanted the rhyming spell in unison.

> 'Solvite! Solvite!
> Keep the paper sticking tight.
> On the ceiling,
> On the wall,
> Do not let the paper fall.'

Decker grimaced, turning his eyes up towards the ceiling and surrendering graciously. His recent attempt to paper the walls of Jason's bedroom had ended in disaster when, overnight, the expensive embossed wallpaper he had applied so carefully slowly pealed itself from the walls and ceiling to lie in eight foot long curls upon the bedroom floor.

'Alright! Alright! So I'm *not* the finest decorator in the world, but I did try.'

'Of course you did my darling.' soothed Helen, 'I shall ask Winnie to cast a special spell for you, just as a precaution. OK?'

'Huh!' he grunted, reaching for the comfort food, a pot of strawberry jam.

'Will you be leaving soon?' asked Helen, her voice sounding unusually innocent.

'About nine-ish.' Decker recognised that tone, 'Is there something you want?'

'It will help if you can drop Jason off at school.'

'Sure, no problem.'

'And are you going to go out just like that?'

He looked down at his clothes. Clean shirt. Trousers pressed. Shoes polished until his face reflected in the shine. He looked acceptable. What *did* she mean? 'Yeah?'

Helen leaned forward. She traced her soft slender fingers down one smooth cheek and then up the other side of his face. They rasped against the day-old stubble.

His hand flew to his face. 'Oh Lord!' he exclaimed, 'I forgot to shave the other side. It's as rough as a badger's ar-r...'

'Ted Decker!' shrieked Helen, 'Really!'

'... a... a... anatomy.' he finished with a cheeky grin.

*

Shortly after nine Decker collected the bell-rope from the Forensic Department. Maddy Gunn was already involved in another urgent project and unable to see him. He scribbled a note to thank her for her help then headed to seek information about the money reported missing from the North Pennine Health Scheme.

'Sorry.' he was told, 'Officially we know nothing about it.'

'But it was published in all the newspapers.' Decker protested, 'Surely there was an investigation. A crime was committed.'

'Technically...Yes.' agreed the detective in the Fraud Squad, 'But the Chairman of the NPHS specifically requested that we let the matter drop. He argued that the resulting publicity from an investigation would damage the scheme far more than the amount of money that went missing. In any event, what good would it do? If Maxwell Bull did steal the money, as appears to be the case, he is now dead and can't be prosecuted anyway. "Let sleeping dogs lie." he said. So we have!'

'Mmmm!' Decker pulled a sour unconvinced face. The Fraud Squad detective looked uncomfortable, glanced carefully around, dropped his voice and murmured in Decker's ear. 'Also we received a message from *on high*… Y'know… the Home Office… suggested we leave well alone. Limited resources and all that bullshit. It would seem your late friend, Bull, had at least one friend in a high place.'

'How did the media get to hear about the missing money?'

'Tip-off if you ask me. From someone on the inside.'

'Any ideas?' the Sergeant enquired.

'Sorry. I haven't a clue.' replied the man with a shake of his head.

'Well, do you know *how* the money was stolen?'

'I can't say for certain but we believe it was through the computer. Y'know, it's how money is transferred these days, electronically, that's how we think it was done. Probably the best person to ask would be the company's accountant. He'll know.'

'I will.' answered Decker. He'd tried once and failed with one accountant. Just suppose the one who *knew* was Harry Radge. Too late there… the man was dead!

'Thanks for your help.' he called as he turned away.

Before leaving the headquarters of the County Police he made two telephone calls, the first to the Queens Medical Centre where Iona Radge had been taken. He asked if she had been released and was told that it was expected she would be returning home on the following morning. His second call was to the Mansion House to enquire a suitable time to visit and speak to Mr Charles Chapling, the accountant. This time his call was successful. Chapling was available. He arranged to drive there immediately.

*

The accountant was years younger than Decker had expected. *Thirty at the most,* he thought, *probably less.* He waited in the foyer of the Mansion House and watched his slight figure walk down the wide elegant staircase from the first floor. Looking up Chapling looked fairly tall, his slenderness giving a false illusion of height, but as he reached the foot of the staircase and stepped onto the bare flagstone floor, Decker realised that he was only about five foot six inches in all. He wore a plain grey suit, a white shirt and a striped tie. His greeting was friendly enough but as he shook hands the Sergeant sensed anxiety in the clipped sentences of the accountant.

'Sorry. Out last time you called. Visiting auditors. Vital. Lots of problems to sort out.' He turned abruptly to the receptionist, 'Keep my phone clear Jane. Anything urgent, tell them I'll call back.'

Chapling led the way to his office, stepping briskly up the staircase with his feet splayed at ten to two and a bouncy vitality in his walk. There was an outer room where two young women and a teenage boy had their heads down working industriously, the ladies on computer terminals and the young man on a printout.

Charles Chapling's inner sanctuary was tiny, a shoebox of a room, scarcely bigger than a broom cupboard. Decker could not believe his eyes.

This man is responsible for vast amounts of money, thought Decker, *The scheme's members contribute millions. Surely,* reasoned the policeman, *his role is of the utmost importance, it carries status... or it should!* Yet here was Charles Chapling tucked away in an insignificant box of a room. Was it indicative of the lack of regard the late Maxwell Bull had for the man?

Chapling's chair was arranged in one corner of the room. His desk positioned diagonally across from the two opposing corners. The chair he offered to Decker took up the remaining space. Despite the confined area the accountant had his tiny office well organised. His files fell readily to hand, easily plucked from shelves to his left and right. A computer terminal and keyboard stood conveniently placed to one side of his desk. He looked brisk and efficient. What can I do for you Sergeant,' he asked.

'I need to know *how* and *when* the missing money was taken,' said Decker, 'Most important, I would like to know at what stage the theft was discovered. I believe you can help me.'

Chaplin's air of efficiency quickly evaporated and a guarded look clouded his eyes. 'Phew! You don't waste words do you Sergeant? He said angrily, 'I was led to believe that the police were not following up their line of enquiry. Our Chairman regards it as an internal matter. He has already explained the harm that publicity about the missing money could do to the NPHS.'

'I recognise that fact,' answered the policeman firmly, 'but now there are more serious issues at stake. Murder for a start.'

'Murder! … You did say murder? What do you mean?' Chapling's face visibly blanched. He seemed to shrink inside his plain grey suit, reminding Decker of a puppet detached from its strings.

'Murder.' Reiterated the policeman calmly, 'The murder of your late Chief Executive, Maxwell Bull.'

'B-b-but I thought... wasn't it… didn't he commit suicide?'

'No Mr Chapling,' replied Decker solemnly shaking his head, 'I'm afraid he did not. New evidence has come to light that suggests otherwise. Now if you would like to explain to me the manner in which the money was taken I would be most grateful. Please keep in mind I am not *fully* conversant with computers, so make it simple. We are not yet certain that his death *was* connected to the theft, but it seems likely. So, if you don't mind?'

The Sergeant spread his hands wide, inviting Chapling to begin. Something like a full minute passed while the accountant composed himself. He picked up a pen and a pad of foolscap paper. 'The scheme has thousands of members,' he began, drawing a large circle in the centre of the paper to represent the NPHS. 'A large proportion of them, roughly one third, pay into the scheme by a Direct Debit from their personal bank account.' He drew lots of small circles around the large one to represent the members. 'Some pay by monthly instalments, some by quarterly ones and a small number by an annual debit.' Chapling drew arrows from the small circles pointing inwards to the large central ring representing the health scheme.

How very clever, thought Decker, *...drawing the diagrams gives him time to think.*

'Once a month,' continued Chapling, still doodling on the paper, 'on the last working day we run an extract of those members whose contributions are due. The information goes onto a magnetic tape, this contains the bank account number of the North Pennine Health Scheme and also the account numbers of all our members paying by this method. The tape is then despatched to BACS – the Bankers Automated Clearing System – where it is processed. On a specified day money is transferred from the members accounts into the Scheme's account. It's as simple as that.'

'What went wrong?' asked Decker.

'The Scheme's account number was changed. A similar number was substituted in its place. All the contributions that should have been paid to the Scheme went into the wrong account. The problem was, that because we were so far behind with our work, due to holidays and being understaffed, the error was not spotted until the middle of December.'

Abject misery showed on the accountant's face. He clearly held himself responsible for his department's failure to pick up on the misdirection of funds at an earlier date.

'Let me get this straight,' said the policeman, 'The account number into which the money was paid was altered. How was that done? Where was it altered?'

'It could only have been changed in *one* place,' explained Charles Chapling, 'in the computer. Everything is processed electronically from then on so it could not have been amended anywhere else.'

'Then you know from the computer what the false account number is?' suggested Decker. Chapling shook his head, 'No. Whoever changed the account number was able to alter it back to the correct one after the debit extraction had been done. The tape on which the transaction was processed was then re-used. All trace of the original information has been obliterated.'

'Who had access to the computer and sufficient knowledge to know what to do?

'Just about everyone,' replied Charles Chapling dejectedly, 'With terminals all over the building it could have been changed by any member of staff. Safeguards are built into the system, passwords, but in this day and age that doesn't mean much. Kids learn about computers at school. They are so damn clever, with a bit of experimentation, who knows?' He pulled a long mournful face at the deteriorating state of the world. 'It might even have been done by someone from outside, a hacker, it wouldn't be the first time that has happened. Hackers have been known to enter the top secret files of the Pentagon, so what chance do we stand?'

What indeed, thought Decker, secretly feeling sympathy towards the young accountant. But someone pointed a finger at Maxwell Bull. Who?

'We did eventually find out the false account number.' continued Chapling. 'It is normal procedure for BACS to send a written report on every transaction that takes place. We keep them on file. The false number was printed on it, as plain as a pikestaff, but it was so similar to the correct number that no one noticed the difference. It was only when our bank statement failed

94

to tally with the money in our accounts that a discrepancy was found.'

'Then presumably the bank can tell you whose account received all the cash?' Decker suggested, looking optimistically at the accountant, 'Whose was it?'

Chapling's face became even more despondent. He sighed heavily. 'It was a new account. Opened in June in the name of Maxwell Bull. As the bank already knew him to be the Chief Executive of the North Pennine Health Scheme no one considered there to be a problem or made any checks. A thousand pounds was paid in to open the account and no withdrawals were made until the beginning of September 1989 – that was shortly after the massive direct debit was collected. Then arrangements were made for the whole of the two hundred and fifty thousand pounds to be withdrawn, *in cash* and collected by Maxwell Bull in person.'

'Good Grief!' exclaimed the Sergeant, 'That's a hell of a sum of money to pay out in cash! Didn't anyone at the bank question it?'

Apparently not.' explained Charles Chapling, 'it appears that Maxwell Bull telephoned the bank in advance and warned them about the money being put into his account. He said it would be required at a specific time and day. The reason he gave was that he planned to bid for some property at an auction. It sounded feasible to the bank because the scheme has recently invested in similar projects.'

Chapling lapsed into silence, waiting nervously for the Sergeant's next question. He doodled on the sheet of foolscap, drawing neat little squares and shading them in with even diagonal lines until they formed the pattern of a chessboard.

What, wondered Decker, *would a psychologist make of that? A worried man with a neat and orderly mind? A man clever enough to steal a quarter of a million pounds?*

'When you found out, what did you do?' he asked Chapling.

'There was only one thing I could do... I reported it to the Chairman of the Board. I don't mind admitting I was terrified. Touch wood, I've never been in such a situation before and I pray to God I'm never in a similar situation again. *It was a nightmare.*'

'What happened when the Chairman tackled Bull about it?' asked Decker, 'Did he confess?'

'Confess! Are you kidding? Maxwell Bull confess! Pigs might fly! No, he denied all knowledge of it. Swore he was in

Scotland on that day. And what is more... *he was!* There is proof that he caught a flight at 8am on Monday 4th September from the East Midlands Airport and flew to Glasgow. He touched down there at 9am and was met at the airport by our Scottish representative. They spent the day together and the rep is prepared to swear on oath that that is what happened.'

'Then how...?'

'On the other hand,' continued Chapling, 'staff at the bank swear blind that a Mr Maxwell Bull called at their premises at 11am promptly on the same day and withdrew the missing two hundred and fifty thousand pounds. They even have his signature on a receipt - Twice!'

'Signatures *can* be forged.' suggested Decker gently.

'Do you think we didn't think of that?' snapped Chapling hotly, 'Of course we did. We called in handwriting experts, four in all, to examine the signatures in detail.'

'*Four* experts, isn't that a tad extravagant?'

'We called two in ourselves and two were called in by the bank.' Chapling explained.

'What did they decide?'

'Decide! Huh!' Charles Chapling tossed his head back in an expression of disgust, 'You may well ask. One of our experts said that the signatures were both definitely those of Maxwell Bull and the other so-called expert declared they were not. One of the bank's experts confirmed the signatures were those of our Chief Executive and the other one... Well! What a waste of time he was. He sat on the fence so bloody long that he must have had an arse full of splinters. He could not be certain either way.'

'Has there been any trace of the missing money?'

'None whatsoever. That is the biggest mystery of all. A quarter of a million pounds, all in brand new notes, it should be easy to trace and yet not one single note has surfaced. Not one. The bank is just as concerned as we are. They kept a record of each and every serial number issued.'

'In large denominations were they?' asked the Sergeant.

'Fifties, every one. Dead easy to spot.' Chapling gave a little snort of frustration, the air whistling down his nose. Then unexpectedly he volunteered a valuable piece of information that Decker had not considered.

'I know one thing, if Maxwell Bull *did* take the money then he *must* have had an accomplice.'

'Oh! Why do you think that?'

'Because he didn't have a clue about computers... that's why. He may have been the Chief Executive of the North Pennine Health Scheme and he may have been responsible for the modernisation of its procedures but when it came down to the nitty-gritty... he was lost. He was never a *hands-on* type. Maxwell Bull was always far too high and mighty to sully his hands with the every day running of the scheme. Employees like Rachel Bergen and Martin Sellaney did the work, they know the systems inside out... but Bull? He wouldn't even know how to log in.'

Sergeant Edward Decker leaned back in his chair and took a long hard look at the accountant before asking one final question. 'Am I right Mr Chapling... are you trying to tell me that Maxwell Bull *could not* have stolen the money, because *he* didn't know how?'

'Something like that Sergeant Decker. But I can't prove it one way...or the other.'

Chapter Twelve.

December 1989

Dimly he became aware of a light shining in his face. A vague far - off sound like the murmur of waves upon a beach. Voices, low, too low for him to understand what they were saying. Movement. He was being carried. Swaying. Side to side. A slight jolt when he was lifted and set down. More lights. Misty. Then he drifted away again. A sea of darkness overwhelmed his conscious thought.

He came to in semi-darkness. How long he had been there he did not know, only that he was lying flat on his back in the comfort of a bed. In the half-light he felt, rather than saw, a small slight figure at the side of the bed. There was pressure around his arm, a tight rubber tube? The sound of air hissing as it was pumped. As his head cleared and the fuzzy edges of his vision sharpened into focus he realised that a young nurse was taking his blood pressure. He heard the sound of a Velcro fastening being torn apart as she removed the rubber tube.

He tried to ease himself into a sitting position using his elbows. The little nurse, aware that he was recovering consciousness, gently pushed him back against the pillows and shushed him to silence.

'You're going to be alright,' she whispered quietly, 'no bones broken, just a case of concussion. Try to sleep.'

Reassured he sank back. There was a clock mounted high upon the wall. Its hands pointed to three-thirty. Three thirty when? What hour? Night? Day? Which day for God's sake? Which *week*? He had no idea. Reality drifted out of range again and he fell into a deep and natural sleep.

*

When next he woke, the clock on the wall showed eleven-thirty. Bright winter sunshine pierced the windows casting long shadows in the ward. Apart from a dull throbbing in the area of his right temple he felt fine. Gingerly his fingers explored the skin close to his eye.

'You'll be as good as new in a few days, I promise. There's some of my best needlework there. With luck you won't even have a scar.'

A pair of bright twinkling blue eyes peered at him over the top of tortoiseshell glasses that had slipped to the end of a rather prominent nose. 'How do you feel? Up to answering a few questions?' The doctor's head cocked enquiringly to one side.

'Questions? … Uh!' Where was he? How had he got there? What had happened to him? A host of questions flooded his mind. What he needed was answers!

He frowned in puzzlement and winced as the stitches pulled at his skin. 'I-I c-can't remember… what happened? … How long have I been unconscious?'

'Mmm!' The doctor pursed his lips and studied his patient thoughtfully, 'What is the last thing you can recall?' he asked.

What *was* the last thing he recalled? He struggled to clear his mind. Slowly, painfully slowly, clarity returned. Driving up the M5 from the Midlands. Lunching with Janice Holly. Leaving Weston-super-Mare. Heading towards the Mendip Hills. Driving… driving… driving where? To see his aunt and uncle, but for the life of him he couldn't remember arriving. His recollections petered out into an empty void.

'Driving to visit relatives,' he answered weakly, 'Friday…Yes… Friday afternoon, about three o'clock I think. I can't recall getting there or what happened next.'

The doctor did not appear too concerned. Temporary amnesia was common in cases of concussion. He hastened to reassure his patient.

'You had an RTA… ran into a tree. Around six o'clock I'm informed. Fortunately, you were wearing your seat belt and escaped serious injury although the police say your car is a write off. Sorry about that.' The doctor's long lugubrious face seemed to express more concern for the defunct vehicle than the living flesh and blood of his patient. 'There is a policeman waiting to see you. Needs to ask about the accident. Do you feel up to it?'

He nodded in reply.

'Good!' replied the doctor, 'I'd like you to stay in overnight, just to be certain. Alright?' He had a trick of peering over the top of his spectacles and raising one eyebrow at the same time. Again he agreed to the medic's request. There was no pressing need for him to return home any sooner than was necessary. How he was going to get there would need consideration.

PC Westcote possessed a rich west-country burr. It coated his questions with the smoothness of honey. He drew up a bedside chair, settled his broad nether regions upon it and produced a compact tape recorder.

'You don't mind if I use this, Sir?' he asked, 'Only the doctor says you've got amnesia.'

'Go ahead,' he indicated, 'but I'm afraid there isn't a lot I can remember. I seem to have lost about three hours out of my life. The accident is a complete blank.'

'Oh! I see.' Westcote's head nodded slowly and sagely, 'That's a shame that is Sir, so it is. Well then, what can you tell me about the car?'

'The Space Wagon! It isn't my personal property it belongs to the firm. It's a sort of *pool* car for general use. It tends to be used as and when the need arises.'

'A pool car is it: and have you used it often sir?'

'Erm! …No. Tell me, why do you ask? Is something wrong?'

'That we don't rightly know.' said the constable, rubbing at his chin, 'Y'see that's a nasty 'ill where you crashed. Real steep that is and with that sharp right 'and bend we thought it a bit odd because there weren't no tyre marks on the road. Usually there's lots of 'em where folks 'ave 'bin taken by surprise and had to brake sharp. So we 'ad a closer look at your car and this is what we found.' He bent down and fumbled about under his chair. 'Now where's that to? He grunted, 'Ah! ''ere it is.' producing a plastic bag from around his ankles. Sealed in the bag was a length of flexible hose with a gland and a locking nut at either end. The brake hose looked to be in good condition until the policeman turned the hose over and pointed to a V-shaped nick in the reinforced material.

'See this sir?' Westcote explained, 'This is the problem. Mick, our mechanic, says this brake hose is pretty new; it ant been fitted more than or week or two. There's no muck on it and the nuts are bright and shiny as a new pin. Now, as Mick sees it this hose could've been got at in two ways. Number one, it's bin chafin', badly fitted and rubbing on the chassis or on a steering arm. Trouble is, with the car so mangled, we can't tell for sure.'

'And number two? What's the alternative?' he asked quietly.

'Aaah! Well! That don't bear thinkin' about Sir.' The constable looked with concern at the man lying in the hospital bed. 'It's possible, just possible, that it was got at with a rasp or file. Cut just enough to cause a slow leak of the brake fluid. Wear and tear would do the rest.'

There was a long silence as he absorbed the consequence of the policeman's words. Was it possible? Was there someone who wanted him out of the way so badly that they were willing to commit... *murder*? No, surely not.

And yet it had been Maxwell Bull who had suggested he use the company estate car. Rachel Bergen assured him that the Space Wagon had been serviced the previous week. Very likely that was when the new brake hose had been fitted. Who had used the car in the meantime? Where had it been kept... and *who* had had the opportunity to doctor its brakes? His head throbbed as he sought to remember.

Try as he may he always came back to the same name...

Chapter Thirteen.

On his way out of the Mansion House Decker noticed a brass plate that he had not seen before. It was set into the stonework to the right hand side of the solid oak door of the building. There were, in reality, two nameplates set one above the other. The upper plate, which was weathered and had obviously been there for some considerable time, bore the legend: **North Pennine Health Scheme.**

The lower plate, shining like a freshly minted coin, was inscribed: **MASECO Ltd** with below in smaller fainter print: Registered Office.

Why didn't I notice it before? Decker wondered.

He prided himself on his powers of observation and could only surmise that on his first visit to the headquarters had only been looking for the North Pennine Health Scheme and so failed to observe the lower of the two plates.

What, and who was MASECO Ltd? Did it still exist? Was there any significance anyway? He set the questions to one side in his mind and headed towards the country house of the late Maxwell Bull.

*

'Sergeant Decker! How nice. Do come in.' Mrs McLean greeted him effusively and held wide the door. It was a welcome in direct contrast to the previous night's cautious reception.

Astonishing, thought Decker, *how daylight changes one's perception of danger.*

'Good morning Mrs McLean, I was in the area so I thought I would drop in. Has everything been all right? No further sign of last night's vandals?'

'No, Sergeant Decker. Thanks to you. You must have scared them off. Miss Bull and I are most grateful for your concern.'

'How is Miss Bull? Is she any better?' he enquired.

Mrs McLean gave him a watery smile. Her expression implied that Marie Bull verged on being a permanent invalid. 'So-so!' she answered nonchalantly, 'Do you want to see her?'

'If it's convenient...Yes I would.' He held out a restraining hand, 'But first, a quick word in your ear. I... er... I'm returning the bell rope. It *is* your property.' he added quickly, 'what would you like me to do with it? I could re-fix it to the bell... that's if you wish?'

He hovered uncertainly, thinking that perhaps the memory of Maxwell Bull hanging from that selfsame rope would be too powerful a reminder of a traumatic event for them ever to want to face sight of the rope again. He was wrong in his supposition.

'Could you? That's very good of you. I'll get you the keys.' Mrs McLean turned towards the kitchen cabinet with its long row of dangling keys. She picked out the long-shafted pair under the label: "Stables" and handed them to the policeman. 'Will you be able to manage on your own?' she asked.

'I should think so.' he replied confidently.

The rope was in the boot of his little green Morris Minor, still coiled in the clear plastic bag supplied by the Forensic department. It was quite heavy but he carried it easily to the stables, unlocked the door and went inside. It was gloomy in the old building and he fumbled about in the semi-darkness searching for the awkwardly placed light switch at the back of the door. He looked up, screwing his eyes against the glare of the naked light bulbs, trying to figure out which side of the loft he needed to ascend to secure the rope once again to the heavy old bell. It was impossible to be certain which side of the loft the bell lever protruded. Decker removed the rope from the plastic bag. He slipped his head and one arm through its coils so that it hung diagonally across his body and left both hands free to climb the rickety wooden ladder. The rungs creaked with his weight as he climbed steadily but the wood was sound and he moved upwards safely.

Once at the top, above the level of the light bulbs, he could pick out clearly the shape of the bell and see the bell lever facing towards the opposite side of the loft.

Damn! Decker swore softly under his breath. Either he had to climb back down again, move the ladder across to the other side of the loft and once more climb up or, he could risk a leap across the intervening space.

It was only four feet. A little under a metre and a half across: barely more than a long stride. A mere nothing at ground level. So why did it look so far from above?

The latch of the stable door clicked and a slim figure slipped inside. Engrossed in his problem Decker failed to notice the new arrival. He slipped the coils of the rope from his head, weighting it in his right hand. His arm swung forward and back, gathering momentum, before lobbing the bell rope with a precise throw to the far side of the loft. Then it was his turn.

There was room for a short run up. Hardly needed. He took two short strides and with a powerful thrust of his right leg leapt agilely across to land with a heavy thump.

The floorboards groaned ominously, sagging and flexing under his weight. At the point where he landed the boards were shorter. Instead of running the full length, from the outer wall as far as the central joist, three of the boards were quite short. They only ran from the outer joist, which they overhung, to the next joist where there was a join in the floor. In effect creating a seesaw situation, except that the inner ends of the boards had been securely screwed down.

'No! No!' a shrill voice cried out from below, '*You* mustn't do that. It's *our* game… *ours.*' There was a child-like petulance to the cry: an echo of immaturity.

Decker peered over the edge of the loft. He recognised the figure immediately. Almost thirty years had passed since the photograph in the house had been taken but it seemed to the policeman that Marie Bull had scarcely changed. From a skinny ten-year old child she had grown into an equally skinny beanpole of a woman.

'Game?' asked Decker, 'What do you mean, *our* game? I came up here to put the bell rope back into place. Just hang on a moment and I'll be right down.'

He turned his attention back to the job in hand. It was a relatively simple matter. The upper end of the rope had been doubled back and professionally spliced to form a loop. It was simply a question of hooking the loop over the bell lever and settling it into a groove. He reached out with one hand to hold the bell clapper and prevent it sounding and with the other tugged firmly on the rope to ensure it was in place.

'You must be Marie Bull.' he said as he stepped off the ladder. She was surprisingly tall, almost equal in height at around five foot nine inches, with large dark luminous eyes that gazed at him with child-like candour. And there, Mother Nature had ceased to hand out her favours. Marie had a generous mouth but the corners turned down in a permanent expression of discontent. Her dark hair hung lank and was badly cut to frame pinched mouse-like features. Puberty had failed to change her body, provide breasts and the soft roundness of femininity. It was as though Marie Bull had remained a child but one who had simply grown older and taller instead of maturing into womanhood.

'You shouldn't have done that,' she said again with sulky petulance still in her voice, 'It's *our* game... *ours.* You shouldn't have jumped across.'

'Are you the one who jumps across the gap?' asked Decker in surprise, 'It's a risky sort of game. Do you play it on your own?'

'With... with...' She stopped short. The big luminous eyes watched him with suspicion. Marie folded her arms aggressively across her flat bony chest and pulled her head down into the fold of her polo-necked sweater like a turtle withdrawing into the safety of its shell, '... with... with... no one! It's *not* your business. It's *our game,* ours.'

She turned away and headed back towards the house with long ungainly strides. Decker closed and locked the stable door and then followed, quickening his pace to match her stride for stride across the yard.

'I'm very sorry. I didn't mean to pry. Was it your brother you played the game with?' he asked. She acted like a child so he treated her that way.

Marie halted in the doorway of the house, standing on the step so that she was taller and able to look down from a position of superiority. 'Well don't do it again.' she commanded bossily. Then in a sudden change of mood her expression turned to one of dreamy sadness. 'I *always* played with Maxwell... and little Malcolm... but now they've gone away... gone away...' Her lower lip trembled, pushed outwards in a truculent gesture of defiance. With a sudden movement she stepped into the house leaving Decker standing helpless and confused on the step.

*

'She has been that way from a very early age.' explained Mrs McLean as they sat together at the kitchen table over a pot of tea. 'I thought she would grow out of it, but she never has. It's like looking after an eternal child.'

'What does she do all day?' asked Edward Decker, 'Doesn't she have a job?'

'A job! She's had a few. Marie's not stupid. In fact she is quite intelligent really, just hopelessly immature. The problem is that she can't stick at anything. Her mind is like a grasshopper, leaping from one fancy to the next all the time.'

'What sort of other things has she done?'

'Oh! A *lot* of night school courses. Marie is very good with her hands. See there.' Mrs McLean pointed to a sideboard upon which rested two delicately carved wooden animals. One was a simplistically designed beaver and the other a sleeping cat.

'Marie carved those. They aren't just good to look at but also tactile. Try one for yourself, particularly the beaver, you'll find it's quite sensuous to the touch.'

Decker cradled the carvings in his hand, running his fingers along the surface of the wood. It felt silkily smooth and the grain of the timber had been cunningly used to give life and colour to the animal.

'She has also been to cookery lessons, painting in oils, flower arranging, even a course on car maintenance for a while. She was very good at that, but...' Mrs McLean spread her hands in a gesture of despair, 'It's all to no avail. Marie finds it impossible to stick with anything.'

What a tragic waste of talent, thought Decker, *ability without commitment.* In the real world it was an unacceptable combination. A recipe for disaster. He rose to leave. 'I'll drop by again,' he promised, 'Deter the vandals.'

Chapter Fourteen.

December 1989

The train service on Sunday was terrible. There was nothing before midday and then a seven-hour long journey requiring three changes before he arrived at the nearest station to Rowell at eight-thirty in the evening. Rachel Bergen met him at the exit. He had telephoned her from the hospital to explain what had happened to the Space Wagon.

'But are *you* alright?' was her response. He sensed genuine concern in her voice, far more on the telephone than he would have been aware of in a face-to-face situation. 'Are you sure you are well enough to travel? I could come and fetch you?'

'No. I'll be fine. I can't ask you to waste your Sunday by collecting me. If you can just run me to the Mansion House to collect my car from the park, I'll be fine.'

'Are you sure?'

'Positive.'

Afterwards he could have kicked himself. It was one more opportunity missed. He knew he would have enjoyed the company of Rachel Bergen on the long drive back. Three hours... alone... together! They had so much in common and conversation never flagged on the rare occasions they had spent time in one another's company.

She was as lonely as he was. He was quite certain of that, despite the fact that she lived with and cared for her elderly parents. Yet neither of them was able to find the words or the courage, to speak out openly of what was in their hearts. Perhaps both feared rejection. So many times he had longed to reach out and just touch her. He never did. It would be easier to thrust his hand into a burning flame.

Rachel watched while he manoeuvred his car out of the car park. Then she locked the gates and gazed forlornly after him as he drove away. She already knew what was about to happen on the Monday morning. It was unfair, grossly unfair. Part of Rachel's duties was to sit in on the quarterly Board meetings and take the minutes. She was a highly competent shorthand typist.

She was also discreet. It placed a burden of knowledge upon her slender shoulders that at times was impossible to bear.

*

Monday 11th December 1989

'The Board has decided that we no longer require your services.' announced Maxwell Bull with an air of fabricated sympathy.

'What!' His head jerked up from the report he had been given to read. Basically the report told the truth, but a truth loaded and presented in such a way as to give a totally biased and distorted picture of events as they had happened. *It was a stab in the back!*

A mortal wound inflicted by a supposed friend. He was still recovering from the shock of seeing that it had been compiled by Rachel Bergen. The anger welled up inside him until the quiet voice of sanity prevailed. Rachel, he knew, had not initiated the report. It bore the stamp of Maxwell Bull. She had merely done what many others had done before her; written into it what Maxwell Bull wanted to read. It was the *only* way to survive!

'What?' he repeated, 'What did you say?'

'You're fired!' said Bull bluntly, 'It is the decision of the Board of Directors. A direct result of the investigation by the DTI.'

'What!' he exclaimed again, 'Exactly what do you mean by that? It isn't my fault, or that of my department, that the scheme ran into financial trouble.   The Claims and Membership Department hasn't spent one penny over its budget. You know that as well as I. The level of claims is well under the target I predicted.' He lifted his eyes towards the ceiling, looking to the upper floor where, until recently, the over-staffed, over indulged, extravagant Marketing Department had been allowed to run riot with the company's funds. He jabbed a stiffened forefinger upwards and shook it angrily. 'That's where all the bloody money was spent... and you damn well know it.'

Maxwell Bull's face went white with fury, his eyes narrowed into slits of hostility.

'It *is* a Board decision,' he hissed, 'They are the ones who decide who is responsible... and it's you. Now clear out your desk and leave the building. *Immediately.*'

How he contained his rage he never knew. It seethed within him like a witches' cauldron. He could feel his fists clenching until the knuckles gleamed white beneath the taut skin. He longed to smash those selfsame fists into the smug sickening face before him. To batter away until the full lips split and the fleshy nose was flattened into pulp. To see fear and pain reflected in Maxwell Bull's selfish uncaring eyes.

But he had planned for this day knowing it would come. And there were better ways to get revenge. Above all he wanted to leave with dignity. To show to the world the qualities Maxwell Bull would never possess: self-control, integrity, and above all else, the respect of his fellows.

Keep your cool, he told himself, *and don't let yourself sink to his level. All your life you have set your own standards, now is not the time to let them slip.*

Calmly he handed back the report. His hand was as steady as a rock. Only he knew the effort of will required to prevent it from shaking with fury. Slowly, easily, he rose from his chair, head held high, shoulders so firmly squared that a crease of material ran down from below his collar to the small of his back.

'If that's the way you want it... so be it.' he replied in the softest of voices. He nodded in the direction of the damaging report. 'I shall need a copy of that for my solicitors.'

Then with all the dignity he could muster he walked out of the door.

*

Molly watched him clear out his desk with bewildered eyes and growing horror as it slowly dawned on her what was happening. It took a matter of minutes to sweep his meagre personal belongings into a plastic carrier bag. She crept into the room. An unholy fear that she was responsible crept over her.

'I-I-is it my f-f-fault?' she asked in a trembling voice, 'B-because of what we did.'

He raised enquiring eyebrows.

'Y'know,' she said, 'what happened in the vaults.' Her long eyelashes swept downwards, looking towards the floor, 'Down there. You and me.'

He had to smile and shake his head at the incongruity of her words. If only it was that simple. 'Did you tell anyone?' he asked.

'Of course not.' She replied a shade too quickly for the truth, 'I didn't tell a soul.'

Apart from the girls in the ladies' toilets, who in turn would have relayed the lurid details to everyone else in the Mansion House.

'Then *you* have nothing to worry about,' he reassured her, 'My lips are sealed.' He laid a comforting arm around her shoulders and gave an affectionate squeeze, 'Don't fret Molly, it really isn't anything to do with you. It's all part of God's great universal plan.'

'God?' she echoed vacantly.

'Yea God!' His head jerked in the direction of the first floor, 'Yea! ... that God... the one in the office up there. Lord of all he surveys... Maxwell bloody Bull, the Almighty... the man who *never* makes a mistake. The man who does *not* have the guts to shoulder the responsibility for his own cock-ups. Him!'

He picked up his plastic carrier and turned to leave.

'Bye Molly.' he said. He didn't trust himself to speak to anyone else. Just left his keys at the reception desk and walked away from five years of hard work, trust and responsibility. Walked away with his dreams and his hopes and a few forlorn belongings in a cheap plastic bag labelled "**MASECO**".

Chapter Fifteen.

Decker sat outside the Bull house for a further fifteen minutes allowing his presence to be felt. He scribbled busily in his notebook and in addition drew a sketch of the house, the garden and the position of the stables showing the front and rear doors of both buildings. Next he pencilled in lines to show all the possible alternatives of moving from one to the other.

Mrs McLean had discovered the body of Maxwell Bull within minutes of his death. Say, three, possibly five at the most, and Decker himself had been at the scene by twelve minutes past midnight. Whoever else had been there, the person who had switched off the light had had only seconds to slip away, or risk discovery. If Mrs McLean had approached the stables by the front door – it being the logical way, the shortest distance from the house and the one lit by the street lamps – then the unknown person would have exited by the rear stable door, slipped around the back of the house, hopped over the garden wall and been away unseen. But who had it been?

And whoever it was would have needed a car for none of the suspects on Decker's list lived within walking distance.

*

He was just about to drive away when he noticed the workman. Cars and lorries flashed by with monotonous regularity discharging pollution upon the rural scene. Pedestrians, fearful of inhaling their poisonous fumes, plodded along the same stretch of highway with less frequency, and thus were all the more memorable.

The young man looked to be about twenty-five years of age. He wore dark blue overalls powdered with cement dust, boots encrusted with a layer of reddish clay and a woolly hat that failed to conceal a head of naturally curly dark hair.

Decker was certain that the man had already strolled past the house twice. Now he was edging past the building once again, leaning to peer over the garden wall and towards the front door of the house, darting little quick furtive glances as though he were afraid of being spotted.

'Can I help you?' asked the Sergeant, easing himself out of his car and stretching up to his full height. The sudden appearance of a uniform paralysed the young workman whose eyes widened perceptibly while his lower jaw worked like a pair of disconnected bellows unable to pump air to his vocal chords.

'B-b-b-b-barrer!' The word suddenly popped out of the workman's mouth in a small explosion of sound. 'Barrer! ... L-l-los-lost it.'

Decker realised that it wasn't fear of him or a sense of guilt that was responsible for the stumbling explanation. The young man suffered from an uncontrollable stammer.

'You've lost your barrow.' interpreted the policeman, 'and you think it's here?'

'W-w-w-w-working.' Again the explosion of sound followed the tortured working of the mouth and throat, 'L-l-l-last w-w-week.' His arms gesticulated in the general direction of the house.

Decker looked. Closer inspection revealed a plethora of reconstruction work. There was a familiarity about it the policeman found hard to place. Extensive repairs to the tall stone chimneys had been made. Blocks of newly worked masonry in stark contrast to the older mellowed stonework. There were new tiles on the roof, the gleam of replaced guttering and the neatness of fresh pointing between the rows of rustic bricks.

Other refurbishment had been done. Old windows replaced. Painting both externally and indoors. A discarded washbasin, bath and lavatory bowl bore testament to internal renovation. That was unless the occupants had ceased to wash and defecate.

*

'Billy. Where the bloody 'ell yer got to?' bellowed a voice, quickly followed by its owner, a stocky man with florid features. Builder was written all over him. From the top of his weathered balding head to the welts of his brick-dust impregnated working boots. On a cold January day with the temperature hovering in single figures the man wore an open-neck check shirt stretched tight across his barrel-like chest. 'Oh!' The man stopped short at the sight of the policeman, then launched a verbal attack.

'Huh!' A short contemptuous snort preceded the man's words. 'About bloody time too. Trust a bleedin' copper to turn up when it's too bloody late. Yer should 'ave bin 'ere afore they took the bloody thing.'

'Are you referring to your missing barrow?' asked Decker coldly, 'If so then I've only just heard that it is missing. Young Billy here...' he waved a hand in the direction of the young workman who was trying to sidle away unobtrusively, '...has just informed me of its loss.'

'Has 'e? Well bully for 'im.' One massive hand passed across the builder's head, brushing down hair that had long disappeared. Then with its short stubby fingers spread wide the hand slowly travelled down the contours of his face, in one motion wiping away his rage and frustration to reveal an expression of resignation. The massive head shook from side to side.

'It's Decker ain't it? Sergeant Decker from Briseley T'ill. I should 'ave recognised you afore. Sorry.' He wiped his hand on the seat of his pants and held it out. 'Sam Taylor. I've played cricket agin yer, remember, Kirk Loscoe, last year?'

Of course, now the face clicked into place. Decker remembered the burly builder who had batted with more enthusiasm than skill.

Sam Taylor turned to the young workman and ushered him away. 'Off yer go Billy. Yer know damn well the barrer ain't 'ere... and *she* ain't around neither.'

The lad slouched away, trudging with abject dejection in the direction of the Mansion House. Taylor watched him go and then turned his attention back to the policeman.

'Soft little sod,' he remarked, 'Moonin' about over a tart as is twice 'is age. 'E's 'ad a lucky escape if yer asks me. Dead lucky... but 'e can't see it.'

He pumped Decker's hand up and down as though priming a well. 'Now, abart that barrer ...'

The Sergeant scribbled a list of items the builder reported as missing on a clean page of his notebook. Both men knew it was a futile exercise. One builder's barrow looked very much like another. The likelihood of achieving a positive result from an investigation was as remote as a blue moon. Too many thieves regarded building sites as fair game. Decker even recalled reading an article in the Police Gazette written by a contractor who readily admitted his own business had been founded upon stolen equipment.   Perhaps Sam Taylor had prospered in the same way...?

Edward Decker was far more interested in Billy. He listened to the builder with half an ear until an opportune moment arrived and then slipped in the question.

'Are you telling me that young Billy there,' he jerked his thumb in the general direction of the Mansion House, 'is keen on Miss Bull? She's hardly his type?'

'Naw! That's wot I thought. Told young Billy many a time as 'e was wastin' 'is time and effort on 'er. Nutty as a fruit cake she is.'

Sam Taylor folded his arms across his barrel chest and put on his reflective look. It was the pose he used when asked for an on-the-spot estimate. One could almost visualise brain cells clicking into place like gears. Then he slipped into his second phase, the confidential word-in-ear pose, which he firmly believed persuaded his customers that they, and they alone, were getting an extra special deal.

'Ter tell yer the truth,' his voice rumbled in Decker's ear, 'I might 'ave bin wrong. Fact is, they got on like an 'ouse on fire. We've bin workin' on the 'ouse all summer, that and the Mansion House, it's all part of the same contract. 'E's a good lad, Billy, a good worker, bloody brilliant on the stonework. That's 'ow she come to know 'im, when 'e was workin' on the chimneystacks. Took quite a shine to 'im she did, the silly cow. She even follered 'im up the bloody ladders wi' mugs of tea. 'Ad me shittin' bricks she did. There's enough bloody accidents on building's site as it is wi'out moonstruck wimin makin' matters wus. I 'ad ter 'ave a word wi' 'er brother. Put a stop to it. Yer know wot I mean?'

Taylor's beefy elbow nudged the policeman in the ribs. Decker looked up at the tall chimneystacks towering like stone fingers into the January sky.

'It must be forty to fifty feet up there,' he said, 'Wasn't she afraid?'

'Naw! Climbs like a cat that 'un. Never batted an eyelid.' Taylor paid grudging tribute to Marie Bull's agility, adding, 'Strange yer know, when she and Billy were together 'e 'ardly ever stammered at all. Seems like 'e were more relaxed wi 'er. Gawd knows wot they talked about.'

'And did he' asked Decker, 'put a stop to it? Her brother, Maxwell Bull, did he break up the relationship?'

114

'Yer bet 'e did. No two ways about that. Tore inter young Billy like a bloody 'urricane. Vicious 'e wor. Warned 'im off good and proper. Felt sorry for the lad. There were no need for 'im ter be so nasty. Reckon 'e enjoyed it. Bloody Bull'

'I take it you don't think highly of the late Mr Bull?' probed Decker.

'Huh! No. Yer can say that agin. Bloody bighead. Thought 'isself too good ter speak ter the likes o' me.' Sam Taylor's massive head waggled from side to side as he mocked a hoity-toity manner. 'Does orl 'is business through a bleedin' Harchitect don't 'e.'

The policeman reflected upon this piece of information for a few moments, then asked, 'Tell me, did you have any problems getting paid?'

'Paid!' The builder's head jerked suspiciously. He looked through narrowed eyes at Decker. 'Paid? Course I got bloody paid. Made certain o' that. Cash up front fer the materials, and stage payments along the way. I ain't bloody daft yer know.'

'I'm sure you are not.' replied Edward Decker. He turned to leave.

'Hey!' Sam Taylor called him back, 'Tell yer one thing, that Marie Bull ain't never 'ad a man in 'er life. Poor old cow! Come ter that, young Billy ain't never 'ad a woman neither. Ha! A fine bloody pair o' virgins they were tergether!'

Chapter Sixteen.

Twelve young cricketers in dazzling white flannels seemed a touch incongruous in the middle of a dank January afternoon.

'I insist upon it,' explained Martin Sellaney, 'it's a question of setting a standard. If they dress right and feel right then it will boost their confidence, and confidence is half the battle, as well you know.' He leaned towards the policeman with a knowledgeable air. Ted Decker thought otherwise. He recalled a former county player, a crafty old slow bowler who had taught him a trick or two. In his later years Stan Canto had turned out for the Briseley T'ill cricket team. At the end of one season he had stuffed his flannels into a sports bag and they had remained there until the first match of the following season. Unwashed, un-pressed, Canto had pulled them from his bag, creased beyond recognition, smelling decidedly fusty and tainted with mildew and put them on.

He had then staggered onto the field with all the athleticism of an arthritic pensioner wearing his disreputable gear. The first ball he bowled dropped onto a perfect length and his five wickets for twenty-five runs ensured the team a winning start to the season.

There is no set pattern for a cricketer. They are all cast in individual moulds. As Canto proved... some being mouldier than others!

Decker enjoyed the coaching session. The boys, between the ages of ten and twelve, were full of enthusiasm. From the beginning Sellaney imposed strict discipline. He laid down his ground rules in an uncompromising manner. The fee was £1.00 per boy per session and anyone caught fooling about was banned for a month.

'Why only twelve boys?' asked Decker, 'Wouldn't it be profitable to take more?'

'I could, but it wouldn't be wise. With a larger number it's impossible to keep an eye on all of them. With a dozen boys I can pair them off, or split them into groups of four or two teams of six. It enables me to spend time with individuals if I feel they need it. Besides, it keeps them on their toes knowing other players are waiting to take their place.'

Decker could see the reasoning behind his argument.

Sellaney began with a short warm-up session. First, a dozen circuits of the sports hall taken at a steady jog, then a series of stretching exercises followed by competitive games. The boys were paired off and with one throwing a ball and the other retrieving it they raced to outdo one another.

'The secret is to keep them moving.' explained Martin Sellaney, 'they have boundless energy at this age, more than enough. Keep them on the go and retain their interest all the way.'

'Why use tennis balls?' asked Decker.

'It helps to build their confidence,' replied Sellaney, breathing heavily as he moved rapidly between the groups, 'It was an idea picked up from the great Garfield Sobers. They can play their shots without fear of injury. Also, at this stage, there is no need for protection and that allows them greater freedom of movement. Mobility, that's the key. Later on of course, when the boys are properly padded up, we switch to cricket balls. By then they will have learnt the basic skills and are better able to take care of themselves and take the inevitable knocks.'

'Mmm! I take your point.' Unconsciously Decker rubbed at his thigh, reflecting ruefully on the numerous bruises he'd suffered throughout his cricketing career.

'Care to join in and help?' asked Martin.

'Sure. Why not.' He could not have been asked a better question. The policeman had been itching to take part. 'What do you want me to do?'

'Nothing too complicated.' Sellaney explained with a grateful smile, 'We're going to teach the boys their first shot. What I would like you to do is to feed the ball to the batsman. I'll show you what I mean in a minute. Usually I have to get one of the boys to do it but it's much better when done by an experienced player.'

'Oh! Why is that?' he asked the coach.

'Consistency. To teach anyone a particular stroke it's essential that they play it to the right type of delivery. That's where you come in. I'll show you what I mean.'

Sellaney broke off and moving to the centre of the games hall clapped his hands loudly to attract the attention of the boys. 'Right boys,' he called out in a loud clear voice, 'Gather round and listen. We are going to learn to play the pull shot. This is what you have to do.'

Sellaney took a piece of chalk from his hip pocket and marked out positions on the floor. First he drew two footprints to show the position of the batsman's feet as he stood to receive the ball. Then he drew another set of footprints to show where the batsman's feet should be on completion of the stroke. About three metres in front of the batting position he drew a chalk circle. This was the target area in which the ball had to pitch. He drew a cross a further three metres in front of the circle and in a direct line with the position taken up by the batsman.

'Right boys, listen carefully. This is what you have to do. I want you to form up in three groups of four. You all have a number, One, Two, Three, Four,' Martin Sellaney quickly divided the boys into squads and allocated each boy a number. 'Now! Number one is the batsman. Number two feeds him the ball. Numbers three and four act as fielders, retrieve the balls and return them to the feeder. OK? This is how the shot is played.' The coach took up his stance, raised a cricket bat high above his head and played a determined looking pull shot against an imaginary wall. The he nodded to Decker to tell the policeman to pitch a tennis ball in his direction.

'Don't bowl it,' he instructed, 'Throw it hard down at the spot I have circled on the ground. Before you throw, call, "Bat up."... Got it?'

Decker nodded in the affirmative. He took up a position on the cross, gripped the ball firmly in his right hand, called out, "Bat up." and hurled the ball down at the circle of white chalk.

With fluent grace Sellaney moved into place, chest on to the policeman, his feet landing almost exactly upon the second set of chalked footmarks. His bat swung round in a ferocious arc and cracked the tennis ball in the direction of the sports hall wall. There was a loud "Thwack!" as the ball struck the brickwork and rebounded towards the line of boys facing the wall.

Instinctively, one twelve year-old cupped his hands, pouched the ball effortlessly and lobbed it back into Decker's hands.

He was most impressed.

'Okay!' called Sellaney, 'There is a line on the wall. If you hit the wall below the line, it counts as two points. Right. So aim your shots *down*.' He moved to the wall and made two chalk crosses, one at a right angle to the batsman's stance and the other at a right angle to the feeder. 'That's your target area, if you hit the ball to strike *between* the crosses…you get another two points. Each batsman has six chances. Count up your points. The one with the most points is the winner. Begin!'

Decker's group could barely wait to start. They were well into the first round long before Martin Sellaney had set up and started the two remaining groups of four on their practice sessions.

Hitting the ball against the wall allowed the young players free rein for their enthusiasm without putting anyone at risk. It was a simple but brilliant idea.

After two or three rounds of practice Sellaney returned to each group. 'Gather round.' he instructed them again, 'Here is a tip. Play the shot with your arms at full stretch. That way you will get more power into the stroke, like this.' He demonstrated the meaning of his words and then moved on to the next group of boys.

Three times in all Martin Sellaney returned to each group, each time passing on a new tip, demonstrating it to the young players and then moving on.

'The technique,' he explained to Edward Decker, 'is to teach them *one* point at a time and then let them practice it. That way their minds don't become over cluttered.'

*

The first hour of the coaching session passed quickly and Martin Sellaney called the boys together on one last occasion.

'It's time for a game.' he announced. There was a buzz of excitement. The boys rolled out a matting wicket and set out stumps mounted upon a wooden base. Sellaney divided the boys into two teams, selecting each boy carefully to ensure an even balance of skills. He appointed two captains and tossed a coin.

'Heads.' Called the fair-headed twelve-year old who had fielded the original shot played by Sellaney. 'Good! We'll bat first.' he decided without a moment's hesitation as the coin fell in his favour. Off he went to plan the tactics of his team.

The sports hall, part of the University complex, was spacious and airy, fully sixty metres in length and some forty metres wide. A wide variety of sports were played upon its hardwood block floor. Tennis, badminton and netball courts were marked out in lines of different colour. Two sets of half-height goalposts at either end of the hall were used for six-a-side football.

Decker was appointed as one umpire and Martin Sellaney took on the role of the other. Sellaney explained the special rules that applied to the indoor game. Two runs if the ball struck the sidewall and four if it hit the end wall behind the bowler. Batsmen could be caught out from a ball bouncing off the wall. A player had to retire after scoring twenty-five runs and the games duration was twelve overs per innings.

The rules were designed to ensure that each and every boy had an opportunity to participate. A sound idea, judged Decker, who knew from experience that in a real game of cricket the participation of players was all too often disproportionate. It is a problem that frequently causes resentment.

The result hung in the balance until the very last over. Despite his impartiality Decker found himself drawn into the excitement of the game. The enthusiasm of the boys was infectious. If the cricket bug had been measles the policeman would have been smothered in red spots! When, with just three balls remaining, the smallest boy in the team jubilantly smashed the winning shot against the brickwork of the end wall, Decker clapped and cheered along with the rest of the victorious team.

'Well done! Well done!'

'That's it lads.' called out Martin Sellaney, 'Time to pack away the gear.'

'Aaaaaw!' A concerted groan of disappointment went up. 'Please sir, can we come next week?' A babble of requests echoed around the hall. There was no doubting the success of Martin Sellaney's coaching course.

*

'Enjoy it?' asked the coach, towelling away the sheen of perspiration on his brow.

'I did.' replied the policeman, 'Most enjoyable, and energetic. I'm fair blown.' Martin Sellaney laughed easily, 'It certainly keeps one fit.' he replied.

And fit he certainly is, thought Decker, *He must be at least fifty, older than I and yet the man has danced around the sports hall on the balls of his feet for close on two hours.*

Retired on the grounds of poor health? It was an obvious lie. Sellaney had more energy than a man half his age. On Decker's list he had to be the number one suspect. First he was the most recent casualty of Maxwell Bull's paranoid behaviour. He had the motive and the opportunity. His alibi for the time of Bull's death was laughable. Secondly he had the knowledge and imagination to set up the computer fraud, though exactly how he could have done it the policeman was not yet sure. Finally he was convinced that Sellaney had the nerve, the cool self-control to carry the burden of a desperate enterprise like murder. And yet... Decker was far from convinced.

Some people are givers and some are takers. Some create and some destroy. Very rarely did the two conditions exist side by side in the one person. A man who gave so much of his time for the benefit of young boys without thought of reward.

Could he also be a taker... a destroyer?

It was a quandary which racked Decker's brain as he followed the car of the cricket coach to his home in the darkening January gloom.

Chapter Seventeen.

'He tried to kill me you know.' There was an uncharacteristic whine to Martin Sellaney's voice. Decker was undecided as to the predominant emotion; a sense of astonishment or one of resentment.

'He tried to kill you? Who tried to kill you?' he asked

'Bull of course. Who else? Maxwell Bull tried to kill me, he did. I'm convinced of it. How else can you explain what happened?'

'I don't know what happened,' replied Decker, 'Perhaps you had better tell me about it.'

They were sitting in the study of Martin Sellaney's house. Mrs Neighbourhood Watch had noted their arrival. The Sergeant was certain of the fact. He had seen the lace curtains of her front room window twitch as he parked his car.

I'll bet she knows everyone's business, he thought, *the nosey old cow, but a nosey, old cow who may well prove useful. When I have the opportunity I'll have a little chat with her.*

'I took a day off, as holiday,' Martin Sellaney was saying, 'To visit my only living relatives. Well, they *were* my only living relatives, now, sadly, they are both dead. I'd had a message to say that my aunt was dying. She had cancer and wasn't expected to last more than a few days. To my surprise when I asked for a day's leave, he, Bull, offered me the use of the company runabout. It's a large estate car. It was totally unexpected and right out of the blue. I was asked to drop off some of the scheme's latest literature at the home of the Area Sales Manager. She lives in Weston-super-Mare in the West Country and my aunt and uncle, that is my *late* aunt and uncle lived in the same part of the world. Naturally I accepted the offer, it was too good to miss. It saved wear and tear on my old banger and the Space Wagon is a much more comfortable vehicle for a long journey. It was only *after* the accident that I began to have my suspicions.'

'Accident! What accident?' Decker asked sharply, 'What do you mean by "Your suspicions"?'

'I was involved in an accident, apparently the car's brakes failed on a steep hill and the car ran off the road and crashed into a tree. It was a write-off and I was lucky to escape with my life.'

'Apparently…?'

'So I've been told. Y'see I can't remember a thing about it. I was knocked unconscious in the crash. Concussed. It completely wiped out my memory of the visit from around three in the afternoon until I recovered consciousness in the early hours of the following morning. You can imagine how dreadful I feel about it. My aunt died that very night and *I* can't even recall saying goodbye to her for the last time. The terrible thing is that I'm not sure whether to be relieved or upset. On the whole I think I have to feel relieved.'

'Just a minute!' interrupted the Sergeant who was having a problem following Sellaney's train of thought, 'If you can't remember what happened, how can you claim that Maxwell Bull tried to kill you? What exactly do you mean?'

'I was taken to the local hospital and kept in overnight. That's where a constable by the name of Westcote interviewed me. He was the one who suggested that the accident was not all it appeared to be. The problem, he said, was that there was a doubt about the evidence. It was *not* conclusive.'

'What sort of evidence?' Decker asked.

'The hose, the brake hose, the way it had been damaged. The police mechanic could not say for certain whether it had been deliberately weakened or whether it had been badly fitted and had been chafing against part of the chassis.' Sellaney ceased speaking abruptly, leaned across towards an office-type desk, pulled open the lower right hand drawer and took out a polythene bag with a press-seal top.

'Look! See for yourself what I mean.' He handed over the bag for the Sergeant to examine. Decker pulled apart the neck of the bag and took out the hose. At first sight it looked to be brand new and in perfect condition. Then he turned it over and saw there was a deep v-shaped groove some forty millimetres from the locking nut. It would not have been easy to cut for the flexible hose was reinforced with a network of steel wire. A triangular shaped rasp was the most likely tool, Decker decided. Even then it would have taken considerable effort. Either that, or, as the police mechanic had suggested, the hose had originally been very badly fitted and allowed to chafe against the metalwork of the chassis.

'Could I take it with me?' he asked, 'I'd like to get an expert opinion.'

'Yes. Of course.' answered Sellaney, nodding vigorously, 'you believe me then?'

'I didn't say that.' replied Decker cautiously, 'It could be that the accident *was* down to bad workmanship. You can't really expect me to take *your* word for what happened can you?' Martin Sellaney's face fell. He shook his head resignedly.

'No. I suppose not,' he acknowledged, 'but I checked, and *you* can do the same. The Space Wagon was serviced less than a week before the accident at Bladon's garage in Rowell. I made a point of speaking to the mechanic who serviced it. He remembered fitting the replacement brake hose and assured me that he made a proper job of it. What is more, I believe him. Bladon's have been looking after the company vehicles for years. There has never been a problem before. All their mechanics are properly qualified and very experienced.'

'Even the very best can make a mistake,' said Decker pointedly, 'They *are* human.'

'Agreed. But there's more to it than that,' said Sellaney forcefully, 'The car was collected from Bladons by Maxwell Bull whose own car was there for a week. He owns one of those fancy foreign jobs and it had a gearbox problem. Bladon's foreman told me it took over a week to obtain the parts. In the meantime Bull used the Space Wagon. He covered a lot of miles in it so if there had been a fault with the hose then the chances were that he would have copped for the brake failure and not me.

'See what I mean?'

'Yes but…?'

'No one else had the use of the car until Maxwell Bull offered it to me. It was either at his home or he was using it.'

'Mmm!' Decker meditated on the man's words, trying to find a flaw in his reasoning. 'But you drove all the way to Weston-super-Mare, then on to your uncle's place in the Mendips, why is it that the brakes didn't fail until you were on the way back? Why so long…? After all you would have been travelling at a fair lick on the motorway wouldn't you? And using your brakes a lot?'

'That's true, except for one small fact. I am not your average driver.'

'You're not?'

'No. I'm not. I have this - this obsession if you like to call it that, about driving economically. It dates back many years ago to a funny old chap who taught me to drive. He showed me how to control the speed of the car by changing down through the gears and thinking ahead. I hardly ever touch the brakes except in an emergency and to come to a halt. He argued that by changing down a driver is always in the right gear to pull away again. It's true. And makes for safe and economical driving. Racing drivers use the technique all the time...believe me...even on the motorway going there I barely used the brakes. So you see... ' Sellaney's voice tailed away letting Decker judge the logic of his argument. If true, the facts were undeniable!

*

Much later, in the evening, Decker showed the damaged brake hose to Helen Argosy and explained its history. *She* was his expert. An unlikely one but non-the-less one well qualified to advise him. Helen's father owned his own repair shop and from an early age Helen had worked with her father in the business of servicing every make of car imaginable. Had she been a boy she would have followed him into the family business. Only the protestations of her mother had caused her to turn to the second love of her life for her career... art.

'What do you think?' Ted Decker asked. He watched Helen examine the hose thoroughly, flexing it backwards and forwards between her hands so that the v-shaped groove opened and closed. She was effectively simulating the kind of movement that the hose would be subjected to with the car in motion.

'I think Martin Sellaney is right. The hose *has* been tampered with... deliberately I would say. Modern cars are designed using computers. Problems such as the brake hose rubbing against the chassis, or say, a steering arm are extremely unlikely. My guess is that the police mechanic was just covering himself, playing safe.' Helen shook her head slowly from side to side in unspoken comment.

'There's something else?' Decker recognised the signs.

'Mmm. Ye-e-es.'

'What is it?'

'Well if it had been me I wouldn't have tried to cut through the hose, they are very tough you know, it would have taken a lot of effort. I would simply have slackened off the locking nut. See here…' Helen pointed with a slim finger to the rounded end of the hose. 'this end fits into the connection on the brake cylinder and tightens up against a gland. To form a seal one tightens the locking nut against the gland. Me, I would have loosened the locking nut to the limit of its thread and pulled at the hose to break the seal. When the brakes were applied the constant pressure would gradually have forced all the fluid out of the system. Eventually, brake failure, and there would have been nothing obvious to show for it except a nut that had not been sufficiently tight.'

Helen looked into his face with her clear grey intelligent eyes. 'The person who did this knew something about vehicles, about how an hydraulic system works, but they were *not* an expert.'

It fitted. Martin Sellaney was right. If he was also correct in his assertion that Maxwell Bull had been the *only* person to use the Space Wagon between it leaving Bladon's garage and Martin himself taking over the estate car then there was only one conclusion to be drawn.

Maxwell Bull had tried to put him out of the way… *forever*!

Chapter Eighteen.

Sergeant Edward Decker sat alone in the study. It was a masculine room, but tidy. The coach had offered him coffee and the policeman accepted. The rattle of cups and the *gloop-gloop* of a coffee percolator could be heard faintly from the direction of the kitchen.

Decker looked around the study with interest. A man's possessions yielded clues to his character. Rows of books, like silent sentinels, filled the shelves of a large bookcase made of highly polished beech wood. Next to the bookcase was a matching desk with a personal computer and printer standing upon it. The policeman eased himself to his feet, drifted towards the bookcase and began to read the titles. Roughly the books could be divided into two categories; a wide range of popular fiction and a whole series of books about sport. Decker picked out the names of many of the great cricket writers; Neville Cardus, John Arlot, Jack Fingleton, E.W.Swanton, and a host of lesser writers too numerous to recall. There was little doubt where Martin Sellaney's interests lay.

'If you'd like to borrow one, you may.' offered Sellaney as he nudged open the door with a knee and entered the room. He carried a small tray upon which two cups of coffee, a jug of warm mild and a sugar bowl balanced precariously. 'Help yourself to milk and sugar.' The rich tangy smell of percolated coffee filled the room arousing Decker's appetite and reminding him that his evening meal was still a long way off.

'I may take you up on that.' answered the Sergeant as he busily stirred milk and sugar into his coffee. He waved a hand at the computer, 'Do you use this thing?'

'All the time.' enthused Sellaney, 'mainly the word processing facility. Computer games aren't my scene at all, can't be bothered with them. But yes. I find the word processor a great help. It's much better than my old portable typewriter.' A sheepish expression spread over his face as he admitted somewhat reluctantly, 'I've put together a book, a coaching manual for boys. It's a project I've been working on for months. Just an idea I had, there seemed to be a gap in the market for a book of that type.

I've already got a publisher lined up. They expressed an interest in my idea, asked me to send them a synopsis and to my complete surprise I received a letter back advising, "Go ahead." I finished it last week, posted off my typescript and now I'm waiting for the verdict. Believe me, it's more nerve-wracking than facing up to a fast bowler on a bumpy track.'

A flush of excitement suffused the man's face.

'Good luck!' Decker wished him, 'I hope your project is a great success.'

'Thank you.' replied Sellaney, the sheepish expression turning into a look of gratitude, 'It's been a lot of hard work, a long haul, but I *have* enjoyed doing it.'

'Why would Maxwell Bull want you out of the way?' asked Decker, quickly switching the subject back to his investigations. Martin Sellaney had a very mobile face. It expressed his feeling as clearly as though they had been written down on a postcard. The expression of gratitude swiftly turned into a look of pure scorn.

'I *knew* too much.' He spat out the words, 'Far too much for the comfort of our late beloved Chief Executive. That's why.'

'Wouldn't other employees also have known as much?' the Sergeant asked.

Sellaney looked at him and slowly shook his head. 'Didn't you make a list of all the past employees?' he asked. Decker nodded.

'Well there you are then. That's your answer. Maxwell Bull made damn sure to get rid of anyone who knew too much about his dealings. There isn't a single person still working for the company who was there when I joined. If they didn't leave of their own accord they were either *nudged* in the right direction or life was made so unbearable for them that they left to escape the pressure. Either that… or sacked.'

The policeman tried another tack.

'What do the initials M.A.S.E.C.O. stand for?'

'Oh God! Don't ask about MASECO, that's at the root of all the trouble.'

'But what is it, or was it?' pressed Decker.

'A bloody great white elephant, that's what!' Sellaney swore vehemently, 'A bloody great white elephant that was at the bottom of all out troubles.'

'But what was it?' asked the Sergeant again.

'MASECO? It stands for - Medical and Sports Equipment Company – Maxwell Bull's personal brainchild. The company that was supposed to make his fame and fortune, only it didn't bloody work did it?' An angry red flush suffused his cheeks as his indignation rose. 'It should have, but it didn't.'

'Why was that? Was there something flawed about the company?'

Sellaney paused to think before he answered the question. Some of the rage drained from his face as he struggled to present a fair and equitable argument.

'Basically the idea of the company was a good one. The concept being that the North Pennine Health Scheme already had a network of private medical outlets, places where its members went for treatment. It meant the new company had a ready-made market, a place at which it could offer alternative equipment. Places where it already had a foot in the door, so to speak.'

'Sounds reasonable,' said Decker, nodding his understanding, 'So what was wrong about it?'

'Oh dear!' sighed Martin, 'It's so hard for an outsider to understand. Unless one actually worked for Maxwell Bull, came to know what he was like. Lord! How can I explain?' His hands flopped about in a gesture of hopelessness.

'Try me.' Decker replied, hardening his voice. Sellaney shot him a wary look, then continued, 'In essence, MASECO was alright. To create and build a successful new company takes time and effort. No one achieves a fortune overnight, or fame for that matter. Oh yes, you hear about such things but looking deeper into the background what does one find? That success has been built upon hard work over a long period of time. And that's the hub of the problem.

'Bull wants it all... NOW! He is so impatient. He doesn't... can't... work to a long-term plan and build up the business sensibly and steadily over the years. Oh no! He wants an overnight killing: instant success, instant fame, and a quick profit. He looks for shortcuts. Takes gambles. Plunges into deals without stopping to think, and then of course he comes unstuck.'

'That's all very well,' acknowledged the Sergeant, 'but it still doesn't satisfy me as a reason for wanting you out of the way, permanently.' He looked enquiringly at Sellaney and commented, 'After all a man can run his own company as he wishes, spend his own money any way he wants. Just because he is a fool...?'

129

'Ha!' Sellaney gave a short contemptuous laugh, 'That's the crunch. It wasn't *his* money was it? It was *never* his money. Never his right to use as *venture* capital was it! It is the members' money. *Their* contributions, money they believed they paid into the scheme to insure themselves for the cost of medical treatment.

'Their safeguard against the future ...'

'But money *has* to be used,' Decker pointed out quietly, 'It has to be invested in order to accumulate. Everyone knows that, what was so wrong about the way Bull used it?'

'Investing money is one thing, all the schemes do it, they all invest their revenue in safe sensible share holdings. But not Bull. That road was too slow for him. He's a typical gambler. Rash. Impulsive. Always looking for the fast buck. He ploughed money into the stupidest ideas one can imagine. Looking back it seems almost any clever conman could talk him into a deal. It was unbelievable. He never ever took a step back and took a long hard dispassionate look at the propositions put to him. If he had he would have seen that they couldn't possibly work.'

'Name one,' said Decker, 'Tell me about one of them.'

Sellaney looked thoughtful, chewed on his bottom lip while he considered the policeman's request. Finally he decided.

'We tried out a scheme for sportsmen and women. Everyone said it was a good idea. A medical insurance scheme to protect them against an injury sustained either playing sport or in training. *It didn't work!*'

'Why not?' asked the policeman, 'It sounds a good idea to me. Surely there must be a need.'

'Oh but there is, there certainly is a *need* right enough. Everyone agrees on that. What they don't want to do is *pay* for it. I know because I had to administer the "Sports Plan" as it was called for all of the two years it was running. It became a nightmare. The only ones who joined were "*sickies*" ... members who already had a problem. The cost of claims always exceeded the amount of contributions paid in.

'Initially it appeared to work for about three to four months. But that was simply because there was a waiting period. A member was not allowed to claim for a pre-existing condition or until they had been in the scheme for three months. That was the theory. But in practice I soon became convinced that a large number of the members simply joined the plan in order to claim for existing injuries, what is more, and I regret having to say this, the medical profession helped to connive in the deception.'

'So what happened next?' asked Decker, 'Surely the plan was withdrawn.'

'Oh! It was.' replied Sellaney with an air of despairing scorn in his voice, 'but only after *two* years. By which time tens of thousands of pounds had vanished down the drain.'

'Didn't you warn Bull?'

'Warn him! Christ! I drew it to his attention *every* month for two whole years. Each month the situation worsened, and each month I put in a report detailing the income from the members' contributions and the amount paid out in claims. The gap grew wider and wider. It was madness. But would he listen? No! The man was as stubborn as a mule... and about as stupid. God only knows why he allowed the plan to run for so long, I don't. Perhaps he expected a miracle.'

'It does seem unwise.' Mused the Sergeant thoughtfully.

'Unwise? Downright foolhardy if you ask me,' raged Martin Sellaney, 'but there is worse to come. Maxwell Bull didn't give up on an idea that easily. The next thing I knew was that he was talking to a couple of really smooth characters... con-men if ever I saw one. They were promoting another form of sports insurance with a membership card that was renewed on a yearly basis. It covered the holder against the loss of their sports equipment, theft and so on, and for injuries like... er... the loss of an eye or the use of a limb. It also included a member's death. Half a million pounds, it stated, would be paid out in the event of a member being killed whilst playing sport.' Martin Sellaney shook his head in disagreement at the folly of it all. 'It could never have worked.'

'But there are such schemes,' protested Decker, 'perfectly aboveboard and respectable.'

'Oh there are,' agreed Sellaney, 'Always provided there are vast numbers of members involved to spread the risk and to generate the funds required. Also the organisation running the scheme needs the financial muscle to back the insurance cover in the event of a disaster. The idea of starting such a scheme from scratch with little or no resources is madness. Just one death, just *one*, that's all it would have taken. It does happen you know, far more frequently than people imagine. So-called dangerous sports like boxing were excluded from the cover but deaths occur in all types of games. Even in cricket, a game I have played all my life.

131

Cricket is considered to be a gentlemanly sport but I know of at least one player who was killed during a match.'

'Mmmm! So do I.' The Sergeant nodded agreement, remembering the tragic death of a young player some years earlier. The man had run full tilt into a ball being returned from the boundary. At first he had appeared to be merely stunned, but later died from a brain haemorrhage.

'Can I ask what happened to the scheme?' enquired Decker.

'Huh!' Sellaney snorted, 'It sank without trace. Our sales reps sold a few hundred membership cards, the scheme handed over the premiums less a percentage, the two con-men said "Thank you very much"… and vanished off the face of the earth.

'Of course it wasn't Bull's fault was it? He put the blame onto the shoulders of the Sales Manager and booted the poor sod out.'

'What! Just like that?' exclaimed Decker.

'Exactly like that.' Martin Sellaney nodded his head emphatically, 'I can give you his name and address if you like. Go and see him for yourself. The poor sod didn't know what had hit him. All he had done was to follow instructions. Doing what he had been told to do.'

'How did Bull get away with it?'

'Oh, in his usual way. He set the whole deal up then passed on the responsibility to the Sales Manager. When the bubble burst poor John Cook was the one left with egg on his face.' The former Claims and Membership manager broke off momentarily, turned towards the beech-wood desk with the computer on it and opened its bottom drawer. There was a neat pile of folders in the drawer, all carefully labelled. On top of the folders lay a notebook approximately fifteen by twenty-two centimetres in size. It had a black cover with red binding. Sellaney took out the notebook, flicked quickly through its pages then offered it to the policeman.

'Here.' he said, 'Have a look through this. It's a record of events at the NPHS and MASECO. I started making notes of everything that took place soon after Marianne Ortega was fired. That really shook me, opened my eyes so to speak of the kind of man Maxwell Bull really was. I had the idea that one day, if I kept an accurate record of what happened, I could use it to defend myself if it should happen to me.' He gave a helpless little shrug, almost apologetic in its manner. 'But I never did. When *my* time came it just didn't seem worth the effort.' He looked at Decker with sad and mournful eyes, his head cocked to one side and added, 'Of course you have to realise that it only gives the facts as I saw them. I wasn't in a position to know everything. A strange man, our late Maxwell Bull. At times he was obsessively secretive and then later his massive ego would get the better of his sense of judgment and he could not resist the temptation to boast. It was his unfailing weakness.'

Sergeant Decker's head bobbed in silent understanding. He was only half listening for his eyes had already picked out some interesting information from the pages of Sellaney's notebook. He paused, and with a finger in the page, asked a question.

'It says here - April 1985 - that you were made responsible for the installation of the membership computer. Is that right?'

'Yes. I was.'

'Then you're knowledgeable about computers?'

'Computers? Hardly. Not then I wasn't. They were new to me, as they were to everyone else who worked for the North Pennine Health Scheme. The truth was that no one there knew a damn thing about computers. But despite that everyone recognised and agreed that it would be beneficial for the scheme to have one. As it turned out, it was. Six months after it was installed there wasn't a single employee who wanted to revert to the old method of working. It was amazing how quickly we all adapted after some basic tuition from the suppliers.'

'Including yourself?' Decker asked with a watchful eye, looking for the man to lie.

'Yes, including myself,' replied Martin Sellaney, 'It was a gradual process, learning step by step and as I learnt and became aware of its vast potential and what one could achieve with a computerised membership so I was able to develop new ways of processing the members contributions.'

'Like... by Direct Debit?' ventured Decker.

'Yes. That was one of my ideas. My brainchild, so to speak, I was the one who suggested to Maxwell Bull that we encourage members to pay into the scheme by that method rather than the roundabout route of payroll deductions. For one thing it meant that a member who changed their employment could remain within the scheme without needing to take any action. The same arrangement applied when they retired.'

'So you knew... *know*, exactly how the Direct Debit operation is run?'

'Oh yes.' Sellaney answered, the faint traces of a smile beginning to edge the corners of his mouth. It was as though he could see the next question coming. 'In fact it was *my* job to run the monthly Direct Debit tape. It became my responsibility and it was successful. Income by that method increased from a few hundred pounds a month to nearly a quarter of a million. Not a bad achievement don't you think?' The twinkle of amusement spread to his eyes.

He's laughing at me, thought Decker, *Damn well laughing. He knows that I can't prove a thing because there is no evidence… no firm evidence… it was only circumstantial.*

'Charles Chapling, the company accountant, told me that the money taken from the NPHS was transferred into an account opened in the name of Maxwell Bull. An account which had a number so similar to that of the scheme that for some considerable time no one was aware of the error.'

'Was it indeed?' Sellaney made the comment in a casual offhand voice, his eyebrows raised in secret amusement as though enjoying a private joke. 'You do surprise me. Now who would have thought that our late Chief Executive could be so dishonest?'

'But was he?' Decker hardened the tone of his voice, 'Was he? Charles Chapling also intimated that Maxwell Bull… the *late* Maxwell Bull,' emphasised the Sergeant watching Martin's eyes for a flicker of betrayal, '…did *not* have the know-how to alter the account number in the computer and then correct it after the transaction had been made. He said that in practical terms Bull didn't understand computers at all. In fact, he wouldn't even know how to log in. Am I right?'

Sellaney's arms spread wide and his shoulders lifted in an expansive shrug. If he knew the answer to the question he was not about to give anything away.

'Whoever changed the account number,' continued the policeman, '…had a detailed knowledge of how both the computer and the Direct Debit system works. Only a very few people within the company have that kind of knowledge… and *you* are one of them!'

He watched Martin Sellaney with accusing eyes. The secretive smile still lingered. The casual air of innocence did not crack.

Damn the man, thought Decker, *He is either a very fine actor or he is totally innocent. But which is it?*

'Sergeant Decker,' replied the former Claims and Membership Manager with a sad little shake of his head, 'I'm mortally wounded by your insinuation. I loved the scheme. Worked for it night and day. It's a fine scheme, based upon fine ideals. I would never do a single thing to harm it.' He placed a theatrical hand over his heart. 'I swear to you *I* haven't stolen a penny of the scheme's money. Nor would I.'

There was such a ring of conviction in his voice that despite his doubts Decker believed him. But where did that leave the policeman? Back to square one?

He badly needed a lucky break.

Chapter Nineteen.

Billy was drunk. Hopelessly, helplessly inebriated for the very first time in his young life. There were two reasons for the drunken stupor into which he had fallen – depression, and bad friends!

It didn't make sense did it, this love business. What was it all about? Hadn't he done everything she had asked him to do? Hadn't he obeyed her every command, followed her instructions to the letter? Yes, of course he had. He still loved her with all his heart and mind, worshipped the ground she walked upon. Yearned and yearned and yearned for her with a vast empty longing in his soul. So why now, when the obstacle to their love had gone for ever, did she refuse to meet him? It did not make any sense.

Previously, before her brother had warned him off, she had taken every opportunity to meet him. Slipping away to find him. Bringing him little gifts. Cups of tea, coffee, a cake or two, an apple or a pear, sweets, chocolate to nibble, but most of all... herself. Theirs had been a beautiful relationship, so pure and innocent, a meeting of unblemished minds, of two lost souls seeking and finding one another.

And they had talked. Oh, how they had talked to one another, as though never before in the entire history of the world had two human beings conversed together. They talked of their dreams, their aspirations, their hopes and their despairs. They talked about their homes and their parents, their families and their upbringing. Above all they talked about themselves and about each other. Of what might be and of what might not.

For Billy it was a new experience. To be listened to... properly. Trapped by the disability of his uncontrollable stammer, he had never been able to express himself freely. No one had had the patience to listen before. But she listened... Marie.

And because she listened, patiently, unhurriedly, without ever prompting him with words as so many people did, trying to be helpful but only compounding his tension, Billy found the words begin to flow easily. His stammer virtually disappeared.

He talked about his childhood, the lonely empty days, many of which were spent reading. It was his greatest pleasure and filled the countless hours his parents were out working. A neighbour with children of her own kept a watchful eye on him. He could have joined in their games but they mocked his stammer with unfeeling cruelty, totally unaware of the damage they were causing.

It was when Marie talked of her own childhood that he learned about the tragic death of Malcolm, the infant boy who had died at the age of four.

Although Marie was the eldest by a full year it was always Maxwell who was the leader. Maxwell was at the top of the family pecking order. He asserted his power from a very early age and decided the games they would play. His obsession with the Wild West had taken root early. Invariably their amusement followed the pattern of the latest Western movie Maxwell had seen. He always played the fearless sheriff in their childhood version of "High Noon". It was little Malcolm who bit the dust time and time again in his many various roles as the villain.

In Maxwell Bull's version of the battle of the Little Big Horn it was General Custer, in the persona of Maxwell himself, who triumphed against overwhelming odds while the leader of the Indians, Sitting Bull, played by Malcolm, who was shot and scalped with gory relish.

Marie couldn't remember the name of the insignificant film that led to the tragedy. It was one of many, trading on vicarious violence, which flooded out of the film industry at the time. Her recollection of the plot was sketchy. It was one of a mass of heaving longhorns pounding across the screen in a cloud of swirling dust, of men on horseback shouting and screaming as they herded the cattle across a seemingly endless prairie. A second group of men armed with guns and also on horseback raided the herd to try and steal the cattle. There was shooting and fighting. Squealing frightened horses rearing in terror, cattle stampeding and men falling to earth to be ground into pulp beneath the pounding hooves. How one could tell friend from foe in the endless swirling dust she did not know. All was confusion, a blur in her mind.

Just one scene stood out starkly in her memory; a vision of a hard-faced man with a voice like broken glass, the rancher, exacting retribution. He leaned over the pommel of his western saddle, regarded the captured rustlers with merciless eyes and in the scintillating dialogue of the 'B' movie drawled, 'String 'em up.'

The sentence was carried out without more ado. The traditional rough justice of the old West. Two hapless men were hauled onto the back of a flat horse-drawn wagon. There was a shot of the two men's straining faces, their eyes rolling in terror as the noose was put around their necks, of the rope being flung over the broad branch of a tree. A wild cry and the cracking sound of a bull-hide whip. The wagon hurtled away and the final frame of the scene dwelt upon two pairs of twitching legs kicking and dancing wildly as the rustlers met their violent end.

Maxwell was fascinated. He chortled gleefully at the sight of the doomed men's rolling eyes and laughed out loud as their legs kicked futilely at the air.

What fun! What a glorious game it all was. The reality of it escaped him. He lived in a world of pure fantasy.

*

At the time of the tragedy the Bull family lived in an old rambling house with a large garden. At the farthest end of the garden was a mature orchard. It was the children's playground. A safe haven and secured by high walls. At least, it was safe from the outside world. No one considered that danger would come from within.

Intermittently, as the family finances permitted, work upon modernising the Victorian house was progressing. The workmen, in the casual manner so typical of labourers, had left their tools and equipment lying around in the grounds of the house. Maxwell found a long coil of wire with a covering of thick black rubber. In the absence of a proper rope it would suffice.

*

'Ma-axwell! I don't like this game.' wailed Marie unhappily as she and little Malcolm stood precariously on the garden bench which their brother had positioned beneath the largest of the apple trees in the family orchard. 'Please… can we play another game?'

'Don't be silly.' Maxwell bullied them in his aggressive overbearing manner, 'You are the rustlers who stole my cattle…

and I am the rancher. They always string 'em up. It's part of the game.'

'But Maxwell, it hurts my neck. The rubber feels sticky, it makes my skin itch. It's horrible. Oh M-a-a-a-xwell!'

'Shut up Marie,' screamed back Maxwell, nipping at her legs with vicious fingers, 'Shut up... or I'll tweak your leg until it bleeds. Pretend it's a *proper* rope can't you? A proper rope.'

Innocent little Malcolm stood quietly on the bench. What was Marie whinging about this time? It wasn't every game that Maxwell allowed him to join in. Being left out made him feel miserable. He had learned better than to argue.

'Ya-a-hoo!' Maxwell let loose a wild rebellious yell. He made a loud cracking noise with his mouth to imitate the sound of a bull-hide whip, seized the end of the bench and in one violent motion whipped it away.

Marie, with her long skinny legs, tumbled towards the ground. The rubber covered wire rope stretched fractionally and tightened around her slender neck. A frightened croak escaped from her lips. But her feet kissed solid ground... just! The balls of her feet helped to ease the weight of her body from the tension of the rope. Terrified sobs burst from the young girl's mouth. Her hands tore uselessly at the sticky black gripping rubber and in her efforts to keep her balance she teetered wildly. Twisting. Turning. Spinning around until she faced her little brother.

There was a moment of intense shock and then a loud piercing shriek split the air. Its shrill sound reached the ears of Nanny McLean as she worked in the house.

Malcolm's little legs trod the air in a frenetic dance of death. His chubby baby hands clawed uselessly at the choking black rubber. His innocent baby blue eyes bulged outwards from a face screwed into an expression of intense agony, a face turning purple as it was deprived of oxygen.

Lost in his fantasy world Maxwell hugged himself with glee. He chortled with insane laughter. This was great. It was just as it was in the film; the dancing legs, the popping eyes, the swollen child's tongue, protruding in an obscene gesture of rebuke.

Mrs McLean, much younger then, flew out of the house with frantic haste. There was still time to save the child's life. Marie's shrill screams struck into her brain like daggers sending an urgent message, spurring her into action. She raced down the steps at a reckless pace without thought or care for her own welfare. Across the garden path lay a discarded metal tube of scaffolding. One hurrying foot came down squarely upon the pole. It skittered away causing Nanny McLean to lose her balance, stagger and plunge headlong into a pile of the builder's rubble.

Her outstretched hands took some of the impact of her fall, but not all. The jagged edge of a house brick gouged viciously into her head. For vital seconds she lay stunned. Blood oozed in a sticky trickle through the torn skin of her palms and flowed in a crimson veil from the gash upon her forehead, down into her eyes, matting the soft hairs of her brows and blurring her vision.

The first numbing shock of her fall eased. Her brain once again began to function. Waves of stabbing pain racked through her body. She knelt in agony, staring at the upturned claws of her hands, at the grit and sand imbedded in the torn flesh. The injury to her head was severe but the greatest pain coursed in waves from her palms making her dizzy and sick from the agony.

The shrill screams persisted. Their imploring message pierced once more into her brain, forcing her to her feet, forcing her to stagger down the path towards the orchard, towards the apple tree with its dangling burden of grotesque produce.

*

Despite her courageous efforts Mrs McLean was too late to save the little boy's life. At the inquest the coroner ruled that Malcolm's death had been the result of a child's game that had gone tragically wrong. He warned parents against the danger of young children being allowed to play alone, unsupervised and praised Nanny McLean for her valiant efforts, saying, that had her unfortunate tumble not occurred, then the boy's life may well have been saved.

Because of his age Maxwell escaped censure. The unspoken verdict saddled Nanny McLean with the burden of guilt and the halter of scapegoat. The early lesson Maxwell Bull learned was that retribution could be avoided if the sword of justice was deflected towards another... to anybody, friend or colleague. It never concerned Maxwell.

*

When Billy first heard the story from Marie he was shocked into silence. It aroused his protective instincts towards the immature older woman. It was as though the years between them suddenly disappeared. *He* became the adult, her guardian and protector. What he failed to realise was that he also became her slave.

Now she avoided him. Remained in the house. Stayed in her room. She shut herself away and had other distractions. It was as though he had never existed. Never been a part of her life. And they had never been in love.

He hung about the house day and night. Sneaking away from his work at the Mansion House whenever the opportunity occurred. He threw pebbles at her bedroom window to attract her attention... all in vain. At times his despair turned to rage and in one fit of temper he had hurled a broken house brick against the doors of the stable, shattering the window frame and glass. But still she had not appeared. Instead a burly policeman had arrived and he had been forced to run away and hide in the bushes of a nearby garden to watch and wait... but nothing. Nothing!

*

'Come for a drink with us.' invited Gobbit. They were his workmates at the Mansion House. Gobbit and Bodger worked as a team; Bodger being a highly skilled bricklayer and Gobbit acting as his labourer. Billy barely remembered their real names. They had been introduced to him as Gobbit and Bodger when he joined the little specialised building firm run by Sam Taylor. So Gobbit and Bodger they had remained, stuck for the rest of their working lives, labelled by the peculiar twisted humour of the working man.

It came as a surprise to both men when Billy accepted. Work had finished for the day. In the winter months their hours were short; as long as the daylight lasted, which today meant four o'clock. As soon as they had downed tools it was the custom of the two older workmen to head for the Charter Inn. To take time out for a couple of pints before they wended their way home to an evening meal.

'Yer wanna come?' exclaimed Bodger in surprise, 'Yer really wanna come?'

'Y-Y-Y-Yea!' The word exploded from Billy's mouth, his curly head beneath its dusty woollen hat nodding vigorously, 'P-P-Please.'

'Christ!' profaned Gobbit, 'Wonders never cease.' The eye on the blind side of his face winked knowingly at his partner. 'Yer sure yer can tek it Billy?' he jibed, 'Aint yer allus bin teetotal? Signed the bloody pledge din't yer?'

An angry flush coloured the young man's cheeks. Coming from strict Methodist parents he had never taken alcohol in his life, but now was not the time for him to admit that fact. Just wait. He would show them. His mouth worked frantically, the air rasping in his lungs as he fought to eject the words. 'M-m-m-my r-r-r-round!'

He grasped the arms of his workmates and dragged them after him.

*

The Charter Inn stood endways on to the main road that ran through the village of Rowell. It was an old stone building, partially renovated, the work grinding forcibly to a halt due to a lack of funds on the part of the owner and landlord. He had bought the "Free House" some eighteen months previously in a fine flush of enthusiasm, taking on a mortgage that was fast becoming insupportable as interest rates rose.

His dream of wealth and riches turned slowly into a nightmare of despair. The old, listed building, being a money pit soaked up cash like a gasping sponge. He worked every hour that God sent... and more. Served all and sundry without question, the sheer necessity of his need blunting his judgment.

The landlord watched Billy with some concern. He was aware that the young man with the dark curly hair wasn't a regular drinker. He had also noticed that Billy's two companions – what were their names? Bobbit and Godger... No! Stupid names... that's it ... Gobbit and Bodger, had spiked the boy's drink. One had distracted his attention while the other had tippled a full measure of vodka into his glass of beer. An experienced drinker might have known but Billy was far too green.

'It's an acquired taste, beer. After first few pints yer won't notice taste.' urged Gobbit, 'Gerrit down yer. C'mon, keep up wi' team lad.' The burly labourer tilted his head back and poured beer down his gullet in an unbroken stream. One moment his glass was full... seconds later, empty.

Manfully Billy struggled to empty his glass. The taste gagged in his throat. He had not expected the flavour to be so sharp, so sour and bitter… so… so hard to force down. A wet sheen of perspiration broke on his brow. He felt dizzy. Sick. The room and all its occupants receded from him then came rushing back in a babble of noise and confusion. There was a churning feeling in his stomach. Someone was making sour cream down there, down in the bowels of his body. A bitter, sour, churning, cream that threatened to regurgitate up into his throat. He fought to hold it down.

*

'Same again Landlord.' It was Bodger's round. He slouched against the bar waving a crumpled fiver under the barman's nose. Hesitantly the man spoke.

'Hasn't he had enough, your young friend?' giving a concerned nod towards Billy.

'Nah! S'early yet. Don't thee bluddy fret Landlord. We'll tek care on 'im' Bodger's stubby workman's fingers spayed around three brimming glasses and carried them to the table without a drop being spilt.

Now they were tormenting the lad. Winding him up over some woman. Leading him on with jeering jibing remarks. He could hear their sneering laughter over the hubbub in the bar.

'…and I bet yer gin 'er a few good 'uns dint yer Billy boy?' Gobbits coarse laughter followed his crude remarks, 'That snotty bint at the big 'ouse. Ode bluddy Maxwell bluddy Bull's sister. Slipped 'er a few inches did yer? Is it true wot they say, "Nearer the bone, the sweeter the meat." Yer near the bluddy bone there cocker, ain;t yer? Ha-ha. Bluddy skinny bint.'

Billy rocked to and fro at the table, shaking his head from side to side in slow ponderous movements. He strained to force out the words, fought to protect her reputation, to defend her: Marie.

'N-n-n-never! N-n-never d-did it. N-n-no.' A vacuous dreamy expression flitted across his face as he contemplated what might have been. 'S-s-she w-wasn't like that. P-p-pure. S-sh-she's l-lovely.'

'Pure! Hah! Pull the other leg.' sneered Gobbit, 'Yer can't kid me Billy boy. All that time yer spent in loft wi' 'er. Yer can't tell me yer din't 'ave a leg-over wi' 'er in the 'ay. Ain't bluddy natural not to.'

'No! No! No!' Billy screamed at them, pounding the tabletop with his pint mug. Beer slopped out of the glass and splashed across it polished surface. A sly fearful look came into his eyes and he asked, 'H-h-h-how? H-h-h-how d-did you know?'

'Saw yer slippin' in there, inter stables wi' 'er in tow, secret like. It were one lunchtime as we come outa Charter Inn. Din't we Bodge? We saw yer. New Year's Eve it wor.' Gobbit swayed against his workmate, jabbing his elbow with suggestive little movements into Bodger's ribs. 'I said to 'im "Eh! Look there. Who'd a thought it, young Billy slippin' off for a bit o' lunchtime nookie. Tastier than a sarnie... eh! Ha ha!'

'N-n-no!' Billy began to shake his head again in further denial, realised the futility of trying to convince the two men of his innocence and changed the movement into a drunken nod. A lie was easier. A lie was what they wanted to hear. A lie was better than Gobbit and Bodger finding out what he had really been up to in the stable on New Year's Eve.

*

Suddenly the sour churning mass in Billy's stomach reacted violently. He clapped one frantic hand across his mouth and the other pressed against his belly to ease the griping pain. The landlord moved quickly.

'Get that lad out of here.' he shouted at Gobbit and Bodger, 'If he pukes all over my bar then you're all bloody banned.'

There was a hurried scraping of chairs, a rush of movement towards the exit. Gobbit and Bodger seized Billy by the elbows, half dragged and half carried him out of the Charter Inn. They draped Billy over a garden wall and watched him vomit painfully into the flowerbed of the nearest house.

The colour had drained from Billy's face leaving it a pale greenish hue. His eyes rolled upwards in his head as he panted for air. He felt helpless, all the strength washed from his body. Weak as a baby... and lost!

'That's it lad, gerrit up.' growled the voice of Bodger. He thumped Billy between the shoulder blades, pounding blows that did not help at all. 'Yer'll be alright now. T'is best to gerrit orl out lad.'

144

Then they left him.

They walked away to their homes and their evening meal and callously put him out of their unimaginative minds. Perhaps they really believed he would be safe. After all he *was* a grown man of twenty-five. Old enough to take care of himself... *in theory*.

Chapter Twenty.

Objectivity, Decker murmured fiercely to himself, *I must retain my objectivity.* It was all too easy to allow one's personal feelings towards an individual to cloud one's judgment. He could sense that that was what was beginning to happen where Martin Sellaney was concerned. The man had natural charm, a charisma and enthusiasm that was already rubbing off on Decker. They had an affinity for cricket, and when two people share the same passion a bond is inevitably created. Added to that Decker had to admit to himself that he liked the man. But logic should, *must,* prevail.

Facts are what matter, he reminded himself, *only facts.*

He hesitated outside the drive of Sellaney's house, looked back toward the building and then across the road to where Mrs Neighbourhood Watch kept a beady eye upon the activities of her fellow citizens.

Mmm! He murmured thoughtfully to himself, *She's a dour old battleaxe, but who knows, who knows, she may have something useful to add.*

Logic told him that Martin Sellaney was the prime suspect. He had motive, a very powerful motive, especially if, as he also believed, as he undoubtedly did, that Maxwell Bull had tried to kill him. He had had the opportunity and he had the nerve. Decker was certain of that.

If I knew someone was trying to kill me, mused the Sergeant, *wouldn't I try to act first. Get in the first strike, so to speak? No! Perhaps not but then I'm thinking like a law-abiding citizen... and that's a mistake. Criminals don't think that way. They don't have a conscience.* And they don't always look evil either. Some of the worst criminals on record are handsome, dressed in Savile Row suits and have engaging personalities.

Decker braced himself, approached the front door of Mrs Neighbourhood Watch and raised his finger to press the doorbell. He barely touched the button. The door was wrenched open and he was confronted by the quivering bulk of the householder.

'Yes!' The word snapped out belligerently. A forefinger jabbed aggressively towards his nose. 'I know you, you're that policeman… name of Decker. Right? Sergeant Decker, I know you see… I never forget a face.'

He was about to ask politely if he might come in when she pre-empted his request, seized his arm by the sleeve and dragged him forward.

'Come inside.' commanded the woman, 'don't stand there like a turnip letting in the cold air.' The door slammed shut behind him and he was trapped. A captive audience now and Mrs Neighbourhood Watch was not about to let him escape easily.

She was a model of belligerence. Born that way, Decker surmised, long, long before feminism had taken hold. She had an uncompromising face, bulging fierce blue eyes, a loose mobile mouth outlined by a faint unsightly moustache. There was a dark brown mole just above the right hand corner of her mouth. Even the mole seemed to bristle with an independent righteousness of its own.

Decker found it impossible not to be intimidated by the woman and wondered about her husband. An image flashed through his mind of a small mild man who left early for the office and worked late into the evening to delay his return.

'I wanted to ask you about New Year's Eve…' he began.

She pounced immediately, cutting into his question with rising indignation. 'And about time too.' She snapped out, 'I don't know what you've all been messing about at. We pay our taxes you know. We deserve better than this. A bit of service would not come amiss.' Her head shook, her jowls quivered and the brown mole flashed its own independent message of righteous anger.

Sergeant Decker was baffled and totally in the dark. What in God's name was the woman talking about? Sympathetically he ventured, 'Perhaps you would like to tell me personally… at *first* hand, so to speak. I find it easier to appreciate that way… so much better than reading a report.'

'Again!' she blustered, 'Again. What is there to tell? That damn, great bus caused all the trouble. You know what it's all about. Didn't I give all the facts to your constable? Didn't he write them down in his notebook? He spent enough time piddling about, pacing out the distance from our drive to the bus and back. Though what good he expected that to do I just do not know.'

'There was an accident?' suggested Decker, cocking his head thoughtfully on one side and trying to appear intelligent.

147

'No! No! No!' Mrs Neighbourhood Watch berated him, 'There wasn't an accident, although there could have been. Don't you know anything? Obstruction! That's what it was. Obstruction! On New Year's Eve! Right opposite our drive it was. Parked outside Mr Sellaney's house, blocked *his* drive completely. He couldn't have got his car out even if he had wanted to … Poor man.'

Her arms folded angrily across her chest like a fortified barrier. She fairly bristled with indignation. 'And,' she continued, '…and it was parked half on the pavement.' Her forefinger jabbed towards his face with the threat of an Exocet missile. 'That's illegal.'

'Ah!' mused Decker pensively, 'It was there some time I seem to recall.'

'Until one o'clock in the morning. One o'clock! I ask you, is that right? It was there when my poor husband had to struggle out with the car and it was still there when we returned after midnight. Bullet's Buses, that's who they were, a coach party celebrating at the Chardonay Restaurant. Noisy beggars. I gave them a piece of my mind when they came back to the coach. Told them what I thought of them, singing and chattering away enough to wake the dead. It's outrageous. Outrageous!' Her finger tapped on the policeman's chest with the ferocity of a woodpecker seeking breakfast. Her loose mouth working angrily as she spat out the words. The dark brown mole bristled, her whole body breathed indignation... a formidable woman.

'Bullet's Buses! Bullet's Buses! I gave them something to think about. I gave them a bullet of my own, up the backside! Told their Managing Director exactly what I thought. Told him I had reported his bus company to the police. So what are *you* doing about it? Eh! What are you doing about it?'

Decker reeled back against the door, staggered by the ferocity of her onslaught. What could he say? It wasn't really his patch.

'Hmm! Hmm! I'll see to it myself... personally.' he promised weakly.

He though about the real problems the police faced; the muggings, the inner city violence, the armed robberies, the rapes and sexual assaults, the burglaries, the hooligans joyriding in stolen cars and the personal danger to his city colleagues. Where did Mrs Neighbourhood Watch's petty complaint come on their list of priorities? Around about bottom!

Buried under a landslide of criminal activity. There was no comparison.

'I'll see to it,' he repeated, edging towards the door, '...right away.'

'I should hope that you will.' Her voice ascended the decibel scale, soaring to new heights of vituperation. 'I should hope that you will,' she repeated, 'We pay our taxes you know. Pay our taxes and what do we get? Very little, I can tell you, very little. Look out for criminals we do. Organise a neighbourhood watch. We report it to the police and what happens? Nothing. Now it has been suggested that responsible citizens patrol the streets. Patrol the streets! What next? What next? We'll be doing your job for you. That's what is next.' She was back to the woodpecker technique again, her finger beating a tattoo upon his chest.

'Yes. Yes.' Decker nodded vigorous agreement, 'Can you tell me one more thing? Can you tell me... was Mr Sellaney's car trapped in his drive for the entire evening? Was he in fact *in* the house all the time?'

Just for a moment she hesitated, pausing to think before answering his question.

'Of course it was. It was visible in his drive all the time. And so was he. I could see him when we left, tap-tapping away on his processing thing, in his study.'

'On his word-processor.' corrected Decker.

'Yes.' she confirmed haughtily, 'On that thing.'

*

'Phew!' Outside the house the policeman breathed a huge sigh of relief. Thank the Lord that a woman like that was a rarity. She didn't appreciate just how fortunate she was to be living in a peaceful suburban road. But damn it, her evidence had shattered his pet theory. Without the use of his car Martin Sellaney could not possibly have been in Rowell at midnight on New Year's Eve.

So where to next?

Chapter Twenty-One.

I'll try the hospital, decided Decker, glancing at his watch. Although now dark the time was only five o'clock. It had been a long day, so much packed into it, so many twists and turns. His call on Mrs Neighbourhood Watch had been brief, had only taken ten minutes, but had seemed to drag on like a lifetime in Hell. What an unpleasant woman! Now he had another unpleasant duty to perform. He needed to talk to Iona Radge, the widow of the former NPHS accountant. The man who he *knew* had committed suicide. Would it be worth it? How much bearing would it have on the case? Would she even be in a fit state of mind to answer his questions?

There was only one way to find out.

He drove northwards around the Nottingham ring road, took the left filter approaching the QMC and was lucky enough to find a parking space on a road at the rear of the hospital. He backed his dark green Morris Minor into a space between a Cavalier and a mud splattered Range Rover, locked his car door and headed for the entrance.

*

'You must be the policeman who discovered my husband,' said Iona Radge, 'I'm very sorry… it must have been very traumatic.' She looked at him with sympathetic eyes, deep brown pools reflecting infinite sorrow.

Despite himself Decker was very moved. *She* was the one who had just lost her husband and yet was apologising to *him*

'I was far too late to save him,' he replied with compassion, 'I am sorry but he had been dead for several hours by the time I arrived.' He lapsed into silence for a moment, trying to think of something consoling to say, then added, 'It may sound a strange thing to say, but, well, I believe he was trying to be considerate when he… the way he did it.'

'Yes, that was Harry. Even… even in those circumstance he would have tried to be considerate. It was Harry's way…' Her large brown eyes stared at the bedcover, not seeing, looking beyond… looking far beyond, back into the past, to better days, to much happier memories. Her auburn hair glistened in the bright hospital light, clean, shining as though it had just been washed, in sharp contrast to the pale ravaged face with the sad brown eyes it encompassed. She had never been beautiful, her nose was too prominent for beauty. But, Decker suspected, in her younger days she would have had a vivacious personality. An attractive warm-hearted woman and with that flaming auburn hair, been the centre of attention.

'I feared it would happen,' murmured Iona in a low voice, 'I feared it… and yet was powerless to do anything. He was *so* depressed, so down. Nothing I said or did could lift his spirits. He struggled so hard and for so long and got nowhere. In the end he just gave up. He… just… gave… up…' She gave a little lift of her shoulders, the faintest of shrugs to emphasize the depths of her despair.

'It's a hard world,' remarked the Sergeant solemnly, '… a very hard world for those who are unemployed, especially for a man the age of your late husband. Even in their thirties people are considered as being too old. So what chance does a man in his fifties stand?'

'That is precisely what I said to the Inspector, a young woman, rather hostile I thought. She didn't seem to believe me, thinks that people want to be unemployed. Her attitude implied that it was their own fault, which of course it is not.' She peeped at him from under lowered eyelashes. Her sad brown eyes seeking approbation.

'She's young,' excused Decker, 'you must forgive her. She is only doing her job. It is not an easy one, especially in a big city. A policeman, or woman needs to be tough. It's the only way to survive.'

'Yes.' She replied looking at him shrewdly, 'I can see that, but… erm… well, you have a different approach, totally different, yet I'm willing to bet that you are just as successful… yes?' He squirmed uncomfortably on the hard plastic hospital chair, embarrassed by the keenness of her perception.

'So why did you really call to see my husband?' asked Iona Radge, 'I don't for one minute believe you wanted his financial advice as the Inspector said. Harry just did not possess that kind of expertise. It wasn't his field. So what did you really want?'

Decker looked at her long and hard, weighing up the situation. He did not want the reason for his enquiries to become public knowledge, remembering the Chief Constable's warning to be discreet. On the other hand Iona Radge was too shrewd a person to be fobbed off with any old story. He would probably learn a whole lot more by being frank. He smiled warmly at her.

'You *are* right, of course,' he said, 'I wanted to ask your husband about the North Pennine Health Scheme… and about the late Maxwell Bull.'

He saw the anger start to change her face, the hard glint appear in her eyes, the tightening of the muscles around her mouth and an involuntary clenching of the teeth. She controlled her anger well, taking a slow deep breath before replying.

'I loathed that man for what he did to my husband,' her voice was tightly constrained and very low, 'Loathed him. Poor Harry, he was only there for six months you know… just *six* months, yet it was long enough to destroy him. He gave up a good job to go there, persuaded by Bull, promised a better salary, an opportunity for better things, a chance to grow with the company Bull said.'

'Do *you* know what went wrong?' asked Decker.

'Oh yes! I know what went wrong… supposedly. Harry had no secrets from me. He told me everything.' Iona Radge tossed back her mane of auburn hair, the light catching her eyes with the sudden movement. Colour returned to her sallow cheeks and fire to her eyes, a fine spirit re-awakening.

Edward Decker waited patiently.

'I know Harry was not perfect,' she continued, 'He had his faults. He was a vain man, and a bit of a hypochondriac. A bit lazy as well, the sort of man who needed to be pushed, but he was not dishonest. He wasn't a crook as Bull implied. He was just… struggling… just struggling to cope…'

'Struggling?'

'Sorry, I'm not explaining the situation very well. Harry was striving to find a way to sort out the scheme's main financial problem. There wasn't an easy solution. Martin Sellaney tried to help, in fact it was Martin who first drew the problem to Harry's attention. He pointed out what was wrong and why. They worked together looking for an answer but there just didn't seem to be one.'

'What exactly was the problem?' asked the policeman, a puzzled frown knitting his brows, 'I don't understand. Where was the difficulty? Surely it's straightforward.'

'That's what everyone thinks,' replied Iona, 'but it's *not* the case. Harry explained to me that a contributory scheme is far more complicated to run than one might suppose. In one way it is like an insurance company, only the manner in which an insurance company does its business is simple by comparison. Let us suppose you insure your car, or your house, your life, or almost anything. How do you go about it? You pay an annual fee, receive a receipt and your policy and you are covered for the year. A simple process, a single transaction and then in a year's time they send you a reminder and the process is repeated. Simple!

'Now in a contributory health scheme the members pay into the fund on an ongoing basis. Some weekly, some monthly, some quarterly and just a small minority by an annual payment.'

Decker nodded his understanding but his eyes pressed for more information. Iona continued, 'Harry said that the membership is volatile, meaning that it is constantly changing. That's what causes the problem. Maxwell Bull pushed the Sales force to the limit. If, in his view, they were not recruiting enough members, then out they would go. Fired! Who can blame them if on occasions they were less than economical with the truth. A lot of people joined in the flush of excitement at recruitment talks, then, when they had time to consider quietly they changed their minds and cancelled their contributions, perhaps a week, perhaps a month, perhaps six months later. Just consider what that entailed, around *fifteen to twenty thousand new members every year.* But almost as many members cancelled as joined out of a total membership of a quarter of a million people. Every person's contribution required checking at least once a month otherwise how would one know who was a genuine member and who was not? It was a colossal task... and still is. It's virtually impossible to keep on top of.' She paused, her head moving from side to side as she recalled the predicament of the late Harry Radge.

'But it can be done,' prompted Decker, 'Banks, Building Societies, etcetera, they all have to handle many thousands of transactions every day. They manage.'

. 'Of course they do!' Iona's eyes scorched him with a flash of scorn, '*They* have vast resources to do it. Modern computers, ample staff, branches all over the country, of course they can cope. People don't change their bank after a few days, do they?'

She's magnificent, thought Decker, like a tigress defending her young, a loyal wife, even now. The late Harry Radge had been a very lucky man in his choice of partner.

'When Harry started at the North Pennine Health Scheme, they were so old fashioned it was unbelievable, like something out of a Dickens novel. They were in the throes of putting all their membership onto a computer. What a farce that was. There were members who were dead, members who hadn't paid in for years, even members who had left the country and yet still appeared to be claiming benefits. Poor Martin Sellaney, as the Claims and Membership Manager, had to cope with a lot of unpleasantness from angry claimants who had been robbing the scheme blind for years. They *did not* relish being found out. Martin went through a nightmare period. There were even a couple of court cases, one against a medical practitioner who was supposedly treating a patient who wasn't even in the country. Martin discovered the woman had emigrated to Australia two years previously. Can you beat that?'

He could, but he didn't say so. Decker had long since ceased to be surprised at the vagaries of human nature. Instead he asked,

'If your husband and Sellaney were working hard to put things right, why did Bull sack him? What did he do wrong?'

'He was too blunt. Too outspoken. That was Harry's trouble.' A tinge of regret touched Iona's voice as she continued her explanation, 'Harry had already rubbed Maxwell Bull up the wrong way by trying to put a damper on some of his madcap ideas. He said the man was on one big massive ego trip. Mad for power and attention. Wanted to build an empire and couldn't wait for success. He had the crazy idea that any problem could be cracked if enough money was thrown at it. Only it wasn't his money, it was the money ploughed into the health scheme by its members that he used as venture capital. One of Bull's ventures was MASECO, the company he founded to sell sports and medical equipment. It ran for two years and was soon in deep financial trouble.'

'Why was that?' interjected Edward Decker.

'Why? It was new. Untried. Its products were too dear to enable it to break into an established market. The Sales people had no faith in it. They weren't fools, given a choice between selling MASECO products and recruiting members for the NPHS they chose the latter. There was more commission in it... and commission, as you know, is the lifeblood of a salesman.'

'What brought events to a head?'

'There was going to be a Board meeting. Bull asked Harry to prepare a financial report that would show MASECO in a favourable light. He was also told to calculate the resources available to the NPHS and present a projection of the scheme's income over the coming year. It wasn't the first time Maxwell Bull had raided the scheme's funds to prop up MASECO and I don't suppose it was the last.'

Iona Radge eased herself higher in the hospital bed, repositioning the pillows to give herself better support. She shook out her long auburn tresses with a toss of her head, a proud mature woman.

'Harry decided it was time to make a stand. At the meeting he proposed to advise the Board to close down MASECO altogether, he could never see it succeeding, to concentrate all their energies upon developing the health scheme. Somehow, in some way, Harry never discovered how, Maxwell Bull found out what his intentions were. He called Harry into his office and sacked him on the spot.

'We heard later, that at the Board meeting Bull informed the Directors that Harry had been sacked for incompetence. That he had completely fouled up the accounts, that his calculations were hundreds of thousands of pounds in error and that, as a result, he, Bull, had been forced to take immediate action. It was typical of Maxwell Bull he came out of it smelling of roses, presenting it as a fine example of his masterful leadership. Ha! Leadership!' Iona's scornful barking laugh expressed the depth of her feelings about the late Chief Executive.

'But surely your husband took action.' Decker suggested, 'He could have written to the Chairman for example.'

'Oh but he did.' exclaimed Iona, 'That's *exactly* what he did. But Harry was foolish. He wrote his letter in a fit of rage. It was full of passion and anger, a wild letter that accused the Directors of stupidity and blind incompetence, unable to see what was going on under their very noses.' Iona Radge heaved a sigh of regret, 'He was always impetuous, rushing into things with rash enthusiasm. When he was young it was a part of his charm, one of the reasons I fell in love with him. On this occasion it was totally the wrong course to take. He should have written a calm logical letter, one setting out the facts. But he didn't. That was my Harry, poor man. I am going to miss him so much.'

Tears welled in the corners of her large brown eyes. The lively animation in her face died like the fading embers of a fire. The love that had fuelled her life had gone.

'Did you have any children?' asked Decker gently.

'Yes.' Came the soft reply, 'Two daughters, one of them has a baby son. Why do you ask?'

'The only kind of immortality any of us really has is through our children. Part of Harry lives on in them, in your daughters and in your grandson. Remember that.'

She stared at him thoughtfully for a long time, eventually said, 'You're very kind and clever. There is more to it than this, isn't there? What is it? What do you really want to know?'

'Where was Harry on New Year's Eve? Did you go out to celebrate? Were you together?' His eyes watched keenly for any trace of dissimulation.

'New Year's Eve?' Her brows knitted together in puzzlement. He could see the thoughts racing, recollection coming back, awareness dawning. 'New Year's Eve,' she repeated slowly, 'Wasn't that when Maxwell Bull hanged himself? Wasn't... Oh my God! He didn't did he... commit suicide. He was... he was murdered? Is that it? And you think... you think... Harry?'

'I *have* to look at every possibility,' replied Decker firmly, 'there were so many people with a grudge against Maxwell Bull. I need to eliminate as many as I can.'

'New Year's Eve...' murmured Iona Radge reflectively, 'New Year's Eve ... Mmm! We didn't do anything special. In fact I went to bed early. Took a sleeping pill. Harry could have been anywhere... I just *don't* know. He had taken to going out at night, when it was dark, going out for long walks when no one would see him. He became quite obsessive about Bull, had developed a deep loathing for the man. It wasn't just because he was sacked. It was more than that... he came to believe that Bull had gone further, had deliberately spread the word around about him, had deliberately made it impossible for him to secure another job.' She looked at the policeman with panic in her eyes; distress creeping into her soul and aging her before his very sight. It was painful to watch.

He could have done it, Iona whispered to herself, *'He could have done it.*

*

He slipped away wordlessly. What could he say? What could anyone say to a woman with such terrible doubts in her mind, a woman whose beloved husband may, or may not, have committed murder.

Impulsive, she had said, a rash impulsive man who acted on the spur of the moment. Could such a man wait for over two years before exacting retribution? Edward Decker thought it was unlikely, but one never knew... one never knew!

Chapter Twenty-Two

Deserted! Damn well deserted! How could they? How could they just abandon him? Sick... lonely... tormented. How could they leave him draped over a garden wall outside a house near to the Charter Inn?

First Marie, the woman he loved. And now his friends, his workmates, his colleagues, people he thought he could trust and rely upon. They had just walked away and left him.

The nausea had receded. His head was still spinning as though his brain had tilted on an axis and the world was out of alignment. The stonework of the garden wall struck cold, hard and very uncomfortable. In the distance, it seemed impossible for Billy to judge accurately, a worried female face stared at him from behind a lace curtain. The householder, an elderly woman mouthed soundless admonitions and her frantically waving hand urged him to go away.

Nobody wanted him.

Marie had cast him off. His friends had cast him off. And now in his time of need this silly old woman wished him gone. His self-pity turned to resentment and his resentment grew into anger. A burgeoning rage against the world in general and against the people of Rowell in particular.

Billy heaved himself upright. There was a foul taste in his mouth, the lingering sourness of vomit in his throat and nostrils. He spat into the garden, wiped his mouth with the back of one sleeve covered hand and took his first tottering step. He would show them. He would tell them all what he thought. He would shout his rage to the village, to the four winds so they would carry his message out... out... out, across the length and breadth of the land. He would tell the entire world.

But first he had to get to the church, to a high place. To stand where he could be seen by one and all. To be seen... and to be heard!

Billy staggered across the main road and towards the village church, lurching from side to side with the ponderous deliberate steps of the very drunk. His destination fixed immovably in his mind.

*

St Martin's, the parish church of the village of Rowell was a fine Norman building of unusual design. It had a crenellated clock tower but the spire, instead of rising up from the battlements, had been positioned to one side of the tower. It was as though the hand of God had taken the spire and placed it carefully to one side, saying, 'Stop! You are getting too close to Heaven. This is as far as you go.'

It was still a beautiful old church. Time and pollution had left their mark, causing the stone to crumble and decay, spoiling the exquisite carving and graceful curves over the solid oak door of the main entrance.

St Martin's stood on high ground at the centre of the village. It overlooked the market place, the High Street, the Mansion House, the sweeping expanse of the park. It was visible from almost every part of the village and a source of pride to the people of Rowell. That pride was reflected in the contributions made by the villagers to the church restoration fund, the fund which was finally paying for the battered stonework to be repaired or replaced. A framework of scaffolding fronted the clock tower rising to the full height of the battlements. There was a wooden platform positioned just below the level of the clock face and a long wooden ladder lashed firmly to the tubular construction. The base of the scaffolding rested upon the cobbled road leading to the church and a cobbled path encircled the building. Due to the unevenness of the ground, segments of flat stone had been wedged under the bottom ends of the upright tubes of steel to ensure that the construction had a solid foundation. It was to this erection that Billy was heading.

*

Inside the church sat the verger. He rested his tired body on the back row of pews in the centre next to the aisle. It was his favourite place from which to admire the altar and the fine stained glass window that towered above it. Almost half a century ago he had been instrumental in replacing the original window that had been shattered by the blast of the only bomb to fall upon the village of Rowell during the six years of World War Two.

159

Mr Seamark was seventy-five, a lean sparse man, fit for his age, who had formerly been a highly skilled glazier until his retirement ten years previously. Now his life centred round the ancient building of which he was the unpaid verger ever since the death of his wife. It gave him a purpose in life, some meaning to an empty existence that did not quite replace the loss of his partner or the departure of his family.

Every evening he inspected the building after the workmen had finished for the day. He checked the doors were secure, the windows intact and the most sacred religious treasures, accumulated over the centuries, all in place. Many of them were irreplaceable, the ornate silver cross, the highly burnished plates which gleamed like gold, though in fact they were merely brass, the vestments and the fine rich trappings of religion. He guarded them all with the omnipresence of a watching archangel. It was *his* kingdom.

Mr Seamark dozed gently on. He had only intended to rest for a few moments but the peace and tranquillity of the old building had lulled him to sleep. It was cool in the vast cavern of the church and the sound of traffic from the main road through the village was but a background murmur. Fortunately he was warmly clad in a long woollen overcoat, fur-lined gloves and a brown felt trilby hat.

A sudden noise jerked him into wakefulness. Where was he? Ah! Yes. Now he remembered, he was in the church. Alone. All was quiet. No! There it was again, a sound from the outside of the building, a strange metallic sound.

Vandals! The thought came to him in a rush. Seamark hated vandals with a fierce intensity that was strangely at odds with his Christian beliefs. It was many years since St Martin's had been vandalised. Not once during the years he had been the verger. His regular patrols had proved to be an effective deterrent.

The sound came again; a rattling noise from the direction of the clock tower. He cocked his head to one side in an effort to pick out the cause. Someone was climbing the scaffolding, hauling themselves up the ladder lashed to the metal tubing, climbing slowly, ponderously, as though handicapped. Whatever they were about to do, Seamark knew he had to stop them.

*

160

There was no reason for Billy to pick up the sledgehammer. No firm motive in his mind. He just did it because it was there. Because it represented power, because power and strength was what he needed just then.

With the sledge tucked into the crook of his arm Billy hauled himself laboriously up towards the wooden platform. His progress was slow and painful but such was his determination that eventually he reached the top of the ladder. He heaved the hammer onto the platform and pulled himself up after it. From his vantage point Billy was able to see the entire village laid out before him like a map. Below, and to his right, was the Mansion House with its twin stacks of tall chimneys pointing like stark bare fingers into the night sky. Further away to his left was the Manor House where Marie lived. It also had tall twin chimney-stacks, he knew both sets well for he had worked repairing and replacing the damaged stonework of both buildings.

Billy clutched the sledgehammer in his right hand, holding it just below its head. His left hand gripped a vertical pole of the scaffolding that projected upwards from the wooden platform. He stood triumphant, poised like an Olympic champion on the podium or a mountaineer on the summit of Everest.

'L-l-listen!' he bellowed, 'L-l-listen t-to m-me. A-a-all of y-you… Listen.' Billy swayed precariously on the narrow wooden platform. The world was none too steady. He had never had a naturally powerful voice, rarely shouted, it surprised him how much effort was required. Why did no one seem to hear?

'L-l-listen t-to me,' he screamed again, 'I w-want to t-tell you about Marie and m-m-me. I love her. L-love her. D-do y-you hear me? Love her. A-a-and s-she has c-cast me aside. M-me… after what I did for h-her. I w-want t-to tell you what I did.'

Billy's mouth worked painfully as he tried to force out his confession to the world. The air rasped in his throat, his vocal chords ached, yet still the world ignored his cries. 'T-t-terrible things, t-t-terrible things I d-did f-f-for her… for her.' Tears of frustration streamed down his face as he fought in vain to make himself heard.

'K-k-killed for her, I d-d-did. K-k-killed. A-a-and now s-she doesn't w-want me… want me…' His voice trailed away. It was futile. Futile.

Far below him, set one to either side of the church tower, were two floodlights. Their beams had been set to illuminate the clock face making a focal point for the village and highlighting the church to its community. An automatic time switch controlled the lights, which suddenly blazed on with blinding intensity. The figure of Billy was thrown into stark relief against the white metal face of the clock. He threw up a protective arm to shield his eyes from the painful glare. Staggered dangerously close to the edge of the wooden platform. The entire structure swayed precariously. Billy recovered his balance, turned his head away from the hurtful light and looked towards the clock face. It stared back at him. Huge. Impassive. Silent.

There was a sudden click and the minute hand juddered forward to tick away a further sixty seconds of his life. Billy stared at the white metal face of the huge clock.

If only, he thought, *if only time could run backwards. If only those enormously large hands could be turned back... minutes... hours... days. Back to the good times. Back to when he had first met Marie Bull. Back to those tender moments of discovery.*

There was a madness in Billy, a raging anger in his head. He let go of the upright stanchion with his left hand. Seized the heavy sledgehammer in both hands. Raised it high to strike at the clock face.

'No-o-o!' An anguished cry reached his ears, 'No! No! No!' It was the frail voice of old Mr Seamark. The verger gripped the corner stanchion of the scaffolding, his feet scuffed against the flat stone placed under the base of the metal tube. At that precise moment Billy swung the hammer, his movement transferring the downward weight of the construction to one side. Relieved of any pressure the levelling stone squirted away to leave a gap of several inches below the base of the pole. The structure became unstable like a table with a missing leg. It rocked dangerously.

At its base the movement was minimal but high up, forty to fifty feet above ground level the shift was accentuated. Billy staggered and lost his balance. The hammer's great head crashed against the clock with a resounding clang. Its reverberation echoing across the rooftops was heard all over the village. Faces appeared at windows, lights flickered on and the villagers came out of their houses.

Billy had achieved his aim... but at a cost.

The jar of the heavy sledge striking the metal face jerked the hammer from the young builder's grasp. It handle performed a lazy parabola as the weighty tool hung momentarily in the air.

Then head down, it plummeted towards the ground. Drunkenly Billy reached for the upright stanchion, but misjudging the distance, his clutching hand grasped only air. Suddenly the entire scaffolding structure canted violently over to one side throwing the young man forward and over the edge of the platform. A hoarse cry of terror burst from his lips. His hands clawed at the air, stretching frantically for a hold. Briefly his fingers seized a tube, then slid down and away from the cold metal as the weight of his body became too much. Down he plunged in a whirl of flailing arms and legs.

The old verger died instantly, the fourteen pounds of the sledgehammer crushing his skull as easily as one cracks the shell of an egg. The soft grey mass of his brain oozed bloodily over the cobblestones, trickling inexorably towards the gutter at the edge of the path. Quite literally, his life trickled down the drain.

Billy was less fortunate. The young man lived for over an hour. His spine was shattered and almost every bone in his body broken causing massive internal injuries. Blood seeped from his mouth but he was still conscious when the first horrified villager reached his side.

Chapter Twenty-Three

'Edward!' Helen Argosy's voice had that imperious tone which signalled trouble. 'Are you going to read those notes *all* evening? Dinner is on the table.'

Decker heaved a sigh and put down the notebook given to him by Martin Sellaney. His nose had been stuck inside its pages for an hour and a half. He had found its contents fascinating... and more than a little revealing!

'Sorry!' he murmured. Helen *always* used the formal version of his name as a chiding reminder when she was annoyed. She had taken the trouble to cook him a tasty *moussaká* and served it piping hot. A cloud of steam rose from his plate. He blew vigorously onto a forkful of food. 'It's red hot... I almost burnt my mouth.'

'You wouldn't want it cold.' scolded Helen, then she instantly relented and asked sympathetically, 'Is something the matter?'

'It's this Bull business,' explained the policeman, 'The more I find out about the man the more impossible it all becomes. There are so many people with a grudge against the man, so many he wronged, that almost anyone could have killed him.'

'Are you quite certain he *was* murdered?' asked Helen, playing Devil's advocate, 'You could be mistaken? Is it possible he really did commit suicide? Is it even possible it was some kind of bizarre accident...?' Helen's voice held an apologetic note as she made her final suggestion.

'No! No!' Decker shook his head vigorously, 'He was murdered. I'm absolutely convinced of that. Murdered!'

'Well, what about his family? Haven't you always maintained that the vast majority of murders are domestic. After all... *they* are the ones with the most opportunity.' She raised enquiring eyebrows. Decker's mouth curved in sardonic humour as he considered Helen's argument.

'Possible, I suppose,' he reflected aloud, 'But hardly likely. First, because he only has one sister, and she's as batty as a fruit cake. Second, the only other person close to him is the former nanny, now the housekeeper, Mrs McLean. She has been devoted to the family for years. Frankly I can't see her in the role of an avenging killer. Finally… well! What possible motive could there be? Certainly not a financial one. They had nothing to gain by his death. In fact they will both be a damn sight worse off now than before.'

'There are other motives,' Helen Argosy pointed out, 'as well you know. Love. Jealousy. Resentment…?'

An image of Marie Bull flashed into Decker's mind. The skinny shapeless flat-chested bony body, the plain face with its sullen downward curving mouth and the lank badly cut hair. Only her eyes had impressed him, those dark luminous orbs shining from her spinster features. She had, by all accounts, been attracted to the young builder, Billy… until her brother Maxwell Bull had put an abrupt end to their relationship.

'Nah!' he exclaimed, 'Never. That dried up old spinster.'

'You just can't tell,' warned his partner, 'you should remember what they say about still waters. Inside every dried-up spinster there is a passionate woman fighting to get out.'

'You have to be joking,' he replied, bursting into outright laughter, 'A warm passionate woman… inside Marie Bull. Hah!'

'Ted! It's not like you to be so intolerant,' Helen shook her head in dismay at him, 'You're usually so generous towards people.'

Her comment stopped him in his tracks. Made him think again. Helen was right, as usual, one should *never* judge a person by their outward appearance. He knew that frustration at his failure to make any progress was clouding his mind and affecting his judgment. An imp of mischief gleamed in his eye.

'Perhaps you're right. Perhaps I *should* get to know her better.' A teasing note crept into his voice, 'Passionate is she? Mmm! Perhaps we could have a secret love affair…?' His voice trailed to a murmur.

'Don't you dare!' flashed Helen, then she grinned dangerously, 'How would you like hot moussaká down the front of your trousers?'

'No! No! I was only joking.' He fended her off as she advanced around the table. With a sudden change of tactics he rose to his full height, swept one arm under her legs and the other around her body. He held her slender frame easily against his chest. She was a very special person to him. 'There's no need to worry,' he said, pressing his nose into the soft fragrance of her hair, 'I'd always come back to you.'

165

Crushed against his broad chest Helen's tiny fist had little room to move effectively. 'So you should, you great bear!'

*

They tidied up together. She washed, he dried and young Jason slept peacefully in his bed. They were a complete team, a family in all but name.

'What did you learn from Sellaney's notes?' asked Helen when they were finally settled down. The crockery had been washed and put away, the table cleared and they sprawled comfortably together on the sagging old settee in the kitchen diner.

'Too much if anything,' sighed Decker, 'If only half of it is true then the late Maxwell Bull was nothing like his public image. Reading between the lines I get the strangest impression that it wasn't so much the dodgy business deals that Maxwell did that upset Martin Sellaney as the way in which he treated the employees who worked under him.'

'Give me an example.' said Helen, burrowing comfortably into the pit of his arm. An arm that wrapped around her slender body holding her close and secure against his broad chest. Decker's free hand held the notebook, flicking the pages over with an agile finger.

'Well! See here,' he said, 'One of the products Bull took on to sell through MASECO was an insert which slips inside a pair of shoes. It's called Solex Six. It is designed to absorb the shock of an athlete's legs constantly pounding the ground. It's ideal for marathon runners, sportsmen who spend a lot of time on their feet, or anyone else for that matter. Sellaney tried out the inserts himself and believes they are an excellent product. They could have done well except that Bull, as always was too greedy. He did a big deal with a company, bought a massive amount of stock and was then caught out when the company he was selling them on to went bust. Typically of him he had rushed in without bothering to check out his buyer. Seems they had been on the verge of bankruptcy for a year. MASECO was left with around twenty thousand pounds worth of useless stock which it could not shift. According to Sellaney's notebook Maxwell Bull *borrowed* from the NPHS charity fund to bail himself out. On paper the health scheme bought the inserts from MASECO and donated them to a third world country as a charitable gift. I ask you, what

166

use would they have been to the people there? They weren't edible!

It was an outright fiddle, especially as the money to buy the damn inserts originated from the NPHS in the first place.'

'But that's awful.' commented Helen, listening intently.

'Yet strangely,' continued Decker, 'Martin Sellaney seems to be far more upset over the treatment of Rosie Jay than over the misuse of the charity fund money.'

'Who is Rosie Jay?' Helen Argosy questioned.

'Patience, I'm coming to her,' admonished the policeman as he wriggled into a comfortable position and continued with his story, 'Rosie Jay was a young woman set on by Rachel Bergen. She suffered from cerebral palsy and was severely handicapped in one arm. It was just about useless. But that apart that she was a bright cheerful girl and by all accounts a willing worker. She was employed there for eighteen months, not doing anything really vital, just looking after the post room, doing the photo copying, that sort of thing. Then one day, out of the blue, Bull instructed Rachel Bergen to get rid of her. He said the Board wanted to improve the company's image. Rachel Bergen protested, naturally, but she was left with no choice. She had to dismiss her.'

'The poor girl, what a shocking thing to do.' Concern for a person she had never known came naturally to Helen Argosy. 'I can see why Martin Sellaney was upset by it, any decent person would be.'

'Yes.' agreed Edward Decker, 'Especially when Maxwell Bull made such a great show of presenting the NPHS as a caring and concerned organisation. It reveals how big a hypocrite the man is... *was.*' he corrected himself.

They sat in companionable silence for a while, each one wrapped in their own thoughts. Decker started to say, 'Of course it doesn't help...' when the phone rang.

'Hello! Yes ...Yes...' Helen listened patiently, the expression on her face turning from polite interest to one of extreme gravity. 'Yes, I have that,' she repeated, 'I'll let Sergeant Decker know immediately.' She replaced the receiver very gently and raised troubled eyes in the direction of Decker.

'What's wrong?' he asked, levering himself from the sagging furniture.

'There's been some kind of accident, at Rowell, at the church. One man killed and another badly injured. It appears that one man fell from the scaffolding around the clock tower. Vandals, they think.'

'Oh my God!' Decker was up in a flash, pulling on boots, fastening buttons on his tunic as he raced upstairs to collect a powerful torch from their bedroom. Helen was ready with the car keys in her hand, the door ajar, as the burly policeman pounded down the narrow wooden staircase of their tiny cottage. He paused to kiss her briefly.

'See you… when I see you.' he called vaguely.

'Take care… for God's sake… and for mine.' Helen's anxious eyes followed the car as he sped away into the January night…

Chapter Twenty-Four

A considerate villager, or a squeamish one, had covered the verger's body with a worn tartan car blanket. Decker lifted one corner. It tested his willpower and self-control to the full not to visibly flinch and draw away from the sight of the shattered skull with its oozing grey matter. He let the blanket fall back into place.

'Did anyone see what happened?' he asked looking round at the circle of stricken faces. From the plethora of answers which swamped him like flood water he deduced two clear facts. Almost everyone had heard the sound of the sledgehammer striking the face of the clock but not one single person had actually witnessed what happened. They had all emerged from their homes moments too late.

Billy lay on the ground uncovered. He was semi-conscious, moaning and muttering unintelligible words. In the minds of the villagers he had been instantly identified as the villain. No one had moved to care for him, to cover his body against shock or support his head with the comfort of a makeshift pillow.

Decker stripped off his overcoat and wrapped it carefully around the broken body. He glared accusingly at the circle of faces, saying little, thinking that whatever the young man might, or might not have done, he was still a human being. Feet shifted uneasily, eyes lifted to look at the damaged face of the church clock with its broken minute arm, bent and misshapen like a fractured limb. He brought it upon himself, said the accusing eyes as they adopted a protective air of self-righteousness.

'An ambulance, has anyone phoned for an ambulance?' asked the policeman. A grim-faced villager nodded in the affirmative and showed belated concern for the young victim.

'It's Billy Reason, ain't it? Is he gonna be alright?'

Beneath the healthy tan, acquired from years of working out of doors, Billy's face was deathly pale. A sheen of perspiration glistened upon his skin which felt cold and clammy to the touch. He shivered violently and little bubbles of blood-flecked foam came from the corners of his mouth.

'He's tryin' ter say summat.' remarked the villager, 'Wot's 'e tryin' ter say? Eh!'

'Move away please.' commanded Decker, 'I'm trying to hear.'

They shuffled back a few paces. One or two of the less morbid began to drift away, back to their cottages, back to the warmth and security of their homes. The crowd visibly thinned. Decker knelt awkwardly on the cold hard cobblestones, supporting the young man's head with one arm, bending low to bring his ear close to the trembling lips. Flecks of blood splashed against his cheek as Billy struggled to speak. The pain-wracked words burst in tiny explosions of sound from the dying man.

'H-h-have... to... tell... y-you w-w-what... happened. W-w-what... I-I ... d-d-did.'

'Easy Billy,' soothed the policeman, 'easy. The ambulance is on its way. You're going to be alright.'

'N-n-no! H-h-have... t-to... to speak... have to... t-t-tell you... Please.' There was a desperate eloquence in the fading eyes, a burning determination to explain. Decker bent closer. His ear brushing the young man's faltering lips. Only *he* could hear what was being said. He concentrated hard, straining to catch the stammering confession. They became as one, alone in a world apart, joined together as a priest and supplicant are joined in the privacy of the confessional.

*

'Shall I take over now Sergeant?' A concerned hand fell upon Decker's shoulder and a competent voice spoke into his ear. The policeman had been concentrating so hard that he had failed to hear the noisy arrival of the ambulance or be aware of the busy approach of the yellow-jacketed paramedic.

'He fell,' Decker explained briefly, glancing up at the tower of scaffolding, 'All the way.'

'We'll do what we can.' said the paramedic, weighing up the situation at a glance. The tone of his voice was comforting but the fleeting expression he was unable to hide spoke otherwise. Working as a team they edged Billy gently onto a stretcher, eased his broken body into the security of the ambulance. An oxygen mask was placed over his nose and mouth. A needle slid into a vein. The doors of the ambulance slammed shut and Billy was whisked away.

*

It was midnight before Decker arrived home. The valiant efforts of the paramedics had proved futile. Billy Reason died in the ambulance on the way to the hospital and was certified *Dead On Arrival*.

Quietly the policeman eased back the catch, slipped into his darkened home, ducking instinctively under the low beams as he made his way to the kitchen. Helen had left milk in a saucepan, chocolate already in a mug. It would take him two minutes to heat up a bedtime drink. He looked at the utensils with tired appreciation. Shook his head wearily. He was too shattered in body and spirit to bother.

Helen had been right. His investigation had been leading him in the wrong direction, a veritable paper chase of red herrings. His entire strategy needed a rethink. But tomorrow... tomorrow... he would sort out the mess... for now... bed!

He tiptoed up the narrow wooden staircase in stocking feet. Undressed in the dark. Slipped between the sheets to snuggle close to the pool of warmth created by Helen's slumbering body. And was asleep in seconds...

Chapter Twenty-Five

'You're very quiet this morning,' commented Helen Argosy over the breakfast table, 'Is anything wrong?'

Ted Decker smiled ruefully, reluctant to admit he had been wrong.

'On the contrary, it's all beginning to come right.' His strong white teeth crunched on a slice of toast and marmalade. He masticated slowly, ruminating as thoughtfully as any cow chewing on its cud.

'Well! Are you going to tell me what happened?' Helen was pop-eyed with curiosity.

'I might… later!' he teased, 'When I've checked out a few facts.'

'Ted!'

'Alright.' he relented, 'you were right and I was wrong. It's beginning to look as though Bull's death was unrelated to the North Pennine Health Scheme. It was much closer to home than that. A personal…'

'Didn't I tell you.' burst in Helen, spluttering crumbs across the table in her excitement, 'didn't I tell you it was a member of the family. Didn't I?'

'Whoa! Steady! Hold your horses. I haven't proved a thing yet and even though I may have found the answer to how Maxwell Bull died there is still the missing money to account for. Where that ties in I just do not know.'

'Oh dear!' Helen clapped a hand to her mouth in sudden dismay, 'I completely forgot, there was a message for you. It was late yesterday afternoon. I meant to write it down, then the telephone rang again and it went right out of my head. It was about the missing money. A woman rang, said her name was Rachel Bergen. She said she was the General Manager of the NPHS. She wanted to talk to you urgently because something very strange had happened and she thought you should know.'

'Did she say what it was?'

'No.' Helen shook her head, 'No. She refused to go into details on the telephone. Said it was a confidential matter. She wanted to speak to you in person.'

'Mmm! I wonder what she wants?' mused the policeman, 'I said things were coming together… perhaps they are.'

*

Wintry sunshine cast a warm yellow glow upon the mellowing stonework of the Mansion House. It was one of those cold clear January days with a beauty all of its own. Decker breathed in deeply, savouring the fresh clean country air, sucking it down to scour out his lungs and clean them of pollution.

From the short semi-circular driveway he could see clearly the battered face of the church clock and the crazily canted scaffolding. If only, he wished, he could clear his mind of the tragic events of the previous evening as easily as he could flush out his lungs. The memory of Billy's sudden demise and the death of the old verger were indelibly etched into his mind, as hard to eradicate as a grass stain on white flannel. He shook off the depressing thought and turned his attention to the Mansion House.

*

Jane, the receptionist recognised him instantly. She nodded cheerfully in his direction. 'Good morning, it's Sergeant Decker isn't it? Ms Bergen is waiting to see you.' She led him up the wide thickly carpeted staircase, past the huge gilt-framed mirror on the landing, beneath the glittering chandelier and into the plain stark office of the General Manager. The petite figure of Rachel Bergen rose to greet him.

It was like meeting another person for it was a totally different Rachel Bergen to the one he had previously met. The tension he had been so aware of on his first visit had gone. A warm generous smile welcomed him and he could swear that the gleam in her eyes possessed a mischievous twinkle.

'Would you like tea or coffee Sergeant Decker?' she asked, offering a friendly hand. His massive paw enveloped her tiny mitt but there was firmness and confidence in her grasp. At last he could see the attraction Martin Sellaney felt towards the woman.

'I'm intrigued by your message,' he began, 'you mentioned on the phone that something very strange had happened. Would you care to tell me?'

173

There it was again, a slight twitching at the corners of her mouth as she fought to suppress an outright smile.

There is a private joke here, thought Decker, *and I am on the outside.* Whatever it was had changed her entire attitude.

'We have recovered the missing money.' she informed him. The delight showed on her face and echoed in her voice. His jaw dropped in surprise.

'How?' he managed to ask.

'It was here all the time. Here, in the building.'

'Here?' Decker echoed, hoping that he did not appear as vacant as he sounded. 'You did say "Here" didn't you?'

'Oh yes! It was here all the time. It was hidden away down in the vault in the basement of the building. I discovered it yesterday.' The gaiety in her voice transformed Rachel Bergen and he wondered how he had ever thought of her as a grey uninteresting little woman.

'But how...?'

'I received a letter yesterday, supposedly from a member of the scheme, in which he alleged that his claim dated 29th February 1989 had been mishandled. It is signed by a Mr Rob Berry and when I entered his name into our membership computer to search for the details there's no such member. Then of course it hit me, there is no such date either. Nineteen eighty-nine was *not* a Leap year so the 29th never existed. It had to be a hoax.'

'May I see the letter?' asked Decker. Fully prepared for the obvious question Rachel Bergen removed an envelope from the top drawer of her desk and handed it to the policeman. He examined the plain white self-seal envelope with its typed address and a Gloucestershire postmark. The letter itself had been produced on a word-processor. Even Decker's untutored eye recognised the fact by its fully justified printing. It had been printed out on ordinary plain white photocopier paper of the type that can be bought at any one of a thousand office suppliers. He held it up to the light and there wasn't even a watermark. No clues there. Clearly the perpetrator was nobody's fool. There was an address, plainly false, in the top right hand corner of the letter and it was addressed, by name, to the General Manager of the North Pennine Health Scheme.

Thieves Cottage
Highwayman's Lane
Gloucestershire

Dear Ms Bergen,

I wish to protest about the amount of re-imbursement paid against my claim for medical treatment received in February 1989. An error has been made in calculating the amount due to me. Please investigate immediately.

I await your early reply

Yours sincerely

Rob Berry

'Rob Berry,' murmured Decker, 'Rob Berry, Thieves Cottage, Highwayman's Lane... Rob...Berry...Rob-Berry ... ROBBERY! It's a joke! A silly hoax! No doubt about it. A rather obvious one.'

'That's what I thought at first,' agreed Rachel Bergen, nodding and smiling happily at the same time, 'But then I thought, perhaps it's also a message, a weird one in truth, but it would not be too much trouble to check it out. So I did.'

'And what did you find?' asked Decker.

'Come and see for yourself,' invited the General Manager, 'Down in the vault.' She reached for a woollen cardigan and drew it around her shoulders. 'It's cold down there, even in the summer. At this time of year, Brrr! It's an icebox!'

She led the way to an ordinary door tucked away under the well of the staircase. When unlocked the door opened outwards to reveal a brick passage and steps which seemingly disappeared into the bowels of the earth.

'Watch your step,' warned Rachel Bergen. She flicked on a light and carefully picked her way down the well-worn steps. The cold chill air had a death-like stillness to it. It penetrated his warm tunic, seeming to eat into his very bones. There was nothing that was welcoming about the place.

At the foot of the stairs a massive steel-plated door faced them. Rachel Bergen took a peculiar key from a pocket of her grey business suit. The head of the key was separated from its shaft and she screwed the two halves together, tightening them with a knurled little wheel just below the handle of the key. The

175

tumblers clicked open with a metallic clunk and Rachel tugged open the heavy door.

There was a single light in the vault, a circular dome of glass covered with a layer of dust and mounted on the wall. Row upon row of Dexion shelving lined the walls of the vault. The shelves were stacked, ceiling high, with the archives of the North Pennine Health Scheme.

'Our claims records are over here,' Rachel Bergen explained, 'We are required by law to keep them for a minimum of six years. I don't know what I expected to find but... well! See for yourself. Once I realised what was there I left everything untouched '

Countless rows of dusty archive bags ranged along the dexion shelving neatly labelled in chronological order. 1987, 1988, 1989, January, February 1st... 2nd... 28th... 29th. - *29th February 1989...* the impossible date! Whereas the claim forms for all the other dates were contained in just one mouldering archive file, for the 29th February 1989 there were *ten* archive bags, all new, all precisely labelled with the date and year.

Decker turned to look at Rachel Bergen to ask, '*Ten* bags... and nobody noticed them before now?'

'Why should they? It's a gloomy old place and the girls don't stay in here a minute longer than they have to. With information readily to hand on the computer, there is very little need for them to come down here at all.' She gave a quick shrug of her shoulders and stepped past him to take down one of the brown manila bags. Her nimble fingers untied the securing knot, pulled the neck of the bag apart to reveal that it was tightly packed with wads of banknotes. 'They are all fifty pound notes in bundles of fifty,' said Rachel, 'There are ten bundles in each bag, ten bags in all, it adds up to two hundred and fifty thousand pounds by my reckoning. Exactly the amount that went missing.'

'But why?' exclaimed the policeman, 'Why go to such elaborate lengths to steal all that money... only to hide it down here?'

'Steal?' remarked Rachel Bergen pointedly, 'Legally if the scheme's money has been on the scheme's premises *all* of the time,' she shrugged, 'Does that count as theft? What constitutes theft anyway? It would seem that there *never* was any intention to remove it.' She looked hopefully into the Sergeant's eyes, a pleading quality in her voice.

'You know who did this.' Decker accused sharply, 'Don't you?'

'No! Oh no. How could I?'

'No, meaning that you have no idea or no, meaning you aren't going to tell me?' probed the policeman. He watched her eyes. Saw confusion there. Saw divided loyalty. Saw her honesty... or loyalty being tested.

'I - I don't *know* anything... not for certain... nothing that I can *prove,* nothing that would stand up in a court of law. It's... it's simply conjecture... supposition...' Her words tailed away into silence as her shoulders slumped dejectedly, 'I wouldn't want to accuse a person who turned out to be innocent, would I?'

'Like Martin Sellaney?'

'I didn't say that.' she retorted sharply, 'I'm accusing no one. I have no proof.'

'No. Of course you haven't... and I doubt you would anyway.' He looked at her long and hard, thoughts racing around in his head with the speed of light. Did any of it make sense? 'Alright,' he said at length, 'without accusing anyone specifically, what do *you* think happened, and why?'

For a long, long time she remained silent, collecting her thoughts, weighing in her mind just how much to reveal of her theory. 'I think whoever did it wanted to bring events to a head. They had no intention of robbing the scheme of any money. I believe it was Maxwell Bull they were getting at. The plan was cleverly designed to implicate our late Chief Executive without damaging the reputation of the North Pennine Health Scheme. It would have worked... but for his death.'

Rachel Bergen broke off abruptly as a new and awesome thought struck her, 'It wasn't connected, was it? His death, with Ma... with anyone here?'

'Obviously you haven't heard about last nights events.' replied Decker, 'about the accident at the church. The young man who fell from the scaffolding, the young man who died.'

It was clear from the bewilderment on her face that the information was new to her.

'I don't live in Rowell,' she explained, 'I live a few miles away in one of the other villages. Can you tell me what happened? I haven't really spoken to anyone today since I came in early. An *accident* you say...?'

'Yes.' Decker spoke briskly, 'It's too early for me speak officially but it now looks as though Maxwell Bull's death is unconnected to the NPHS. It was more of a domestic nature.'

The anxiety in her face fell away. Her features softened perceptibly and the grey eyes fairly sparkled with animation. 'Oh! Thank God! Thank God! I thought... I thought... Oh! I don't know what I thought.' A great sigh of relief escaped her lips and hung mistily in the cold dank air of the vault. She gave a little shiver. 'Can we go back upstairs? I'll ask Jane to make us a fresh cup of coffee.'

*

'Perhaps you could tell me a little more about the investigation by the Department of Trade and Industry?' suggested Decker, 'What prompted it, and how did it end?'

They were seated once more in Rachel Bergen's stark plain office with the policeman balancing a cup of coffee precariously in his lap and facing the General Manager across her neat and orderly desk.

'Our troubles started when we bought this place,' said Rachel who was back to her composed and efficient self. Her eyes flicked around as though she were able to see every aspect of the old house from the comfort of her chair. 'Maxwell Bull dreamed about a place like this, a solid old building, something substantial, to give the scheme an air of timeless stability. He saw it as a symbol of solidarity, a place to impress visitors. He was right. It *does* impress them. It *is* a beautiful old house and because it is a grade two, listed building which had stood empty for many years he was able to buy it for a song. What he failed to take into consideration was the cost of restoring it. Places like this are a money pit. They soak up cash. He did what he has always done... he went overboard. He spent money that the scheme did not have. Plundered the contingency fund. That was when the DTI stepped in. Maxwell was furious about that. He claimed that our new financial director had sold him out. That it was he who reported him. The poor man disappeared overnight, dismissed on the spot. It couldn't possibly have been him for he only started with the North Pennine Health Scheme in April that year and the DTI began their investigations in January.'

178

'Oh!' Decker cocked his head in mild surprise and with an air of innocence asked, 'So who did report Bull to the Department of Trade and Industry?'

'I – I – don't know,' Even though she had been expecting the question Rachel Bergen stumbled over her words, 'No one knows for certain. Although…' she hesitated as though uncertain whether to go on, then continued, ' …Martin and I discussed the situation on many occasions over the year. We were both becoming very concerned about what was going on. In fact…' she hesitated nervously once more, bent an appealing look at the policeman, '…I did try to ring them once and was told that if I wanted to lodge a complaint then it would have to be in writing… but I never got around to doing it.'

'Obviously someone did.' observed Decker.

'Yes.' Rachel nodded her agreement miserably, 'I often wish I had had the courage of *my* convictions and gone through with my complaint. But what good did it do? He still got away with it.'

'What!' exclaimed Decker, 'How?'

'How! How do *you* think? He had friends in high places, or at least *one* friend who must have had influence. He should have been removed from his position as Chief Executive, but he wasn't. It was all hushed up. His misuse of the scheme's funds should have been made public, but again, it wasn't. So much for the DTI as a watchdog! What good were all their investigations when it resulted in a cover-up.' There was bitterness in her voice and a tightening of her mouth as she spat out the words. 'When I think of all the people who suffered as a result of Maxwell Bull's ego, all those innocent victims. And poor Martin, he was *so* dedicated to the scheme.'

She shook the memories away, straightened her back and relaxed into her chair. 'It's all in the past Sergeant… all in the past. One can't pass through life always looking over one's shoulder all the time, can one?'

Chapter Twenty-Six

Sergeant Edward Decker lifted the boot lid of his little green Morris Minor and stared thoughtfully at its contents. It was immaculately tidy. He abhorred those cars that resembled a mobile dustbin. A plastic bag of tools was tucked neatly into one corner. Decker pulled open the bag, rummaged around inside and took out a short stubby screwdriver. It slipped easily into his tunic pocket, creating only a slight bulge.

He had parked close to the all night garage in the village of Rowell. There was a telephone booth nearby from which he put through a call to the County Police Headquarters. Although Decker felt confident in his ability to carry out an arrest it made good sense to call for some backup, a female police officer for preference. In this day and age he did not want to risk an accusation of sexual harassment that may prejudice his case.

*

'Why Sergeant Decker, this is a surprise.' exclaimed Mrs McLean, 'what brings you here? Oh dear! Is it to do with that poor young man who died last night? The one Miss Marie befriended.'

'In a way, yes. But... er... first I wondered if I might borrow the keys to the stables. I've misplaced my torch and quite possibly I left it there when I replaced the bell rope. Do you mind?'

'Not at all.' The housekeeper was only too eager to help. She turned towards the kitchen cabinet with its row of dangling keys, selected the long shafted metal one marked "Stables" and handed them to the policeman. 'Can you manage on your own?' she asked, 'I'm in the middle of preparing a little something for lunch.'

Decker was secretly relieved at her words. He had been struggling for an excuse had she decided to accompany him. 'I'll be fine,' he replied, 'Is Miss Bull around?'

'She's in her brother's room, sorting out his belongings. Do you wish to speak to her?'

'Later.' replied the policeman over one shoulder as he turned away and headed for the stables. The panel of hardboard Decker had secured over the broken windowpane was still in place.

Very likely, he thought, *Mrs McLean is watching the pennies until Maxwell Bull's financial affairs are sorted out.* Jobs like replacing broken glass would have to wait. He unlocked the door and went in. He fumbled for the light switch in its awkward position, found it and illuminated the stable in the harsh light of the naked bulb.

Knowing exactly what to search for made a considerable difference and he found the piece of rope quite quickly. It was about nine inches long and had been fashioned into a slipknot. There was a darkish stain on parts of the rope and at the opposite end to the slipknot, a knotted lump caused by the strands being tied over again and again. Blood, guessed Decker correctly, looking at the dark stain. Whoever had tied the additional knots had intended the slipknot to jam against them and be virtually impossible to release.

The wooden ladder to the loft creaked ominously under the weight of the burly policeman as he climbed cautiously up. He stood on the edge of one side and looked across. The distance across the gap was a mere four feet. A relatively short distance to leap across at ground level. Why then did it appear so much further because it was high off the ground?

It's in my mind, he told himself. Then jumped. The overhanging boards flexed and groaned as he landed with a thump. But they held. He brushed aside loose strands of straw and a layer of dust and felt around with his fingertips, probing tentatively until he located the heads of the screws which secured the inner ends of the shortened floorboards to the joist. His stubby little screwdriver turned easily and within seconds there were four woodscrews resting in the palm of his hand. The screws were all new, one and three quarters of an inch in length, their heads slightly dulled by dirt and dust but otherwise there wasn't a trace of rust to be found. A greasy substance had been smeared onto the threads. Decker scraped with his fingernail and touched it to his lips. The tip of his tongue tasted the substance. A smile of satisfaction flitted across his face. Soap! It's an old joiner's trick. A little soap smeared onto the threads of a screw made it so much easier to insert and to remove.

He was about to replace the screws back into their sockets when he heard the ladder creaking. Coming quickly to his feet he slipped the screws and the short stubby screwdriver into his tunic pocket. To a casual eye the floor of the loft looked normal... with one dangerous exception. The shortened boards at the edge of the loft now balanced on the central joist. Without the screws to hold them in place they would act like a seesaw with the end joist acting as a fulcrum. If a person's weight were to land on the outer edge the boards would tilt and tip whoever landed there over the edge.

The head of Marie Bull appeared. She climbed easily like a cat, her long feline limbs swinging her thin body effortlessly off the rungs of the ladder and onto the floor of the loft. Her large luminous eyes regarded him solemnly, her loose generous mouth, which could have been so attractive, turned down at the corners in a tight expression of anger.

'What are *you* doing here?' she asked sullenly, '*you* have no right to be here. It's *our* place. Ours. Mine!'

'My job.' said Decker in a matter of fact voice. The last faltering words of Billy were still fresh in his mind. At the very least the woman was unbalanced, probably insane. He knew he had to tread warily.

'But you are a policeman.' The words came out like a challenge. They were full of resentment and unsuppressed hostility.

'Exactly!' replied the Sergeant, '... and I'm looking into a very suspicious death.'

The large luminous eyes narrowed and took on a look of animal cunning. Her head cocked suddenly to one side, a queer jerky movement.

'Here? Why here? My brother died here... he committed suicide.'

'I think not.' Decker said quietly.

'What do you mean?' she snapped, 'Of course he did. It was in the newspapers.'

'Well, they were wrong. We were wrong... the police. It happens, but *now* I have new information, information that forces me to believe otherwise. I *know* your brother did not commit suicide... and he didn't die accidentally either, did he Marie?'

'What do you mean? He did. He did. You can't have new information. You can't have. *He* wouldn't tell... never... never! He... he promised me.'

'Who wouldn't tell Marie? Billy? Was it Billy who promised never to reveal your secret? Was it?'

Marie drew back slightly. She seemed to shrink back into herself. He could almost see her animal mind working, looking for an escape route, her large, expressive, luminous eyes flickering around. 'He's dead.' Marie said, 'Billy's dead. *He* can't tell you anything now. He wouldn't have... he loved me.'

'Oh yes! He loved you.' Decker heaved a weary sigh, 'He loved you right enough, too much in fact. But he was dying... and he did not want to die with a guilty conscience. I was with him when he died last night. He told me everything.'

'What did he say? What did he tell you? How do you know it was the truth? How?' Marie's mind was still working feverishly. Still seeking a way out. Still playing for time.

Ted Decker's eyes never left her face for a second. He guessed what she was doing, what she was thinking. This was not the way he had planned it to happen. He needed support. Where was the policewoman he had called for? Where? What was taking her so long? He looked across the four foot gap between the two sides of the loft and realised he was at a disadvantage. If Marie were to make a sudden dash for it she was on the side of the loft with the ladder. He needed to play for time. To delay her until help, in the form of a policewoman, arrived.

'It wasn't the first time you tried to kill your brother was it Marie? But this time you succeeded. Oh yes, and very cleverly you planned it too.' He was playing to her vanity. Flattering her like a spoilt child. Seeking to hold her attention and distract her mind. 'We, the police, didn't know about the games you played... the dangerous games. We never guessed, wouldn't have guessed without Billy's information. You have always played them haven't you... you and your crazy brother Maxwell. The game of "Dare" Is that what you called it?' Decker could see that she was listening intently, see a faint smile of smug satisfaction creeping around the corners of her loose, generous mouth.

'Lots of young children play it don't they? Truth, Dare or Promise - that was what we called it when I was a boy. I played it many times. It was great fun... and fairly harmless. But you and Maxwell took it a stage further... a lot further didn't you? You took it to the extreme limit, to the point where you both put your lives on the line. Why Marie? Why? Was it to prove which one of you was superior? Was it? Unfortunately for you Maxwell always won didn't he? *He always won...* until *you* outwitted *him.* Very clever of you Marie, very clever, outwitting your big brother Maxwell. You won the *final* game. The very last game you ever played.'

She was smiling now, a broad beam of delight. He could see her eyes glowing in the harsh light of the stable's bare bulb. Glowing with pleasure, the pleasure of her success... and glowing with a hint of madness in them.

'Shall I tell you how you did it shall I? Shall I tell you how I managed to work it all out, with Billy's help of course. You were *so* clever. I would never have guessed without the knowledge he gave me.' Decker smiled at her, his warmest friendliest smile. She was hooked, basking in the glow of his admiration.

'It was you who invented the dares wasn't it? You, who thought out the game of leaping from one side of the loft to the other. It was quite a simple game at first, in fact, too easy for someone as agile as you. So then you made it harder. First you had to compete with your hands clasped behind your back. That didn't work too well because it's natural for a person landing to throw out their arms to hold their balance. That was when you cut out a few strands of hemp from the bell rope, wove it into a slender cord and formed a slipknot to hold the thumbs together behind the leaper's back. The contest then was to see who could jump across and keep their balance without pulling free from the knot. Only when the time came *you* made sure that Maxwell would be unable to free *his* thumbs quickly enough to save himself. *You* put extra loops into the cord so that the slipknot jammed, only for a vital second, but long enough to be fatal...!'

'Ha! You've missed the point.' She cried out triumphantly. Decker looked across the gap at her eyes gleaming in the harsh light. Her slender figure, clad in close fitting jeans and a roll-neck sweater was quivering with tension like an over-wound clock spring.

'Have I? You mean the idea of putting the bell rope around one's neck, like a noose... to add extra spice to the danger. Is that what you mean?'

'No. No. Not just that.' Her face had turned sullen again. She hated being out-thought. Her mood swings were quite violent and sudden. 'I mean about the light. You don't know about the light do you clever-dick?' A sneering child-like tone of triumph crept back. 'You didn't know that we jumped across in the dark did you?'

'How...?' Decker leaned out over the edge of the loft, twisting his head to try and see the hidden switch. It was impossible.

'Not that switch you fool.' scoffed Marie scornfully, 'There's a second switch,' pointing to a darkened corner of the loft. 'Over there!'

So much for my theory, thought Decker, *...blown away in seconds.* The possibility of a second light switch had not occurred to him. It should have... and yet he had still been right in his belief that Maxwell Bull had been murdered.

'Ah! Yes.' he said thoughtfully, turning back to look admiringly at Marie's face, 'Very clever of you, *very clever indeed.* In the dark he wouldn't be able to see that the screws were missing from the floorboards. Poor Maxwell... he plunged to his death simply because he couldn't see... didn't appreciate that when *you* jumped across the gap you *knew* where it was safe to land. But when he jumped, the floorboards tilted like a sea-saw, and he fell backwards and down. He tore his thumbs free, that's what made the cuts on the insides of them. He grabbed at the rope around his neck to try and save himself but it was too late. He was too heavy. The slipknot held just long enough. That's how he died... playing one of your games. Your silly... dangerous... fatal... games.'

Decker cocked his head to look enquiringly at Marie. 'Am I right? Is that how you planned it? Is that how you murdered your brother?'

'You can't prove it.' Marie hissed at him. 'There's no proof... no proof.'

'Oh but there is,' replied Decker, '... there is. To begin with there is Billy's confession, the confession of a dying man. A jury will believe that. Then there is the cord that you took from the bell rope. The cord to bind your late brother's thumbs together... it's still stained with his blood. We missed it originally because we didn't know what to look for and it was insignificant amid all the loose hay on the stable floor. I found it this morning. Then there are the screws, the woodscrews which Billy so carefully removed for you and coated with soap. It enabled you to remove them easily… and to refit them in seconds *after* Maxwell had plunged to his death.

'All very clever Marie… very clever.' He paused, watching her across the gap. '…except that you made one little mistake, one fatal mistake. You refitted the screws, came down the ladder and slipped out of the rear door of the stables, made your way back to the house and sneaked indoors at the same time as Mrs McLean used the front entrance of the stables. She switched on the light and found your brother's body.

'*She switched on the light.*' Decker's voice hardened as he emphasised the words. 'That was your mistake Marie. Switching off the lights. Habit, was it? Instinctive? The training of a lifetime? We all do these things don't we… often without even thinking about it. Maxwell couldn't have switched them off could he? Because… he… was… dead!'

'You're bluffing.' She snapped, her eyes hyperactive, flitting searchingly around the loft. 'Bluffing me. No one can possibly know.'

'No one but you and I.' admitted Decker, 'But they will, they surely will.'

It was a fatal admission.

Marie's head snapped suddenly to one side, looking towards the stable door. Without thinking the policeman's head turned to follow the direction of her gaze. In that split second of distraction she leapt. Flew like a panther across the gap to land lightly at his side.

He couldn't imagine where the knife came from. The huge Bowie knife with its razor sharp blade and needle pointed tip. He only knew that it was pressed tight against his throat, the razor edge nicking the soft skin of his neck and the sharp point pricking the flesh under his jawbone.

Marie's body was pressed tight against his own. Her right hand gripped the front of his tunic and her left held the Bowie knife to his throat. He felt her breath in his face; little panting jets of warm air like feathery fingers on his skin.

'Oh no they won't,' she hissed in his ear, 'No one will ever know except you and I… and you are going to meet with an accident. A very unfortunate accident, just like my dear beloved brother.'

'You'll never get away with it.' croaked Decker. He was up on the tips of his toes, head held back as high as he could manage in a vain attempt to escape the relentless pressure of the knife point against his Adam's apple. They were both perilously close to the edge of the loft and the boards flexed and groaned from the pressure of their combined weight.

'But I will.' She whispered in his ear, 'I will... and do you know why? Because you will die the way my brother died and I will tell them that you were trying to reconstruct what happened... slipped... and fell. So tragic! They will *have* to believe me for there won't be anyone else to contradict my story, will there?'

*

She had the bell rope tight around his neck and a length of cord bound his thumbs together behind his back. Perspiration trickled down his face, dribbled in a damp stream inside his collar and traced down his body.

Oh God! He thought, *Helen... Jason... Forgive me for leaving you this way.*

The relentless pressure of the knife forced him towards the dark abyss.

'They're coming,' he croaked despairingly, 'I sent for backup. They're on their way... police colleagues... be here any moment.'

Her large luminous eyes gleamed with triumph, the pupils wide, dilated to an abnormal size with the excitement. The blood raced through her veins, the adrenaline flowing, keying her wiry body to fever pitch.

Jesus Christ! He thought... *she's enjoying this. She's on a high. This is what she lives for... the mad... crazy... woman.*

His feet were on the edge of the boards... slipping... slipping. He felt her hand move to the small of his back to give him one final thrust. To launch him into oblivion...!

*

'No-o-o-o!' A wild cry came from below, 'No Marie... No.' Mrs McLean rushed into view. He glimpsed a dark metallic object grasped between her hands. 'Stop! Marie please stop... don't make me have to shoot.'

The heavy gun wobbled unsteadily in her grasp, its barrel, pointing upwards, traced an erratic arc around Decker and Marie Bull.

187

If she fires, thought the policeman, *the bullet could go anywhere.*

For a brief moment Marie hesitated uncertainly and Decker felt the cord binding his thumbs together give a fraction. It was enough. He twisted his hand and eased his left thumb out of the slipknot.

'Go away!' screamed Marie at the housekeeper and made to push her prisoner to his death. There was a blinding flash followed by the sound of the bell clanging as the bullet ricocheted against the outside metal and deflected to fly between the heads of the policeman and his tormentor.

Marie flinched... and stepped sideways... onto the unsecured floorboards. They tilted in a seesaw action and tossed her into space. A startled cry escaped from her throat. One hand clutched frantically for a hold, found Decker's tunic and dragged him after her.

The Sergeant threw his left arm upwards in a circular motion, winding the bell rope around his arm and clutched at the coarse hemp with tenacious fingers. Instinctively his right hand grasped the woman's wrist. Held it for seemingly endless seconds.

Together they hung there, swinging out over the void between the two sides of the stable loft. The muscles of his arms screamed as their combined weight tore at the fibres and sinews of his body.

It was too much.

Marie's fingers, losing strength, slipped relentlessly down his tunic sleeve. Her slim wrist, moist and clammy with perspiration, slid like wet soap from his grasp. She gave a short sharp strangled cry before crashing heavily onto the cobbled floor.

'Marie! O-o-o-oh Marie.' wailed the housekeeper. The gun dropped from her nerveless fingers. She rushed to kneel beside the still figure lying face down in a curious humped position.

'Help!' croaked Decker, 'The ladder... get... the... ladder...' His fingers were sliding inexorably down the bell rope, its slipknot tightening around his neck. The housekeeper raised startled eyes. For one agonisingly painful moment she remained paralysed with shock and fear. Then she moved. Leapt to her feet. Wrenched the ladder from its position and threw it across the abyss. Decker's scrabbling feet found a rung to take his weight. The ladder held.

Gingerly he removed the bell rope from around his neck. With one hand resting on the shoulder of Mrs McLean to steady himself and the other working to release the noose which had so nearly finished his life. It was the closest he had ever been to death and the experience left him white and trembling from shock. He fought to regain a semblance of self-control, gulping in great breaths of air, sucking it down into his heaving lungs.

'The gun,' he panted, 'How? ... Where?'

M-M-Maxwell... it belonged to Maxwell.' Mrs McLean stammered an explanation, 'I-I-I d-didn't even know it was loaded. Oh my God! Have I killed her?'

Decker shook his head.

'No. The bullet hit the outside of the bell and ricocheted between us... thankfully... but it saved my life.'

A low moan came from the huddled figure on the stable floor. Marie lay face down, one arm stretched out ahead of her as though to fend away the ground and the other doubled underneath her humped body. Mrs McLean hurried towards the stricken woman and gently turned her over.

'O-o-oh!' The air whistled out of her in a gasp of horror. The broad blade of the Bowie knife protruded from Marie's ribs. In the fall she had landed on her own weapon. Blood was seeping through the roll-neck sweater and spreading out in an ominous dark stain.

Mrs McLean's reaction was instinctive. She reached out and plucked the Bowie knife from Marie's body before Decker could prevent her.

'No-o-o!' he screamed in vain. A jet of blood like a fountain spurted from the open wound. He threw himself onto his knees beside Marie's stricken frame and jammed his fingers into the gaping hole. 'Run!' he yelled violently at the badly shaken housekeeper, 'Run like Hell. For God's sake, phone for an ambulance... Get help... And pray to God it's not too late!'

The wound was low down, away from the heart on the right hand side of Marie's body. Her breathing was laboured but to his relief there was no sign of frothy bubbles escaping. The sharp fearsome blade of the Bowie knife had failed to pierce a lung.

Decker's greatest fear was that a main artery had been severed and that Marie would bleed to death before expert help arrived. He fumbled awkwardly in his trouser pocket with his free hand while maintaining pressure upon the wound, found a clean white handkerchief and pressed it against the gaping hole.

Hurry. Please God make them hurry, he muttered under his breath. Another human life was fading before his very eyes and he felt powerless to prevent it.

*

'They're coming... They're coming.' Breathing heavily Mrs McLean returned from the house, knelt beside Marie and cradled the stricken woman's head in her arms. She looked at Decker with wide apprehensive eyes, her white shocked features drained of colour. 'Will she live? Please. Please make her live. It's my fault, all my fault. I should have seen it coming, seen what she was becoming. I've known her all her life... all her life... and I still didn't realise what was happening until it was too late...!'

'You mustn't blame yourself,' soothed the policeman, 'She *is* a grown woman... an adult with a mind of her own. Able to make her own decisions.'

There was silence for a few moments and then he asked gently, 'Why? Why did she do what she did? Why did she want to kill her brother... her *own* brother?'

For an answer Mrs McLean reached for the roll-neck of Marie's blood-soaked sweater. 'She had good reason, a very good reason after what he did to her.' The bitterness was apparent in her voice as she pulled down the material.

Then Decker saw for himself... and shuddered at the sight. There was a circle of raw puckered flesh that ran in a band around her neck. When Maxwell Bull had played out his western game and hanged his brother and sister, young Malcolm had not been the only victim. The rubber-covered wire had cut into Marie's neck, become infected, festered and left a suppurating wound that had never properly healed.

190

Chapter Twenty-Seven

The short cold January days lengthened slowly. February passed and March arrived in a surprising burst of warmth and sunshine for the time of year. The Briseley T'ill Cricket Club held its annual general meeting. Work commenced at the ground to prepare it for the approaching season. Decker helped fellow members to mow the square, the outfield and to roll the wicket. The details of his investigation into the North Pennine Health Scheme and the death of Maxwell Bull began to fade from the police sergeant's mind.

When the telephone rang and Martin Sellaney's voice came over the wire he needed to pause and remember who was calling before he recognised who it was.

'Sergeant Decker? Martin Sellaney, do you remember me?'

'Erm! Er…Yes! The cricket coach… yes… of course I do.' He clicked his fingers in spontaneous celebration. How could he forget? 'How can I help you?' he asked.

'You can't,' replied Sellaney, the good humour obvious in his tone of voice, 'I have something for you. A special gift that I hope you can accept. Would you like to call at my house and collect it?'

'When?' asked Ted Decker, his curiosity was aroused. What on earth could it be?

'Whenever it suits you. Say this morning…?'

'Right. Fine. I'll be there in about an hour. OK.' He put down the receiver thoughtfully, the puzzlement showing on his face.

'Who was that?' asked Helen, 'You look flummoxed.'

'Flummoxed! I'm not flummoxed.' He retorted, 'I've *never* been flummoxed in my life, whatever it means. No, it was Martin Sellaney, the man who used to work for the North Pennine Health Scheme. He asked to see me. He says he has a special gift for me? I can't imagine what it might be.'

'Isn't he the man who was your prime suspect? The man *you* were so certain had murdered Maxwell Bull?'

Damn! Trust Helen to remember. She had a mind like a steel trap. He had the good grace to smile ruefully and admit his mistake.

'Yeah! That's the one. I really thought he did it. It seemed so obvious at the time. How wrong can one get...?'

'But right in the end.' consoled Helen Argosy, 'when it came to the crunch you were the one who was right.' She turned back to her work, concealing the unbounded admiration and pride she felt. He had come so close to death in pursuing his duty. It had disturbed her in a manner she had never thought of as possible. Love, pride, admiration and fear, they were all jumbled together in her heart. Feelings she was forced to conceal.

*

Martin Sellaney greeted him at the door with a warm smile.

'She's slipping,' remarked Decker with a glance over his shoulder.

'Eh!'

'Mrs Neighbourhood Watch, she's slipping. I've been on your doorstep for a full ten seconds and her curtains haven't twitched once.'

'Oh her!' chuckled Sellaney, 'She has her uses I suppose. But you underestimate her, she's away at the moment otherwise you'd have been spotted in seconds.' He threw wide the door. 'Come in. I've got the coffee on.' The smell of ground coffee percolating pervaded the house. Martin led the way to his study, settled Decker comfortably in an easy chair and went to serve the coffee.

'She provided *you* with an alibi.' called out the policeman.

'Did she, when?'

'On New Year's Eve, she's the one who told me about the bus that blocked your drive. It meant that you could not possibly have used your car to drive to Rowell at the time Maxwell Bull was killed. She also confirmed that she saw you working away on your word processor until after midnight.'

'The nosey old cow.' muttered Sellaney as he returned from the kitchen balancing two cups, a bowl of sugar, jug of cream and the pot of coffee on a small round tray. 'When I'm busy,' he mused, 'absorbed in my work I completely forget about simple things like closing the curtains. So yes, she would have seen me.'

He poured the coffee, spooning in a generous helping of sugar for himself and then floating a layer of rich cream on the surface. 'Wicked... all those calories.' He grinned boyishly at Decker and then asked abruptly, 'Did you really think it was me?'

192

'Yes I did,' admitted Decker, 'Especially after you told me about the attempt on your life... after the car had been tampered with. I really began to believe it was you. It seemed logical. You had the motivation, more than anyone else, *and* you had the knowledge.'

'But I wouldn't...'

'Of course not, I know that now.' Sergeant Decker reassured him, 'But *you* were wrong about Maxwell Bull trying to kill you. It was the other way round. It was Marie Bull attempting to kill her brother. She persuaded Billy to tamper with the brakes on the pool car, showed him what to do, except that Billy was ham-fisted and didn't make a very good job of it. Unfortunately for Marie, Maxwell Bull's own car was repaired sooner than expected. He returned the pool car and innocently loaned it to you. You copped for the brake failure... completely the wrong man.'

He shrugged ruefully, 'Sorry!'

'I read about it in the papers,' remarked Sellaney, switching the conversation, 'it was you who saved her life... after she tried to kill you. That's astonishing. I don't know what I would have done in those circumstances. To do what you did, I hope I would have done the same, but who can tell?'

Decker made a nonchalant gesture, brushing aside the mention of his courageous action. Who could foresee what *any* person would do in such a situation. He did not see himself as a hero and felt more than a little embarrassed whenever the subject was raised.

'Wasn't it strange about the missing money? How it turned up again. Seems it wasn't stolen after all.' Decker paused, watching Sellaney's face closely, 'Perhaps the thief had second thoughts... a conscience?'

'Perhaps.'

'The tip-off letter was posted in Gloucestershire and typed on a word-processor,' pressed the policeman, 'I notice *you* have a word-processor...and don't you have relatives in the West Country... the Mendip Hills I think you said?'

'Did,' corrected Martin Sellaney, 'my aunt and uncle lived there, they died soon after my last visit. Once Aunty went uncle seemed to lose the will to live. He died just before Christmas. Left me a great deal of money. I never realised how rich he was.' Martin's head shook in wonderment at the thought. 'He was just Uncle Ben to me, an eccentric man who pottered about in his workshop trying to invent things. It seems that he did, very successfully. Nothing earthshaking, just lots of sensible every day objects that people need and use. He took out a fistful of patents and had a very comfortable income as a result. He left it all to me.'

He looked Decker in the eye with beguiling innocence.

'I've told you once before, I would *never* steal a penny from the scheme... and that's the truth.'

'I believe you.' replied the Sergeant mildly, 'Theft was *not* the intention ... was it?'

No?' Sellaney raised a pair of enquiring eyebrows. Spurious innocence shone from his face. 'What was the intention?'

'To embarrass Maxwell Bull and show to the world the kind of man he really was. That was the *real* motive behind the so-called theft. Am I right?'

Martin Sellaney's face remained impassive. Just the faintest hint of a smile touched his lips.

Damn him. Decker thought, *He is never going to admit he perpetrated the computer fiddle. I know it. And he knows that I know it.* But...Well! Did it matter any more?

'They still think very highly of you.' remarked the Sergeant.

'They...? Who?'

'Who? Why the staff at the North Pennine Health Scheme of course and one of them in particular, Rachel Bergen. She is very concerned about your welfare. She was so relieved when the money was found... so pleased that it hadn't been stolen. It quite changed her personality. Lifted a load of worry from her shoulders.'

'Why should it do that?' Sellaney frowned in puzzlement.

Decker lifted his eyes heavenwards in sheer frustration and sighed, 'You just don't see it do you? She was relieved to know that a person she cared about was innocent. That they - you weren't a thief. She cares about *you* Martin. Cares a lot about you.'

'No! How can she, I mean, well.' There was so much doubt in his face that Decker found it laughable.

'She does, believe me.' encouraged the Sergeant, 'You should write to her.'

'Mmm! No, I couldn't, I've been a bachelor for far too long. It wouldn't work, would it?' He looked at Ted Decker with appealing eyes, seeking conviction. Then suddenly burst into a loud chuckle. 'I never imagined Cupid in a serge blue uniform before, with stripes on his arm. Oh dear Sergeant...' and he dissolved into outright laughter.

'Oh, by the way I have something for you.' Martin said, switching the topic again, 'I nearly forgot'. He crossed to the beech wood office desk in his study and opened one of the drawers. There was enormous pride and satisfaction on his face as he took out a pristine copy of a hardback book. Its cover was in dark green with shiny gold lettering.

'For you.' He said simply, 'It's the very first copy of my cricket coaching manual for young boys. My book. For years it has been a dream and now it has come true. I can hardly believe it myself. The publishers plan to distribute it worldwide. Everywhere the game is played. Australia, India, New Zealand, the West Indies, Pakistan, Sri Lanka, Zimbabwe... the lot.

'They say it should sell very well. I could be even richer. Famous even!' He stood proudly, arms folded across his chest, watching the policeman examine the book in detail. 'Now perhaps you will understand why I wanted Maxwell Bull alive, very much alive. *I wanted him to read about my success.*

'A wise friend once told me that the best form of revenge is to succeed. In my own field, in what I love and do best, I *have* succeeded. My book is about to be published worldwide. For me that would have been far more satisfying than killing the man, however much he deserved it. My revenge was *much* more subtle than that.

'But damn it! He died too soon.'

Acknowledgements

My gratitude goes to all those people who have helped me with the publication of this book. To Ruth E Glover, a friend and fellow author who introduced me to self-publishing and gave me valuable advice on what to do. To Sue Barlow who taught me what precious little I know about computers and helped to set up the cover designs. To Gordon Turner, my oldest friend and severest critic who worked diligently editing my manuscript. Any remaining mistakes are my own. To my artistic brother, Robert, who painted the original picture on which the cover is based. To Geoff Clark, of Clark Associates, who supplied my computer and continues to give support. And to all those friends and colleagues who have encouraged and supported my efforts and finally to my wife, June, without whose patience and encouragement none of this would be possible, goes my undying gratitude.

A well-known author once wrote to me that a novel does not really exist until it has readers. So to everyone who picks up my book, turns the pages and reads the story, may it give you as much pleasure to read as it gave me to write. Thank you.

Also by Michael John Smedley

Fiction

The Sirius Phenomenon
Pools Within The Mind
(Published by The Book Guild)

(The Decker Trilogy)
Late Cut
A Subtle Revenge
Manna From Abaddon
(Last still in progress)
(Published by Lulu Online)